DIE AGAIN TO SAVE THE WORLD

DIE AGAIN TO SAVE THE WORLD

DIE AGAIN TO SAVE THE WORLD™ BOOK ONE

RAMY VANCE

MICHAEL ANDERLE

DISRUPTIVE IMAGINATION

THE DIE AGAIN TO SAVE THE WORLD TEAM

Thanks to our Beta Readers

Kelly O'Donnell, Rachel Beckford, John Ashmore, Larry Omans

Thanks to the JIT Readers

Veronica Stephan-Miller
Deb Mader
Jackey Hankard-Brodie
Zacc Pelter
Dorothy Lloyd
Dave Hicks
Diane L. Smith
Jeff Goode

If I've missed anyone, please let me know!

Editor

The Skyhunter Editing Team

This book is a work of fiction. All of the characters, organizations, and events portrayed in this novel are either products of the author's imagination or are used fictitiously. Sometimes both.

Cover Art by Jake @ J Caleb Design
http://jcalebdesign.com / jcalebdesign@gmail.com

A Michael Anderle Production

LMBPN Publishing
PMB 196, 2540 South Maryland Pkwy
Las Vegas, NV 89109

Version 1.01, June 2021
ISBN (ebook) 978-1-64971-851-8
ISBN (paperback) 978-1-64971-852-5

DEDICATION

To BETA for BETA-ifying the hell out of this story!

—Ramy Vance

To Family, Friends and
Those Who Love
to Read.
May We All Enjoy Grace
to Live the Life We Are
Called.

— Michael

CHAPTER ONE

Reuben—Tuesday, February 14, 9:36 a.m.

Reuben walked to work with an extra bounce in his step. Today he was going to ask Aki Yamashiro out. Sure, she'd probably reject him. Sure, he'd need to find a large boulder to hide under when she did.

He was going to do it anyway. Today he was going to face his fears, step up to the plate, do whatever any other motivational cliché demanded.

Today he was going to take his chance, goddamn it.

As he neared the CIA's offices in downtown New York, he stopped at the corner of Broadway and Thomas and looked up at the five-hundred-fifty-foot-tall skyscraper that was his workplace.

He took a deep breath. "You can do this," he assured himself in a quiet voice. "Yesterday, you had a moment. Valentine's is coming. She's single, you're single. You can *do* this."

A nearby car honked, causing Reuben to jump. "Argh, maybe you can't."

From behind him, he heard a voice. "It doesn't matter. Do it, don't do it. She'll never remember."

Reuben turned, startled to see a homeless man standing a few feet from him. He wondered how the guy got so close.

"Excuse me?" Reuben asked as he instinctively fished around in his pockets for loose change.

The man smelled like mac and cheese and a hint of lilac. "Ask her or don't. She'll never remember. No one will—no one but you, Repeater. You are the only one who can remember. You and you alone."

"Remember what?" Reuben found a quarter. He tried to hand the change to the man.

He looked at the coin like it was diseased. "You are the only one who remembers the Repeats. Some intuitives experience déjà vu, but you, Mr. Hash Brown, remember everything."

Reuben took a step back. "What…what did you call me?"

The homeless man tilted his head. "Repeater."

Reuben shook his head. "No, not that. Mr. Hash Brown. How did you know?"

"Why would I call you something so processed?" The man smiled, exposing two uneven rows of yellow teeth. "Me, I only eat organic."

"No, I distinctly heard you call me by the nickname my mom…" Reuben trailed off. "You know what? Never mind. Do you want the change or not?"

"What I *want* is for you to remember the future and fix it," the homeless man roared, causing Reuben to take two steps back onto the road.

A courier jetted past Reuben, knocking him back onto the sidewalk with a *thump*.

"I don't think you can fix anything." The homeless man waddled away with a cackle. "At least, not this version of you."

Reuben watched him go as he stood, dusting himself off. Not the confidence-inspiring morning he'd hoped for.

If he couldn't stand up to a homeless man or avoid death by bicycle, how would he ever find the courage to ask Aki out?

Before he could talk to Aki, he needed to do his job. Right now, that meant compiling a report for the Division director, Sven Larson, on anyone and everyone who ever came in contact with CIA's hot suspect of the month, a teenager from Iowa named Julian Schaeffer.

Working from an anonymous tip, the CIA had found trace amounts of a manufactured isotope of strontium in a dumpster near his home, along with a bunch of other shit that shouldn't be in any suburb. They'd also recovered a small amount of metal mesh and several damaged microwave ovens —probably not related. The radioactive material had caused major waves in the department, as it should. The department was A, baffled as to how the kid could get his hands on such materials, and B, had no idea where the materials were now.

God help us all.

Instead of arresting him, they'd decided to watch the kid's every move.

Ever watch a teenage boy's every move? They spend ridiculous amounts of time in the bathroom...ah...grooming themselves.

Reuben remembered those days.

Hell, Reuben still lived them.

After three days of twenty-four-hour surveillance, to all appearances, Schaeffer was a normal nineteen-year-old community college dropout who lived in his parent's basement, smoked pot, played video games, and posted ridiculous memes on social media.

No way was he a criminal mastermind building weapons of mass destruction.

That was Reuben's opinion, not that anyone had asked for it.

Reuben glanced at Sven's office as the first report finished loading. What he saw caused butterflies to flit in his stomach.

There she was.

Aki Yamashiro.

They didn't come finer than her. Smart, strong, sexy...she had all the Ss. Not to mention special agent.

So all the Ss and an A.

What would she want with a guy like him?

At twenty-five, Aki was a hotshot agent, a real-life Charlie's Angel. An Asian-American goddess with short, bobbed hair that fell below her chin, framing her flawless, creamy complexion. Petite and athletic, she was slender and curvy in black skinny jeans, thigh-high boots, and a tight-fitting black top. As a field agent, she could dress however she wanted, and she didn't waste the opportunity.

Not like him, with his business-casual tan khakis, blue button-down, and not-really-ironic argyle blazer.

They were the absolute yin and yang of good dress sense.

Reuben knew she'd recently broken up with her boyfriend

Mike Fury, who was currently in rehab for anger management for punching his superior officer.

Who would have guessed a guy named Fury had anger issues?

Now, for the first time since he'd known her, they were both single.

Eh, who was he kidding? He was always single. Except for that time he was engaged. Yeah. Didn't work out. It never did.

Which meant now he had to act fast. For a girl like Aki, it took longer to microwave a burrito than it did to get a date.

What would he say?

"So, you know the other day when I was fixing your computer...maybe I could fix your heart."

Oh, geez. Did I really just mutter that? Who am I, Milton from Office Space*? OK, OK, Reuben, play it cool. You're cool. She's cool.* Reuben groaned internally. *Of course, she's cool. She's always cool. What are you thinking? You have nothing to offer this girl! Other than a year of small talk and one great conversation yesterday, what have you got? A six-year-old Mazda...and, uh...uh...a decent retirement plan? Yeah, how would that go?*

"Hey, you want to go for a ride in my old, beat-up Mazda and talk about 401(k)s?" He could see exactly how that would pan out.

He laughed aloud as he thought about the moment they had yesterday. Her computer had needed a defrag and some software optimizations—nothing fancy. Merely time-consuming. So he'd put on his "Office Jams" playlist on a little Bluetooth speaker while he worked.

Aki had sat patiently next to him, pretending she wasn't bored out of her skull.

Then one of his favorites had come on, and everything had changed. She'd suddenly clicked her acrylic fingernails against the desk and gasped, "You listen to Je Ne Sais Pas?"

His fingers froze mid-keystroke as he glanced down at his phone that now sat in her hands. She had switched from Office Jams to his more obscure playlists.

Je Ne Sais Pas was an underground rock band from Montreal. He'd started listening to them several years ago after his girlfriend left him for an older man who looked exactly like Michael Douglas.

Je Ne Sais Pas, he'd discovered, had the best angry breakup songs.

Reuben had glanced at her and laughed weakly. "Yeah, I've followed them since college, and—"

"Oh my God," she'd gushed. "Me too. All my friends from NYU, we had this tradition to see them at this show once a year at the—"

"May Fest," he'd blurted.

"Yes." The word exploded from her mouth, and her palm hit the desk with excitement. "Did you ever go?"

"I… I…" He'd motioned weakly with his hands. Everyone in the Je Ne Sais Pas fan community knew about the annual May Fest show. Despite being a die-hard fan, he'd never made it to a show. Not once. Montreal had always seemed too far away.

Sitting before Aki, he'd realized that he'd not only missed the chance to see his favorite band but also be in the same room as her. *Damn it.* "No, I never made it. I tried a few times, but, uh…"

"Omigod." She'd sighed and shook her head, her eyes misty with memory. "You should have gone. The concerts were amazing."

He'd shrugged. "I'll keep that in mind, for when I reincarnate as Marty McFly. I'll put it on the list with, 'Don't try to ask Marianna Prescott, the homecoming queen, to prom. It will only end badly.'"

She'd clasped her hands in delight as she laughed. "You're too funny, Reuben."

"Don't be fooled. The cool-guy persona isn't real. It's like Superman—eventually, I have to turn back into full nerd-mode."

She'd laughed again, harder this time. "So, like, at midnight? Do you automatically grow a *Star Wars* robe, don a replica lightsaber and watch *Firefly* reruns on Disney+?"

"The Mandalorian."

"What?"

"*The Mandalorian* is on Disney+, and it's *Star Wars*. You got your nerd stories so mixed up," he'd chided.

"Did I?"

"*Firefly* is Whedon. *Star Wars* is Lucas. Every nerd knows that."

"Humph. You learn something every day."

"I guess you do." He'd smirked and pushed his chair away from her computer. "Done, by the way."

Aki had leaned in to test her computer. "I got the *Star Wars* part right, didn't I? I mean, you're into it, right?"

"Yeah," he'd said dreamily. She was so close he could smell her shampoo. Cinnamon and strawberries. God, she smelled great.

"If it redeems me in your eyes, last Halloween, I tried to get my hair to do those side buns like Princess Leia and wore a sexy robe."

Reuben had given her a coy smile, but inside he thought he might be having a heart attack. Merely the thought of Aki dressed like Princess Leia made every one of his fantasies come true.

"OK," he'd conceded. "But you're on nerd probation. I'm going to have to see photo evidence."

"Photo evidence?" She raised an eyebrow and grabbed her phone off the desk. "Fine. Here's your evidence."

She'd passed it to him. There on her RedBook social media profile was a photo of Aki dressed in the sexiest Leia costume ever.

He'd blushed, stammering, "Ah, that's, ah, a very revealing, ah, hairstyle."

Aki was red-faced with stifled laughter.

He'd handed her phone back and bowed to her. "I guess I could pull some strings. Get you inducted into closet nerddom."

She'd laughed harder. "Closet, huh?"

"Oh, yeah." Then, before he could stop himself, "You're way too hot to be a real nerd."

The comment had fallen hard, and the moment was gone. He'd totally struck out. He'd stood to leave.

Then, she'd surprised him. As he was leaving, she'd smiled. "You're a nice guy, Reuben. Why can't I find a nice guy like you?"

What had he said in reply? "You'll find someone."

Reuben cringed as he replayed those words. That was then. Now he had another shot. What had the homeless guy said? "A repeat?"

Yeah, a repeat. Why not?

All right, Reuben, pull it together. It's now or never.

Pulling his last report up quickly, he readied himself for glory or total failure.

Trying to affect a casual, cool-guy stroll up to Sven's office, he rehearsed what he was going to say. Right now, his best plan was the 401(k) approach.

Sven motioned him in.

Reuben handed Sven the file. "I thought I'd personally bring the Schaeffer report. I knew it was urgent. I also did some digging into the Canadian and—"

"The Canadian?" Sven asked.

"Yeah, ahh... It's an alias, sir. Some gangster that Agent Fury wanted me to look into before, you know..." Reuben turned to Aki and gave her a sympathetic smile.

"He went batshit crazy," Aki said. "No need to pussyfoot around it."

"You're right." Reuben turned to Sven and added, "Before he went batshit crazy."

Aki laughed.

Sven did not. Instead, he touched his swollen left eye. "Right now, all I can manage is Schaeffer. This Canadian bullshit can wait for now. I mean, what kind of criminal alias *is* 'the Canadian,' anyway?" Now it was his turn to laugh.

Sven flipped the file open, ignoring Reuben.

Aki must have noticed the brush-off because she said, "Thank you, Reuben. Excellent work and initiative, don't you think, Sven?"

Sven smiled perfunctorily, engrossed in the report.

"Well," Aki rose from the couch, "I'll leave you guys to it."

"Well, I only came in to drop off the report." Reuben gestured back out toward the hall, but Sven held up a finger for him to stay.

"You know Schaeffer's a threat to national security, right?" the Director asked.

"Yes, sir." Reuben's reply was automatic.

"Don't bullshit me, kid." Sven snorted. "I've been in this business long enough to spot lies. You don't believe he's our guy, do you?"

Reuben wasn't sure how to respond. It was common to ask operatives trick questions. After all, they all worked for an agency built on secrecy, lies, and agents who double-crossed so many times that it would make the average Joe's head spin.

He decided to go with the truth on this one. "No, I don't. I think he's a kid who got mixed up in a game he doesn't even know he's playing."

Sven pursed his lips. "I agree."

"You... You do, sir?" Reuben stammered.

"I do." He sighed and looked up from the report. "Good work, Reuben," Sven added, dismissing him with a raised eyebrow.

Riding high on his success, he spotted Aki. She stood against a window, reading something on her phone.

OK, Sven undid some of the confidence shaking from this morning, he thought as he approached her. *I got this.*

He joined her at the window. "Hey." Reuben gulped. *I don't got this.*

She frowned as she read her screen. "Can you believe this? Schaeffer somehow evaded his surveillance. He flew out of Des Moines in the middle of the night and headed for Albuquerque. What's in Albuquerque?"

"Nuclear testing plants in the New Mexico desert?" Reuben automatically offered. Then he remembered the kid's file. "His aunt."

She sighed. "Which one do you think he's visiting?"

Reuben shrugged. *Smooth.*

Aki sighed. "I hope we can get this guy. We have an agent

in Santa Fe driving out there right now, but Sven wants me out there if he needs backup. So, I'm on standby."

"Right," Reuben replied. "Hey, listen. I know we're all under a lot of stress here with the threat of a possible bomb—"

"Tell me about it," Aki cut in. "You know what sounds so good right now? A long relaxing bubble bath. I don't even remember the last time I did that."

Reuben scratched his temple and tried to fight away the mental image of Aki in a bathtub. "Would you, uh..." The words he'd rehearsed came bubbling out. "Would you, maybe, want to go to a... Or go out somewhere relaxing? I mean, I don't mean a bubble bath. Well, of course, if you wanted to, but what I really mean is like out to drinks or something?"

She cocked her head. "Are you asking me out?"

Reuben felt his face burn. "Yeah. I guess I am."

She eyed him for a long, terrifying second. "You know what? Let's do it."

"Yeah?" His voice rose in shock.

"Sure." She winked and sashayed away. "It'll be fun."

Reuben stood there until she was gone. Had she really said yes? He glanced at his Apple Watch. This was historic, and he had to note the time.

9:47 in the morning. The exact minute of his triumph.

He stood at the window and tried to calm himself down enough that he wouldn't blow it by tripping over his own feet or something equally awkward.

That was when he saw... What *was* that?

"An exploding ball of light?" His eyes grew wide. "Nuclear?"

It wasn't nuclear. A clear wave of energy that distorted

everything around it rushed toward his building as he watched through the window.

"What the..." Reuben froze with fear as the invisible wave passed seamlessly through the glass.

Suddenly, his body was vibrating like a seismic tremor. He felt like he was being torn apart at the atomic level.

His skin cracked. His blood boiled.

He screamed.

He died.

CHAPTER TWO

Martha—Tuesday, February 14, 7:56 a.m.

NYPD officer Martha Dragone crept through the alley, trying not to let the sound of her combat boots alert the target to her presence.

The lone figure—dressed in a cliché bad-guy black trench coat—click-clacked past the back doors of shuttered hipster bars and the rickety fire escapes of the sexy urban-chic apartments of the nouveau riche. Martha struggled to keep up.

The target was Alister Pout. If her sources were correct, the douchebag's alias was "the Canadian."

The Canadian made sense. He was from Carnduff, Saskatchewan.

Founder and majority holder in the social media platform RedBook, the tech investor seemed to have his fingers in every seedy pie in Manhattan. That, and he was connected to several murders.

Since when is being a tech-multi-millionaire not enough?

Charming, devilishly handsome, and loaded to the hilt, the Canadian managed to evade every implication against him.

Those whom he couldn't circumvent, he bought off. He was a venture capitalist who the *Manhattan Scene* recently featured as one of the "Top 35 Under 35." A real mover and shaker. Last year, he'd been voted the most eligible bachelor at a charity auction.

If they only knew about his dark side.

"If only I could take him down. That's all I'd need," Martha muttered under her breath.

Taking him down would be tough. No one believed a rookie cop who'd only been on the job about eleven months. Not when it was someone who funded galas, police balls, and the mayor's campaign.

Besides, while big-city cops knew better than to be openly sexist, they made their opinions known—no girls allowed in this club.

Passive-aggressive little bitches.

Proving that Alister Pout was dirty would change all that. Upgrade her status from rookie to rockstar. That was why, on her day off, she had her back pressed against a dumpster trying desperately not to gag on the collective smell of rancid meat and rotting eggs.

Total rockstar behavior.

She didn't know what Alister was doing here. Murdering someone else? Paying off a business rival? Selling a bomb? One thing was sure. Martha was going to find out.

Alister rounded the corner toward a six-story parking garage. Martha followed him from a safe distance, darting in and out of bushes and behind corners. She caught the reflection of a burly, tattooed night guard watching Netflix on an iPad.

Frasier? *Really?*

When she entered the garage, the morning light glinted

like laser-beam spotlights on the shiny metal of BMWs, Mercedes, and the occasional Porsche or Ferrari thrown in for zesty seasoning.

She slid up to a Jaguar and crouched beside it as Alister entered an elevator. *Frasier* guard stepped in after him.

As soon as the doors shut, Martha made a mad dash to the elevator. She watched the overhead numbers.

One...

Two...

Three...

No, four.

She slammed open the door to the stairwell and bounded up the stairs two at a time, reaching the fourth floor out of breath. Excited, she tried to ram it open.

Locked.

"Damn." She flew down the stairs to the third floor, then burst out of the stairwell, sprinting up the car ramp to the fourth floor.

As she was about to turn the corner, she saw the *Frasier* guard roping off the entrance.

He eyed her with disdain. "Restricted access, ma'am." He clicked a faux-velvet rope into place with a big, meaty hand. "You're going to have to go back down."

"Yes, of course." She thought about identifying herself as a cop. Still, cop or not, following a suspect without going through the proper channels was dangerous.

Best to fly under the radar.

Time to mobilize backup. She headed back down the incline and shot off a text to her partner. She had stumbled onto something. She was sure of it.

She pinned her location and turned the corner, away from the night guard. As soon as she was out of his sight, she leaned out over the third-floor wall. She heard muffled voices and tires squealing.

She leaned farther and could now see the opening to the fourth-floor wall. She surveyed the distance. If she could climb out on the ledge, she could probably see what was going on.

Martha climbed out onto the ledge with careful movements, balancing her weight on one foot. Slowly rising to full height, she steadied herself against a corner.

With one hand on the wall, she reached the other up and...*bingo*. She touched the opening of the fourth story and pulled herself up with both hands.

"Thank you, hot yoga," she whispered.

She hung from the wall like an uncoordinated Spiderman, her legs dangling wildly in the air beneath her.

She could see the fourth floor perfectly.

Two large white delivery vans were parked side by side. Alister stood behind them, a lit cigarette in hand. Around him, half a dozen men scurried around at his commands.

"Unload it already," Alister barked.

One of the men opened the van's side door and nonchalantly began to unload the contents.

"Holy shit," Martha whispered. Her eyes grew wide, and she felt her insides turn cold as she saw what was inside. She knew Alister Pout was into some crooked misdeeds. But this?

"Hey! Who are you, eh?" Alister shouted and looked up.

She realized that in her distraction, she'd gotten sloppy, and the bastard had seen her.

His eyes were cold blue steel, not the dreamy heartthrob that lit up bachelor auctions. "Who the fuck are you?" Before she could react, he pulled a pistol from his trench coat, and with a *zip,* she felt the excruciatingly blinding pain of a bullet piercing her shoulder.

Her hold on the ledge weakened, and…

"Oh fuck," she muttered as she collapsed into a dizzying free-fall.

CHAPTER THREE

Reuben—Saturday, February 11, 7:03 a.m.

"Information for Precinct. Sound of shots fired, 200 block First Avenue, parking lot outside the Tuscan Café. Two shots heard from the east."

"Copy that."

"We're requesting response cars, multiple suspects."

"Copy, requesting response cars."

The garbled noise of the police scanner was the first sound Reuben heard when he came to.

Emphatic yells followed, "Go get 'em, boys!"

There was only one place he'd ever be with a raging maniac yelling at a police scanner. He was safely in his bed.

Wait. *What*?

He had died, hadn't he? Was it all a dream? The explosion. The meeting with Sven. Getting a date with Aki… He *had* been blown up, right?

Reuben recalled the visceral feelings of his insides cooking and his skin splitting open. He shook his head. Had he imagined it all?

No, that was real. It had to be.

"There was a bomb..."

Wasn't there?

He was sure of it. That pain and the invisible wave of energy. Some kind of experimental weapon that cooked him from the inside, like in a sci-fi movie.

But now, here he was in his bedroom with his blankets, his furniture—even his computer running his Je Ne Sais Pas screensaver.

In the other room, his dad ran the police scanner like he did every morning. Some people needed coffee to start the day off right. Others liked workouts or meditation.

His dad preferred the morning's take on murder and mayhem.

OK, Reuben reasoned. *It was only a dream.* An astonishingly vivid one, but a dream nonetheless.

He sat up in bed and threw off the covers. At least he was alive. There was no bomb. The world more or less still existed.

Reuben wondered if asking Aki out the way he had in his dream would work. Maybe in real life he wouldn't do it so awkwardly. Perhaps he'd be super cool.

That was when he noticed the pizza box on the dresser. He'd ordered pizza a few nights ago, but he distinctly remembered breaking the box down and taking it out to the apartment dumpster.

Next to it was an unopened Amazon package.

"The curtains." He jerked his head to the window.

Not too long ago, the city had cut down the tree in front of his window. Now, the incoming streetlight light through the blinds kept him up all night. He'd ordered blackout curtains on Amazon, and they arrived Thursday night. He had spent most of Sunday morning hanging them, and it took him forever. He didn't have the right screws, and he'd had to make not one but two trips to the hardware store. His respect for Martha Stewart had grown exponentially that day, and all he had done was hang some stupid curtains.

Now the window had nothing but bare blinds.

The police scanner continued, *"The suspect has entered the Second Cup Café, and..."*

"Produced a pink baseball bat," Reuben quoted in unison. He froze. "What the hell?" He grabbed his Apple Watch off his nightstand and checked the date.

Reuben yelped loudly. "Saturday fucking February eleventh?"

What the fuck was going on?

Reuben's dad bellowed from the living room, "What the hell you yelling about in there?"

"Nothing, Dad," he replied.

Reuben's pulse quickened. Was he having a mental breakdown? He grabbed the Amazon package and ripped it open. Shrink-wrap still neatly sealed his fresh curtains.

He checked the date on the pizza box—February tenth at 7:30. He flipped it open. One slice remained. He picked it up and took a tentative bite. It was old but edible.

"Certainly not four days old," he mumbled.

"I'm not going to have to have you committed or anything like that, am I?" Reuben's dad called. "Talking to yourself; it's what happens when you sleep alone all the time. You get weird. It's not natural."

That was the last thing Reuben wanted to hear right now. Especially from a guy who yelled at police scanners.

"OK, Dad." Reuben stumbled into the other room and rubbed his face.

Whatever was going on, he needed to start this day. That meant getting his dad to take his meds. He sure as hell didn't need him to have another episode, especially when it looked like he was on the verge of one himself.

The sooner he could get that taken care of, the sooner he could start looking into his mental problems.

His dad sat by the living room window with a morning beer, running the police scanner at full volume. Reuben had taught him how to stream the police feed online, but Marshall Peet insisted on having an old-school police radio.

The living room was as spacious as any city apartment, with hardwood floors, plush orange couches, and a fifty-two-inch plasma TV that was powered off in a rare moment, sparing the room the talking heads on a twenty-four-hour news cycle.

Reuben was particularly grateful for this because if he was in some sort of personal sci-fi-slash-metaphysical experience, the last person he wanted to prove it to him was Bill O'Reilly.

Talk about a "no spin zone."

As Reuben stepped into the kitchen to make breakfast, he passed the frame on the wall. He felt a twinge of sadness over what had been. It was the Medal of Honor awarded to his dad when he was on the force. Next to that was another frame, a mounted Key to the City.

At one time, Marshall Peet had been a cop and a good one. That was before...everything.

"Don't make those damn hash browns, Mr. Hash Brown." Marshall scoffed. "They're shit. You always burn them."

"Don't call me that," Reuben barked. Only his mother had been allowed to call him "Mr. Hash Brown." Not much pissed Reuben off, but his dad calling him that did.

Marshall knew it, too. He waved his hands. "Yeah, yeah," he muttered as he turned back to the scanner.

Reuben considered the past three days, which was somehow the present again, looking for more clues. He remembered that hash browns had been Friday's breakfast experiment, and yes, they were a bad idea. His dad had thrown them out, and Reuben had taken them out with the trash on…

"Monday," Reuben recalled in a whisper.

He took the trash out only on weekdays because it coincided with his morning work routine. With a quick burst, he ripped open the freezer.

The hash browns were still there.

"Nothing like a little murder to start the day, huh?" Reuben had made this joke verbatim the first time he had lived through this day. He wanted to see his dad's reaction to the replay.

"Keeps you straight like V8." Marshall raised his beer to emphasize his comment. His face softened. "Just like when you were a kid, huh? You loved your V8." Then his eyes narrowed as though he remembered he was supposed to be an asshole and he added, "Not that you drink it now. Now, you're too good for V8, aren't you?"

Reuben's mouth dropped. That was the exact response he'd received the first time. He stared at his dad. Marshall paid no attention and instead studied the scanner as new information came in.

"I tell you," Marshall rambled, "these cops these days, they aren't even cops anymore. All these laws, political correctness, pussyfooting around. They don't do shit anymore. Underfunded. Undertrained. Outgunned. It's a shit show."

Reuben steadied himself against the counter. Sure, his dad had the same soapbox issues, but he'd heard this one word for word. He tried to focus on making breakfast. His dad had to have something with his meds, and Reuben needed to make sure he got them before he left. He grabbed some eggs and cracked them open over the skillet.

"They let these damn criminals go wild," Marshall continued. "They're babysitting all those criminals like they're entitled children. Too many criminal rights. Stick to the Mirandas and that's all you get, then lock 'em all up."

Reuben mouthed the last words with him as he sprinkled cheese into the sizzling pan.

"Innocent until proven guilty, Dad." Reuben ordinarily knew better than to interfere with Marshall's rambling. Still, if he was in some sort of time warp, could he change the events?

"Innocent until proven guilty," Marshall scoffed. "It's only a theory. You gotta have instinct, guts, and you gotta know how these sonsabitches think."

OK, Reuben thought, *I changed the order of things, but not the narrative.* Marshall would have gotten to the same rambling nonsense anyway.

He grabbed his dad's pillbox on the counter. He knew it was accurate because he tediously loaded the pills each week and kept up with them. Yep. It was on Saturday's dose.

"You need to eat something." Reuben handed Marshall a steaming plate of eggs and a glass of orange juice. He set the Saturday pills on the table.

Marshall growled. "I'll eat when I'm good and ready."

"Take your meds, Dad." Reuben set the plate down. "Please, humor me so I can get ready for work."

"State Department's working you on Saturday now?"

Reuben's face froze. No, they weren't. However, the CIA was. Not that his dad knew he worked for them. His dad was so unreliable, always blurting things he shouldn't. Reuben told him he worked for the State Department as his cover. Lying to his dad made him feel simultaneously like a real covert agent and guilty.

Still, there was a bigger issue at play. His dad was right. It was Saturday, and whereas many agents were working today, Reuben wasn't.

It was his day off.

He looked down at his clothes and realized that he'd gotten dressed for work, believing it was a weekday morning.

Instead of answering his father, Reuben silently transferred the remaining eggs to his plate.

"Moron." Thankfully, Marshall sat. "Computer science degree from Columbia, but can't remember what day to go to work."

Reuben sat at the table with him. For all of about two minutes, the Peet household had a pleasant family breakfast. Then Marshall grabbed the pills off the table. Reuben tensed and pretended to pay close attention to his eggs but watched Marshall in his peripheral vision. Reuben relaxed when Marshall washed the meds down with orange juice.

"I knew you were watching me," Marshall grumbled. "I told you to mind your own business."

Reuben gestured at his eggs with his fork. "I was eating my damn breakfast, Dad."

Marshall leaned back in his chair. "You don't have to babysit me like a goddamned two-year-old."

"Maybe I wouldn't have to if—" Reuben stopped himself before it turned into an argument.

"If what?"

"Never mind. Forget it."

"Yeah," Marshall muttered.

A silence passed between them, and all that they heard over the police scanner was the sound of forks scraping against glass plates.

"You know, you think you're so hotshot over there," Marshall sneered. "But it doesn't matter what you do up in that office. It's all going to end up in one giant shitstorm—"

"Of a nuclear explosion. You just watch," Reuben said.

"Hey." His dad looked at him, impressed. "You finished my thought. Not bad, kiddo. Maybe you don't have shit for brains after all."

Not that Reuben heard his dad's last jab. He simply couldn't stand it anymore. Either he was going crazy, or some weird shit was happening to him. Either way, he needed to find out. Where could he go for help? Who would believe him?

Then a thought hit him. He knew exactly who might.

Buzz.

Reuben jumped out of his chair and grabbed his keys and jacket.

"What?" Marshall yelled. "I'm sorry, did I insult your little sense of purpose and bruise your pussyfoot self-esteem?"

He bounded down the stairs outside his apartment two at a time. Reuben only wanted to get to Buzz. If anyone could help him get his head on right, it would be him.

Distracted by his mission, he didn't notice Patricia, the apartment owner, and Midge and Sheera at the bottom of the stairs on the sidewalk.

“Shit,” he muttered. Reuben turned to go back up the stairs, but they saw him when Patricia called his name. "Fuckity fuck fuck," he muttered, faking a smile as he submitted to the firing squad.

“Patricia.” Reuben’s voice oozed saccharine sweetness. “How’s the beagle?”

It was a known fact among the residents that they could easily evade any unpleasant conversation with Patricia with the topic of her prize-winning beagle, Bagel, who did somewhat resemble a bagel. However, he knew it wasn't going to work as the words came out of his mouth. After all, it hadn't worked the first time.

“Fine,” Patricia said through pursed lips. “That’s not what I want to talk about.”

Yep. This was unfolding as he remembered it with Midge and Sheera, the hot lesbian banker couple, standing with their arms crossed over their chests. Their eyes bored into Reuben, and he tried not to shudder. He racked his brain to figure out another way to steer the conversation.

“Look, Reuben,” Patricia reasoned in an even tone, “we all respect your father and what he’s done for this city.”

Reuben shifted his weight and held Patricia’s gaze. With big brown eyes and long red hair, in a blue pantsuit and flat black pumps, she was somehow barely shy of pretty. Maybe her nose was too big.

“When he saved those kids from that bus kidnapping…

What was that, fifteen years ago?" Patricia held her hand over her heart. "I was a schoolteacher back in those days, and I had two students who were part of that. He was a hero. None of us could thank him enough. You know all of this. You were on that bus, too."

"Right." Reuben checked his watch. He hadn't liked this little speech the first time he heard it. He liked it even less the second.

"That's why I was honored two years ago when the two of you moved in," Patricia continued. "But…"

Patricia faltered, and Midge blurted out, "He needs to be in a home. If he were my father, I'd get him some help."

Sheera grunted her agreement, and Patricia silenced them with an upraised palm.

"What we're trying to say here," Patricia offered, "is that your father's declining health is having an adverse effect on his ability to live peaceably within the general community."

Sheera snarled, "That's a nice way to put it."

The first time around he'd kowtowed, diverting his gaze and nodding in agreement. The first time he heard it, the comment caught him off-guard. This time, it pissed him off.

"Yeah?" Reuben scoffed and narrowed his eyes at her. "Enlighten me. How would you put it?"

"Oh, you think this is a big joke." Midge laughed mirthlessly, ran her hands through her hair, and turned away from Reuben. "I can't with them. I can't even. I just can't even."

"Unbelievable," Sheera replied. "Do you know what he was doing at two a.m.?"

Any other day, Reuben would have had an answer to that question. Given he had no idea when two a.m. in their reality coincided with two a.m. in his reality, he couldn't say one way or another.

"I'll tell you what he was doing." Sheera swished her hips and wagged her finger. "He was stomping around the floor in what had to have been a circle. I don't know where you were, but he was yelling, and I mean *yelling*, so loud about criminals and Democrats, and I don't even know what else. We could hear it through the windows."

"Before that, at, like, midnight," Midge added, "we had to turn up the TV to drown him out."

"Look." Midge turned back to Reuben. "He obviously has some kind of problem. Get the man some help. Because the rest of us around here would like to get some sleep."

Reuben held out a hand in a calming gesture. "I'll talk to him."

"It doesn't help." Sheera turned to Patricia. "We've heard this before."

Patricia let out a deep breath. "Reuben, I'm afraid if this doesn't stop, we're going to have to start the eviction process on you and your father."

"Oh, Jesus." Reuben rubbed his face. "He won't be a problem anymore. I'll do…*something*."

Even in repeat, he didn't have a good answer. When it came to Marshall Peet, no one ever had a good solution.

"Let's hope so," Midge retorted.

CHAPTER FOUR

Martha—Saturday, February 11, 6:01 a.m.

It was that damn sheep again. Martha lived outside NYC in a small one-bedroom flat in a quaint little subdivision fourteen train stops from work. It was as good a place to live as any. Good locale, cheap rent, low crime rate, lots of green spaces, peaceful.

Well, that was until the new neighbors had moved in with a pet sheep they kept in a shed in their backyard. Seriously, who kept a pet sheep? Martha groaned and rolled over in bed as the bleating got louder.

She glanced at the time bar on her phone.

"Six?" She groaned. "Come on, man." She had looked into the city ordinance about keeping livestock in residential areas. Unfortunately, it didn't consider one sheep as livestock. Couple that with her neighbors' claims that the animal was their support pet, and well, she didn't have a case.

Still, six a.m. on her day off? She was considering shooting the damn thing.

Normally she'd be at work at this time, but she was

nearing the end of her first year on the force, and she had a handful of "use them or lose them" vacation days piled up. It had been too short notice to plan an actual vacation, so she settled for a "staycation" where she could get a couple of extra hours of sleep. Was that too much to ask?

As if answering her question, the sheep got louder.

She moaned and piled pillows over her head. Upstairs, Mr. McClosky slammed open his patio door. McClosky had lost his mind in Vietnam and had been in the building since Reagan was president.

He yelled from the balcony above her window, "Shut that damn thing up, or I'll shut it up for you!"

"Yeah?" the neighbor taunted back in a thick Eastern European accent. "Why don't you come over and make me, tough guy?"

"I think I will!" Mr. McClosky bellowed back. "Just wait until I find my slippers and—"

"Slippers?" sneered his opponent. "Look here, you Hefner-wannabe reject. It's one hundred percent legal for my sheep to bleat."

"I'm gonna beat your ass!" Mr. McClosky retorted.

The two neighbors argued back and forth several minutes longer, and someone else joined the chorus. Meanwhile, the sheep kept bleating.

"Shit." Martha threw back the covers and rose. "I'm up."

She briefly thought about stopping the two from killing each other, but right then, their deaths would be an improvement.

She shook her head, chasing away the thoughts. "Uphold the law, Martha," she chided herself. "That's your job." She resolved that she'd keep an eye on them. If things escalated, she'd get involved.

Stumbling to the shower, she stepped over containers of the takeout she'd eaten in bed while watching *Jimmy Fallon* and the embarrassingly large pile of wrappers from the pre-Valentine's Day chocolates she'd bought herself. She scanned her DVD collection and tossed her extreme yoga workout case onto the wrapper pile.

"Nothing's better at inspiring fitness than National Singles Awareness Day," she declared.

She reached the shower and let the warm water invigorate her senses while she thought about the case she'd been tracking for the last several weeks.

She had multiple suspects in multiple cases, all of whom referenced "the Canadian" because he was super polite and used the word "eh" a lot. None of them knew anything more about him other than that he was the wizard behind the curtain. The more she looked for this guy, the bigger the legend seemed to get.

He was the money behind this or that operation. A voice through a burner phone. What made things worse was that somehow, he always made the evidence disappear.

As she toweled herself dry, Martha got ready to head over to her favorite place for breakfast, Gigi's Breakfast Café. She could always think there.

Looking at her wristwatch, she groaned. "6:40 on a Saturday morning." It would take her just a little bit more than twenty minutes to get there.

She'd muse over everything while having a coffee. Muse and make plans. Plans like how she was going to find this Canadian and nail his ass to the wall.

CHAPTER FIVE

Reuben—Saturday, February 11, 10:17 a.m.

Reuben's Uber pulled up to the brick mansion. There was a circular drive, a bird bath, and an immaculate garden.

Buzz was already outside.

Reuben didn't have many friends he kept in contact with to share his current predicament with. He had a childhood friend in the NY police department, but it had been a while since he'd spoken to her. Besides, there wasn't a chance she would believe him.

Now, Buzz, on the other hand...

Buzz Lugger was the single smartest person Reuben had ever met or even heard of. He was one of those whiz kids who finished high school at the age of twelve and had to wait until the minimum age of sixteen to go to college.

Buzz and Reuben had roomed together at Columbia. Buzz had turned out to be the type of student whose first day in class was usually the final exam. He did, however, graduate Magna Cum Laude with a triple major in engineering, robotics, and computer science.

He'd also authored three books his senior year. One on quantum physics, another on wormholes, and the third had been a surprisingly good erotic novel involving a mad scientist and a robot, titled *Love in Binary*.

Reuben knew it was only a matter of time until that one became non-fiction.

He was also the reason Reuben worked for the CIA.

Out of college, Buzz became the CIA's number one draft pick but turned the gig down, explaining to Reuben that the CIA's glory days were over. "At one time," he'd said, sipping on a beer in an empty bar near campus, "they were at the forefront of science and technology. Ever since the globalization of intelligence..."

Buzz had registered Reuben's disdain and quickly added, "They sold out. Now, it's all about all this Gestapo anti-terrorism. They've lost sight of really pushing science to its limits."

"So you turned down the CIA?" Reuben clarified.

Buzz shrugged. "They keep calling me." Buzz wagged his beer approvingly. "But NYU and their experimental physics lab is where my heart is at."

"Right." Reuben stared into his drink.

"So, tell me," Buzz had asked as he draped his arm around the back of his chair, "what offers have you got lined up for after grad?"

"Uh." Reuben had blushed. "Yeah, you know, I got MCC and all. I think I might do that."

"MCC?" Buzz's brow furrowed. "I haven't heard of them. What's that?"

"It's this, uh," Reuben had stammered, "groundbreaking experimental school. Junior college out in rural Wisconsin. They're looking for an assistant department chair for the technology department. A lot of growth potential, getting back to basics. The city, man, it pollutes the purity of science."

"Right on." Buzz had pursed his lips. "I like it. Experimental. Back to basics."

"Yeah. I think we've both, you and I, been given such a greenhouse experience in the technology field here in the city."

Buzz had stroked his chin as Reuben continued to talk. "This doesn't have anything to do with the fact that you don't have any other offers, does it?"

"What?" Reuben had jerked his head back. "No, of course not. I mean, you know, I've got a lot going on. Hitting the ground running. Strike while the iron's hot."

"Cool." Buzz had sipped his drink. "'Cause I got my recruiter from the CIA practically begging me to sign on. I could slip him your name, you know. See if he's interested. But if you're cool with your back-to-basics nature gig, that's cool, too."

"Well," Reuben had started but abruptly changed his tone. "Please, please, please. I don't want to move to Wisconsin. I'm fragile, and I hate cows."

Buzz had laughed hard and pulled out his phone. "All right. I'll call my recruiter right now."

Reuben recalled how he had rubbed his bloodshot eyes and tried to steady his slurred speech. "Right now? I mean…" He'd gestured toward their drinks. "We've been here a while."

"Relax," Buzz had said as he walked away from the bar. "You think no one at the CIA ever has a drink?"

Buzz had come back five minutes later with a smile on his face. "He's totally into you. He said he'll call you in the morning."

"Oh, my God. Thank you, man. You saved my life." Reuben

had meant it, too. He doubted he could survive rural Wisconsin.

"I did it for the cows."

And that was how Reuben Peet ended up as a tech operative for the CIA.

Now, he was about to see if his best friend could save him from whatever was happening to him again.

He found Buzz standing outside in a blue silk bathrobe and slippers. "Hey, Peet." At twenty-three, Buzz was thin and gangly, with light-brown hair that stuck up in odd places and wire-rimmed glasses too big for his face.

"Hey, there." Reuben greeted him with a hug. "God, it's good to see you. How long has it been?"

Buzz gave Reuben a worried look. "Oh man, this must be serious. You only ever greet me with platitudes when shit has really hit the fan," he said as they entered the house. "Tell me, what's going on?"

Reuben sighed. "I need a drink first."

CHAPTER SIX

Reuben—Saturday, February 11, 11:13 a.m.

Buzz's place took Reuben's breath away every time he walked in. High, vaulted ceilings with frescoes painted with what he was sure was gold leaf and winding staircases, plus marble floors. Buzz had bought it from some millionaire who'd received it in a divorce but then wanted to unload the emotional baggage.

"I'm custom-building my own place," Buzz told him. "Until then, this will have to do."

Reuben chuckled. "Well, at least it's furnished now."

Last time he was out here, the expansive office had taken over the great hall, and there was nothing else in the mansion.

He wasn't even sure where Buzz slept.

And to think all this wealth came from some proprietary 3-D imaging software Buzz had invented that nearly every modern video game console utilized. Not only had he received a windfall when he'd sold it, he received a royalty every time a consumer bought a video game.

Basically, he was set for life.

"Yeah." Buzz laughed. "I found that if you want to get in good with the ladies, they have to be comfortable. So, at the advice of my financial advisor, I called a decorator and asked her what makes ladies comfortable."

"And what did she say?"

Buzz gestured around the softly decorated living room. It was all tan and white and beige, with rugs so thick and plush Reuben could barely see his shoes. A chandelier glittered on low, while small lamps dotted the room, casting a soft and tender glow, and one hell of a well-stocked mini-bar. "She said it's a thing called layering and texturing, as well as strategic light placement."

"Hmmm." Reuben touched some of the couch pillows. They were comfortable, much more comfortable than his flat-bed pillows at home. "Strategic light placement gets you laid?"

Buzz handed Reuben a drink. "That's what she said."

Reuben sipped it and grimaced.

"So." Buzz sank into a beige leather couch. "Drink is in hand. Tell me what's on your mind?"

"Right." Reuben rested his elbows on his knees, then rubbed his palms together and studied Buzz. "Einstein..."

Buzz sipped his drink. "Uh-huh?"

"He wrote that time travel is theoretically possible," Reuben continued tentatively.

"Of course, child's play. It has to do with the properties of time. Mass. Gravity. Space. Time. They are all intricately connected—"

"Right, right," Reuben interrupted. "I got that part. But what if..." He scratched his head for a moment and tried again. "Have you ever heard of someone actually time traveling?"

Buzz rubbed his neck. "I'm... I'm not at liberty to say."

Reuben's eyes grew wide. "You mean it's actually happened?"

"I'm not at liberty to say," Buzz repeated and shifted uncomfortably.

"Fine." Reuben waved his palm dismissively. "I'm not trying to get you charged with treason or anything. But, OK, what if someone had an experience that was similar? Could you advise that person on what science actually knows about travel through time and space?"

Buzz leaned forward, suddenly interested. "What exactly are we talking about here?"

"Well, it's kind of metaphysical…"

"Metaphysical?" Buzz cleared his throat and took on an all-knowing tone. "Like what are we talking, mind-bending, or astral projection? Dissolution of mass that allows beings to walk through walls?"

"Sort of." *Walking through walls? That was happening? Never mind.* Reuben scratched his head, deciding to dive in. "You ever heard of …ahh…" He struggled for the words. "A personal time warp?"

"Time warps?" The side of Buzz's mouth rose in half-smile, and there was a faraway look in his eyes. "Like looping back on your own timeline?"

Reuben nodded.

Buzz frowned. "That's some trippy shit. I've never heard of it in our reality. But, some scientists postulate that it's possible."

"Really?" Reuben moved to the edge of his seat. "Who? What are they saying?"

"Well, it's mainly a cockeyed theory," Buzz said. "Mostly hacks. No one in the scientific community actually takes that seriously."

"What if I told you," Reuben lowered his voice, "that I might be in one?"

Buzz stared down at the floor in contemplation. "Well, it's not the wildest thing I've ever heard."

Reuben rubbed his face. This was going better than he expected. "At first, I thought it was a dream, but there are some things that happened. Things I know I can't explain."

"What do you mean by that?"

"Things that carry over from the dream world into our reality."

Buzz leaned forward. "Go on."

That was exactly what Reuben did. He told Buzz everything, starting Valentine's Day morning.

Buzz stopped him. "Wait, this year?"

"Yes."

"Fuck." Buzz blinked in shock and took a long sip of his drink. "Go on."

Reuben went through everything, sparing no details. The homeless guy, the Julian Schaeffer investigation, asking Aki out.

"So this Aki chick," Buzz interrupted. "She hot?"

"Fucking smoking hot as hell."

"Nice. Keep going."

"So I ask her out, she says yes, and I'm standing by the office window on the twenty-third floor. You know, quietly celebrating."

"You didn't make a fool of yourself, did you?"

"No, I actually kept my cool."

Buzz lifted his drink. "Impressive dude."

Reuben chuckled. "I know. I managed to not make a fool of myself. And then what happened? *Boom*. I died and looped back into myself three days earlier, give or take."

"And you're sure you weren't just stressed by this Julian investigation?" Buzz asked. "Had a headache and took the wrong combination of pills to ease it? Hallucinated the whole thing?"

Reuben shook his head. "Julian's a shitty skateboarder. No way he's behind any of this. My best guess is he's being set up by the real mastermind. That, or he's super unlucky. No stress."

"Still, investigating a possible nuclear threat. It's heavy shit. You sure this wasn't some lucid dream or something? You know how you get. The girl, the investigation. You're many things, my friend, but cool under pressure, not so much."

Reuben considered this. As much as he hated to admit it, Buzz was right. He did tend to catastrophize things a bit. Who was he kidding? Reuben was a master architect, capable of turning any hill into Mount Fucking Everest. See Exhibit A: talking to girls. "I don't know," he said, wanting to believe Buzz. It would make things easier. Maybe he did just dream it all. As for all the precog shit, maybe it was just dumb luck. After all, it wasn't like his life was filled with crazy variables. Marshall, Amazon orders—it was all fairly routine.

"Maybe," Reuben finally said. "But it all felt so *real*. I mean, when the explosion hit, it was like my blood started to boil, but my skin was still all there. It felt like it was drying out, and then...like...my whole body just turned to dust or something."

Buzz's mouth dropped open, "Sorry, say that again."

"It all felt so real."

"No, the part about your blood boiling."

"Yeah, I mean, literally it felt like my blood was bubbling inside me. I thought I was going to bubble over, that my skin would explode and I'd crack open like that fat guy in the Monty Python skit." Reuben shook his head, "Stupid me.

You're right. It was a dream. I mean, of course it was. Me and Aki. Ridiculous and—" Reuben looked up to see Buzz staring at him in utter shock. "Buzz? Why are you looking at me like that?"

"Fuck me up a peach tree," was all Buzz could manage.

CHAPTER SEVEN

Martha—Saturday, February 11, 12:12 p.m.

Martha sat at her cramped cubicle desk in the Precinct Four office, sipped yet another cup of coffee, and grimaced. She had successfully snuck in without being noticed by the captain and hadn't run into any of her fellow officers along the way.

After all, today was her day off. No sense in raising any alarm bells.

What the captain doesn't know won't hurt him or me.

Rubbing her face, she stared bleary-eyed at the same information.

She replayed the interrogation video. She had to put headphones on so she could turn up the volume in the tiny space. A paunchy man in his mid-fifties, covered head to toe in tattoos, sat at a table in a dreary room. He had been charged with the murder of a teenage prostitute and had no real chance of a defense. The only thing he could do now was lessen his sentence by giving information.

In the video, Martha got in close. "Who was it that ordered the hit?"

"I don't know." The suspect sighed. "I told you, it was just some guy who calls himself 'the Canadian.' Everyone else calls him that too. Heck, even the CIA probably calls him that. They probably got oodles of files on him. The way he walks and talks, he's a big deal."

"The Canadian?"

"Yes." His impatience was clear. "That was the only name I ever got from him. We communicated by disposable phones. Phones would just show up in my house, or workplace, or even on my person without me knowing. Then the phone would ring. I would answer it, and he identified himself as the Canadian. I don't know anything else."

Martha stopped the video and went back through the police database again. This was the fifth suspect who had named the Canadian, and there was no one that suggested an actual name of the sort. No first name. No last name.

Just "the Canadian."

How many Canadians were there in New York City? Was she going to have to cross-reference all of them?

She leaned back in her chair. "It could literally mean anything. Where should I even start?"

A young voice spoke up from across the divide. "What?"

She whipped her head around to see Zach, the new kid who looked so young he still had a curfew, pop up like a meerkat over his cubicle wall.

The intern had a fresh-faced smile and a blue coffee mug that read, *Serve and Protect,* and was every bit of the eager wannabe that made real cops want to vomit their Krispy Kremes.

He'd helped her clear a few cases a month back. He was

good. Capable and dependable. But sometimes, she couldn't handle his energy.

Martha gave him an incredulous look.

"I thought you might want some assistance," he offered.

"I'm fine." She wasn't about to accept help from someone greener than her. No way.

"Are you sure?" he insisted. "Because your body language cues are off the charts. You're showing every sign of experiencing frustration and physical fatigue. I've been taking that Reading Body Language course in the precinct training materials. I'm up to part five on that. Man, there is some good stuff. Everyone needs to take those tutorials."

Christ almighty. This kid needed a tranquilizer.

"So we're on the same team here," he said. "What can I do to help?"

Martha rolled her eyes before a thought hit her. "You know what? See what you can find on the alias 'the Canadian.'"

"The Canadian?" Zach repeated. "Sounds pretentious and seriously *un*dangerous."

Martha sighed. "I don't know about either of those things. This guy is an elusive crime boss that no one has ever seen."

"What do we know about him?" Zach leaned against the wall between them and sipped his cup.

Martha popped her back. What the hell? It couldn't hurt to verbally process with the kid. "So far, we know that he's had five people murdered or maimed. His M.O. is to communicate by disposable phone, and no one has ever heard his voice. He, or I guess it could be she, types into a computer and has it speak over the phone for him. He has assistants slip disposable phones into people's pockets or houses for him to call, and then the phone is destroyed."

"Are there any similarities between the phones?" Zach asked.

Martha raised an eyebrow. This kid was better than she gave him credit for. "We've confiscated two Nokia 2720s. But they were wiped before we could analyze the data."

"How many places around here sell those?"

Martha shook her head. "I asked tech for stocking manifests weeks ago. Still haven't heard back."

"Ahh, those guys are losers." Zach came over into her cubicle. He clicked around on the laptop he brought with him. "Besides, that's too broad."

"If you think I didn't try an internet search, you're sadly mistaken," Martha told him. "I did, and found nothing."

Zach swiveled the screen around so Martha could see it. "The five crimes were all committed in this ten-mile radius."

"Uh-huh." Both she and Zach studied the screen. A green-shaded circle highlighted the area.

Martha grabbed the mouse from Zach. "This is just an idea. It might not pay off, but then again, it might. I wonder how many places within *that* radius sell a Nokia 2720."

Zach nodded. "Well, he could have bought them online."

Martha shook her head. "If so, he probably would've used a fake name and credit card. Also, one of the suspects we interrogated mentioned a generic convenience store sticker on his burner phone. Our best bet is to check sellers within that area."

She ran a function that pulled up all the retailers licensed to sell the old, largely discontinued phone within the radius and printed out a report. She handed one page to Zach and took the other. "Just because they're licensed doesn't mean they still carry them. Call them and find out if they have that phone. If they do, try to unearth anything else you can. We need to narrow this down to shoddy places only."

"Got it," he said as he scurried away.

Martha called him back before he left the room. "Oh, and if the captain asks, I'm not here."

An hour later, Zach returned with a report.

Not bad, Martha thought as she read it, her hand hovering over the phone.

She was just about to start dialing when she heard raucous laughter down the hall. Looking up, she saw the other guys on her squad all bunched up in a group.

Tom was in the center of the group, telling some story or other while the others hung onto every word. "So finally, I told the guy, 'Well, if I arrest the ghost, will that help?' And the dude was totally into it. So, I asked him where the ghost was, and he pointed to the kitchen. So, I stood in the kitchen and cuffed the air and led the ghost outside to the car. The dude thanked me and everything."

All the guys laughed again.

She considered walking over but hesitated. She wasn't just a rookie. She was also the only *lady cop* rookie on the floor.

Besides, Jake was there, and that guy was the epitome of intimidation. A decorated Marine veteran, super-nice, and sexy as hell. Martha always stuttered like a schoolgirl around him.

Tom noticed her watching. "Hey, Dragone." He nodded in her direction. "You solved a crime yet?"

She'd made plenty of arrests and solved more than her

share of crimes in her eleven months on the squad. But it was no use explaining herself to those guys. She just smiled.

One of the other officers, a burly man named Dwayne, waved a meaty finger in her direction. "You gotta earn your stripes around here. Maybe then we'll get you a real desk."

They all laughed, and Martha just shook her head. It didn't matter what she did; she would always be the woman. She got on the phone and started calling stores.

"Hi, I'm looking for a disposable phone and wondered if you sold them."

"No," a snobby voice on the other end replied. "Get off probation, loser."

Click.

"Asshole," she muttered.

She powered through the report, disguising her voice so that it sounded less police-like and more discrete, like that of a criminal with something to hide. She hit dead end after dead end. Somewhere near the middle of the page, she got to a dry cleaner called Mr. Sudds.

A dry cleaner selling phones? This had to be a mistake.

But Zach was thorough, so she called the number listed on the report. It was disconnected. She was about to give up and go to the next listing when she overheard Zach arguing on the phone.

"No," he insisted. "I need a Nokia 2720. It's very important. Well, could you have someone look on the shelf? Yes, Nokia 2720… Thank you… No, I'll hold..."

Inspired and somewhat one-upped by Zach's dedication, Martha ran a quick online search for Mr. Sudds. She found no website, but a couple of customer review sites detailed terrible customer service, dirty facilities, and cheap prices, and one review graphically recounted a mugging that happened in the store.

Zach's cell phone buzzed, and Martha glanced over the cubicle wall at him. He held his work phone to one ear and his cell phone to the other. "Yes, Wal-Mart, thanks for calling me back," he spoke into the cell, awkwardly holding up both phones with his shoulders while he grabbed a pen. "Were you able to find one? So you don't have it... Yeah, I'm sure Amazon would be the best bet. Thanks for trying."

Martha continued to browse Mr. Sudds' reviews and then ran across one that mentioned buying a disposable phone. She scanned the rest of the reviews and found no further mention of phone service.

"Zach," she mouthed. "I'm leaving. Keep up the search."

Zach nodded, still on hold, and Martha grabbed her jacket and left. She didn't know if this Mr. Sudds was anything, but she was going to check it out.

"Officer Dragone," her captain Ken Kenneth called.

"Fuck," Martha muttered. She was caught. She turned to face her captain.

Ken Kenneth was in his late forties. He looked like he had at one time been muscular. Years of working a desk job had made him out of shape, but not quite overweight. He had a receding blond hairline and sharp blue eyes that suggested if she had met him twenty years ago before he discovered mustaches and middle management, he would have been quite the heartthrob.

Right now, he stood with his hands on his hips, and his eyes registered pure business.

"What the hell are you doing here on your day off?" he demanded.

"Nothing, Captain. I just missed the gang, you know."

He wasn't buying her bullshit. "Aha, sure. This wouldn't have anything to do with the Canadian?"

Martha pursed her lips and shrugged.

"Where are we on this case, anyway?" he asked.

This was interesting. Maybe the Captain was at least open to her thoughts. "He's elusive, sir, but I've got a couple of leads I'm following."

The side of his lip rose in displeasure, and he looked right past her. "How many man-hours are we putting in on this?"

"Sir, I assure you, I've got this. I can find this guy; I'm right on the verge of a breakthrough."

He raised his eyebrows dismissively. "You're not a detective. You're a beat cop. I need you out on the beat."

"I know, sir. I just need a little bit more time."

"Very little time."

"Thank you, sir." She turned to walk away.

"Dragone." His voice had a contemplative tone.

"Yes, sir?"

"Just so you know, this does count as a vacation day. Last thing I need is HR on my ass because you never take a day off."

"Day off? Crime doesn't take a day off."

"It sure doesn't." He chuckled. "But you're a pretty little lady. Why don't you let the boys around here take the lead for a little while? Go to a spa and get one of those fancy hot stone massages or something? My wife likes those; it relaxes her."

Martha suppressed a sigh. "I appreciate the offer. But I take my work here very seriously. Even on my day off, which, for the record, today is."

The captain raised an eyebrow. "I like that attitude. Either get this thing wrapped up or pass it up the ladder. We need you out on the beat."

She nodded. "Absolutely, sir."

There was no way she was passing this up the ladder.

Martha grabbed a cab and booked it back to her apartment. She needed a credible reason to check out this Mr. Sudds place.

She needed laundry.

Arriving home, she lamented how small her apartment was. So tiny she could use a beach towel as wall-to-wall carpeting.

She had moved here right after she got back from Afghanistan but had never even so much as hung a picture or bought new furniture.

She never told people about her Afghanistan years because it implied something it wasn't. Originally from Virginia, she'd studied art history in college. She found out very quickly after graduation that there was no real career path for that. After a string of entry-level jobs, she'd signed up to work with a global trucking company that ran routes in Afghanistan.

Death would be preferable to taking orders from her new supervisor, whose role models included pop stars with an affinity for cupcake bras and whipped cream-shooting tits.

Rosie the Riveter would be proud.

The job in Afghanistan had nothing to do with the war. But given that it was entirely possible to die in a minefield explosion during a day's work, the pay was through the roof. She made good money, stayed in Afghanistan for a few years, and narrowly evaded death a few times. When she got back home, she missed the adrenaline rush and moved to New York for a career in law enforcement. Now, she was finding the boys' club at NYPD to be a lot harder to navigate than she'd thought. Apologies to Rosie. Maybe a cupcake bra would help.

Martha sifted through the laundry. Her wardrobe consisted of t-shirts, jeans, tank tops, sweatpants, and work uniforms. She finally found a crumpled cotton dress in the bottom of a basket.

"Here we go." She smiled as she shook it out.

It was a black-and-white floral print that she'd bought on clearance. It looked great with combat boots whenever she backtracked to her hipster, art nerd days at UVA. But, when did she have a chance to do that? About a year ago, she'd gone out with a guy who'd tried to impress her by taking her to an art show. She'd fallen asleep.

Martha changed out of her work uniform, stuffed the dress into her bag, and ran downstairs to catch a cab. She didn't know what she might find at Mr. Sudds, but she was out of time on the Canadian case.

She needed to come up with something fast.

CHAPTER EIGHT

Martha—Saturday, February 11, 1:46 p.m.

Mr. Sudds was a corner shop in a seedy part of town. It was a brick storefront building with black burglar bars guarding the grimy windows and the glass door, all of which looked like it hadn't been cleaned in over a year.

The words, Mr. Sudds $1.00 cleaners, were painted in shoe-polish red, and a neat, finger-sized hole that could only be attributed to a bullet glared out of the bottom of the door.

Martha opened the door and a loud bell announced her entrance. The odor was the first thing that greeted her. The whole place smelled like a gas station bathroom. She noticed a wide-open door to the unisex restroom right near the entrance.

In the lobby, the speckled linoleum was chipped and cracked in many places. Three plastic chairs sat against one wall. A pea-green plastic counter with a manual cash register filled up the rest of the lobby.

At the sound of the bell, a wide-eyed man emerged from the back room. He was probably in his early fifties, with stringy dark hair hanging to the middle of his neck. The top of his head was completely bald.

He smiled when he saw Martha. "How can I help you?" His voice was low and raspy.

She pulled the dress out of her bag and shook it out. "I need to get this cleaned."

She held out the garment, and he took it with a quizzical expression.

"It'll cost you $1.00," he told her with a puzzled look.

"Great. I've got a date tomorrow night. I need this taken extra special care of."

He shrugged and grabbed a hanger. "It'll be ready after four."

"All right." She scanned the lobby quickly and didn't see any evidence of a phone. "Oh, I almost forgot. Do you sell phones?"

He frowned, set the dress on the counter, and leaned on his big meaty knuckles. "What does this look like, a Verizon?"

"Uh, I just heard you sell them," she stammered. "I need it for something I'm doing, and I thought I'd ask."

He studied her. "What are you doing?"

She was acutely aware that he hadn't said "no" yet. "I've got a lot of clients. One's gotta protect one's privacy, you know."

"Hmm." He narrowed his eyes. "What kind of clients?"

The creepy way he stared at her made her skin crawl. But, it was just the kind of lead she wanted. She said a silent Hail Mary to Rosie the Riveter, leaned over the counter, and let her cleavage show. "Oh, you know…"

She didn't finish the sentence, but he smiled and clearly took in the view. Then he reached under the counter and twirled a Nokia 2720 flip phone in his dirty fingers.

"These old phones are hardly on the market anymore.

Totally untraceable. Sell for a premium these days. I only have one left. My personal one, but I could give it to you if you give me something in return."

She was still leaning over the counter, letting him see what he wanted. "And what would that that be, exactly?"

"Dinner, drinks. Tonight."

Martha leaned in closer. "Tonight is no good. I've already got plans. Next weekend, however, I could do that." She fingered the phone in his hand. "After all, you'll have my number."

He smirked, and in a slow, deliberate move, he pushed the phone into her bra, his hand giving her breast a firm squeeze on exit. "You have a nice day, Miss…" He looked at her expectantly.

"Rosie," she said as she stood and pulled the phone out of her shirt.

"Rosie," he repeated. "The dress will be ready after four."

"I'll see you then," she said as she turned to leave.

"I bet you will." She saw him unashamedly stare at her ass in the reflection in the window.

She left Mr. Sudds and checked out the alley beside the shop. She saw a white van with a giant marijuana leaf on it. Several crates sat around it, waiting for loading.

Now, this was suspicious.

Not seeing anyone around, she stepped closer to inspect it. There were several crates already in the cab of the van, all labeled with various chemicals for cleaning.

Outside of the sheer volume and the fact that the van was oddly marked, there was nothing out of the ordinary. Maybe this was a delivery van supplying the entire area.

Weed and cleaning supplies. Sounds like quite the niche market, she mused.

Then she saw that one of the crate's latches was busted. She glanced around—still no one—so she hopped inside the van. The inside of the van was grimy and dank, with hand tools and dirty rags.

She stepped around old trash to inspect the busted crate. "Sheets of metal mesh? What the fuck?" she whispered.

"Hey!"

Martha jumped as she heard the shout.

A well-built man who was probably in his early forties was pointing at her. He was wearing a white hoodie with stripes on the shoulders. As soon as their eyes connected, the man said, "Fuck, you're early."

"Excuse me?" The man looked familiar, but Martha couldn't quite explain it. He reminded her of a friend of hers who she'd known since grade school, only older and with a giant scar on his face.

She jumped out of the van to confront him. But before she could get a chance, he pushed her hard to the ground. Without a word, he spun and started running.

With a quick hip flex, she got to her feet and ran after him. For a guy with his kind of bulk, he was fast.

She chased him for several blocks, but when she was sure she had lost him, she stopped, leaning over on her knees to catch her breath.

"Fuck," she muttered. "Fuckity fuck fuck fuck!" She couldn't shake the feeling that she knew him from somewhere.

She returned to Mr. Sudds, but the van was already gone. Either the perp doubled back quickly, or someone else moved it. Either way, her lead was gone.

But not totally evaporated.

She had confirmed two vital facts. One, Mr. Sudds sold the

Nokias, and, two, they were definitely up to something. Although what was up with the metal mesh, she didn't know.

Hailing a cab, she pulled out her phone as she got in and called Zach. As she waited for him to answer, she scrolled through the recent call list on the Nokia, seeing only one phone number. Aha!

"Hello?" Zach answered.

"Zach, I think we have a winner with Mr. Sudds. I noticed an ATM across the street. Can we pull up the CCTV footage for the last two weeks? Also, run a check on this phone number." She gave him the number.

The phone went silent as Zach did his thing. A few minutes later, he said, "The number is for an office building lobby. Some food distribution company. Mostly imports from Canada. As for the CCTV footage, that's going to take some time."

She'd expected as much. "Cool, I'm on my way back to the precinct. See where you can get on the CCTV footage."

"Will do, Chief," Zach said, hanging up.

Chief, huh? she mused. She really liked the sound of that.

CHAPTER NINE

Martha—Saturday, February 11, 3:13 p.m.

Martha arrived back at the police station, and Jake was the first to greet her. Jake was the very definition of tall, dark, and handsome. He was ex-Marine and could probably still run circles around military recruits. His hair was short and close-cropped, and his brown eyes glinted with intensity.

Although he could be hard on her, Jake was one of the only officers she knew that truly valued her insight and grit. He was a good man, and she was glad he was on her side. They were often partners when out on patrol.

"The captain wants to know everything you've got on the Canadian," were Jake's first words. "We're going in on this guy, or we're pushing it up to the investigative unit."

"I'm not pushing this up the ladder." *Hey, I didn't sputter,* she remarked to herself with pride. This wasn't the first time the captain or Jake had told her to 'send it up the ladder.' "Why the sudden interest? Before it was all, 'you're wasting your time.' Now I got the great and all-powerful Jake bugging me." She was finding her courage now.

"Great, yes. All-powerful, hardly." Jake rested his hands on his hips. "Look, Martha, I know you want to be a great cop. I know the guys around here don't make it any easier."

Martha rolled her eyes. "Who said that? I don't need a teacher coming in and—"

"I'm not blind," he interrupted. "These guys are tough. I get it. You want off the Tampon Squad."

Martha held up a hand. "The what, now?"

Jake cracked a smile and stared down at his boots. "I've known these guys for years. They're real good guys once you get to know them, but they can also be massive assholes. We all can. It's an occupational hazard."

Martha snorted. "I don't need your pity, Jake."

"Good, 'cause you don't have it. But what you do have is my experience. You're a rookie, and you're in over your head. Your ego won't let you admit it. It happens to all of us. But you've got to know when to stop."

She folded her arms. "Thank you for the advice, but I'm not in over my head."

He raised an eyebrow and cocked his head. "As to your second question, the reason we're into it now is because of what happened at the border."

"What happened at the border?" she asked.

"Not now," Jake told her. "First, let's get into your notes and see if there's anything there."

"Let's." She led the way to her cubicle and sat at her computer.

Jake stood against the wall and rested his wrist over the top. She could smell his cologne and tried not to let it distract her.

Next to her, Zach pounded away on his computer. As soon as he saw Martha, he gave her a smile that said he had something. Martha shot him a look that said, 'Later,' and to her pleasant surprise, he got it.

Sitting down, she turned to Jake and said, "This is what I've got on the Canadian."

He peered at her screen as she showed him the map. "These are the five places where the related crimes were committed."

"Right." He pointed to crime scenes and recalled the victims' names. "Salinas, Gutierrez."

"Overland, Roberts, and Matthews," they both recited in unison.

"Exactly," Jake agreed. "We know these are all connected because they all have suspects that mentioned..."

"The Canadian," Martha and Jake said together.

Martha smiled. "Now, we know that the Canadian communicates through disposable phones. We confiscated the ones in the Salinas, Matthews, and Roberts cases. They all used the same type of phone."

"Really?" Jake pursed his lips. "I wasn't aware of that."

"Nokia 2720, a disposable flip phone." She brought up the five-mile retail radius map. "These are all the retailers within that ten-mile radius. We figured he was buying loads of them, one for every conversation."

"OK," Jake didn't seem convinced, but Martha kept going.

"Mr. Sudds." She moved the cursor to a point on the map. Then she produced the Nokia from her pocket and tossed it on the desk. "They're a dry cleaner's that sells phones under the table for under-the-table deeds."

Jake looked impressed. "How do you know that?"

"He only gave me the phone once he was under the distinct impression that I needed it for 'clients.'"

Jake raised an eyebrow at her euphemism.

"And check this out..." She flipped open the phone and pulled up the number. "That's to the building of a major food distribution company. A company that distributes maple syrup."

"Fuck me," Jake said, running his hands through his hair. "The border crossing..."

"Excuse me. I ain't fucking anyone," Martha quipped.

Jake ignored her. "You want to know why we're suddenly interested in the Canadian? On Wednesday the eighth, up at the border, there was a shootout with local PD and a bunch of truck drivers smuggling...ahh...maple syrup."

Martha frowned. "Maple syrup? That's the border shit you were talking about?"

Jake nodded.

"Who gives a fuck about maple syrup?" she asked.

"When a cop is killed because of it, everyone."

Martha couldn't believe what she was hearing. The Canadian had to be involved in the shootout. He had to be. There was a dead cop on the line. That meant the brass would be on everyone's asses to get him. Right now, Martha had the biggest lead.

She had wanted to fly under the radar on this, solve it herself, but with everything, this was too close to keep to herself.

She called Zach over, and he sheepishly approached. "What did you find out?"

"In front of him?"

Damn, Zach was loyal. She was starting to like the kid. "Yes, please."

"OK, but you're not going to believe this." He sat and opened his laptop. "I retrieved the CCTV footage from the ATM across the way. This guy shows up."

He fast-forwarded to a guy wearing a hoodie with stripes on the shoulders, his face covered by his hood. Next to him stood another man in a fedora. His face was also hidden from the camera, but not because he was being slick. He was just being annoyingly fashionable.

Next to them was the same van with the marijuana leaf on it. "Holy shit, I saw that van earlier today. That hoodie guy is the asshole who knocked me over."

Jake shook his head. "So what? Delivery vans would show up all the time."

"Not with scarred assholes who hit first and ask questions later," Martha insisted.

"Dude hit you?" Jake raised a concerned eyebrow.

"More like knocked me down, but yes, he didn't want to engage. And he said I was 'early,' whatever that meant."

"Another wacko?" Jake suggested.

Martha shrugged, turning back to the screen. "What else do you got?"

Zach fast-forwarded the footage again. "They chat for about ten minutes, then the hoodie guy hands the other one a burner phone."

"Nokia?" Martha asked.

Zach nodded. "Yep. Then go their separate ways. Hoodie Guy on foot, Fedora Guy gets in a fancy car."

"Did you get the license plate?" Jake asked.

Zach shook his head. "Couldn't get a good shot of it, but I did manage to follow them both using other CCTV cameras around the city. The Hoodie Guy disappears two blocks later."

Martha pressed her lips together. "You think he got lucky?"

Zach laughed at the thought. "No way. No one is that lucky. With those stripes on his shoulders, he ought to stand out. No, either he knew where the CCTV cameras were and ghosted us, or he time-traveled or some shit like that. Now, Fedora Guy, he wasn't so slick. Watch."

The feed followed Fedora Guy's car through the city for about fourteen blocks until it stopped in front of a fancy investment skyscraper with an overblown modern sculpture out front and out stepped Fedora Guy, sans fedora.

"Fuck me," Martha said.

Jake winked and said, "I ain't fucking anyone."

"No." Martha almost didn't believe what she'd seen. "Do you know who that is?"

Jake leaned in to take a closer look. "No."

"That's Alister Pout, the Canadian tech investor and creator of RedBook."

Jake looked at her in disbelief. "No way. No way Alister Pout is the Canadian?"

"He is," Zach confirmed. "I checked."

Martha nodded. "We need to find more proof. Right now, all we have is him visiting a shady place."

Jake shook his head. "For all we know, this guy in the hoodie is his weed dealer. You're going to need a lot more to even open a file on a guy like Pout."

Martha rubbed her temples, groaned, and pounded the desk. "When is there room in police work for instinct?"

Jake stiffened. "There's instinct, and there's insanity. We have to stick to the facts and do the job right. If that doesn't work for you, then you're in the wrong line of work."

"Sorry." Martha felt herself blush and then sat up straighter in her chair.

Jake lowered his voice and forced a smile. "What do you want to do?"

That was an easy question. "I want to track Alister."

Jake cleared his throat. "You aware of what you're taking on, right?"

"We're just watching the guy," Martha reasoned. "We're not issuing a warrant or anything."

Jake thought about it for a moment, then nodded. "OK. What have you got on that?"

Martha turned to Zach. "Zach, what do you have?"

Zach handed Jake a printout. "These are all his engagements over the next three days."

Jake read the printout, then passed it to Martha. "How do you want to narrow this down?"

She scanned the page. "He's not going to make any underhanded meetings publicly available. So, we block off these times and find out where he goes the rest of the time."

Jake studied the ceiling, deep in thought. "The easiest way to do that would be to monitor the surveillance footage from outside his office during this time. We can follow him through most of the city streets, and it will give us an idea of how to give Investigations a better lead."

"I'm not pushing this up the ladder," Martha reminded him.

"With what little you've got," Jake shook his head, "you damn well should."

Jake left with the printout, and Martha buried her face in her hands. She was definitely taking those vacation days. But she wasn't getting a hot stone massage.

She was going to catch herself a bad guy.

CHAPTER TEN

Reuben—Saturday, February 11, 9:00 p.m.

Reuben rubbed his temple around the sensors on his forehead while Buzz clicked around on a laptop. "Are we done yet?" Reuben asked.

Over the last hour and a half, Buzz had hardly spoken to Reuben as he ran a myriad of experiments using equipment that no home should have: MRI scans, blood screening, ultrasounds, and a weird machine that looked like a toy version of the Swiss Hadron Collider.

Even CIA check-ups were less thorough.

"I mean, what's the big deal? I thought you said it was most likely a vivid dream or something."

Buzz responded with a distant, "Um, hmm…" That was the same response he had given Reuben the last twenty times he'd asked.

"Should I be worried?"

"Aha…" Buzz pulled out another needle, presumably to draw more blood.

Reuben shook his head. "If you aha me one more time, I

swear to God, I'll scream. I think I've been a good sport the last four times you prodded me. No more needles, Not until I get some answers."

Buzz shook his head. "If what you experienced actually happened, then you didn't die by a nuclear explosion. You died by microwave incineration."

Reuben's head was still fuzzy. "Like a hot pocket?"

Buzz sighed and sat, looking very disappointed in Reuben. "It's something you wouldn't know anything about. It's not knowledge disseminated among the proletariat. Basically, to break it down...let's see..."

Buzz stared at the ceiling and pursed his lips. He crossed his ankles and shook his foot as he thought deeply. "To break it down, a microwave will accelerate water molecules so fast that they evaporate." Buzz's tone indicated his irritation that he had to leave out so much detail to be understood by the common folk. "That's exactly what you described. The water in your body, and your cells, boiling away."

"Well, that's not so complicated."

"Yeah...not at all. Still very specific. And unusual."

Reuben pushed away his agitation with Buzz's characteristic know-it-all attitude. He needed Buzz, and his arrogance went with him. The best way Reuben had found to deal with Buzz's ego was to feed it. That wasn't difficult in this case because he was genuinely lost on this one.

Reuben cracked his neck. "I mean, how do you know it was a genuine experience? What if I actually saw that on a science show, or heard it in some intel briefing at work and just filed it away, and then it seeped into my subconscious and expressed itself in my dreams?"

Buzz made a face. "It's possible, but not probable. There is a difference in the way the brain recalls experiences versus the way it recalls things we've learned. The things you've recalled relate to your experience. Talking to Sven Larson about Julian Schaeffer was an experience. But your thoughts are different. Besides, your blood has withstood three simulated temporal shifts. That shouldn't be possible."

Reuben frowned in confusion. "Simulated?"

Buzz pinched the bridge of his nose. "Here, let me show you." Turning the needle on himself, he drew a few milliliters of his own blood. "If I put my blood—normal blood—into this capsule and run it through this machine, watch what happens."

He squirted his blood into a plastic test tube and placed it in the mini-Hadron collider.

Reuben narrowed his eyes. "What is that?"

"It's something I threw together to simulate the effects of a wormhole."

"So, it's not a toy Hadron collider?"

Buzz tilted his head in confusion. "No? Why would I need one of those?"

Reuben shrugged. "I don't know. Why would you need to simulate a wormhole in your own home?"

Buzz chuckled. "Good point. But given what may or may not be happening to you, you'll be glad I have this." He turned the machine on. Like the last time, it hummed for about six seconds before he turned it off. Buzz pulled out the vial. "What do you see?"

Reuben held up the vial. It looked empty. Impossibly clean, actually. "Nothing."

Buzz pointed at him. "Exactly. Every time I run organic material through that thing, the result is always the same. It disappears."

"Where does it go?"

Buzz shrugged. "Another dimension, a parallel universe, back in time, forward…a hell dimension? I don't really know." Buzz took the vial back then pulled out another needle. He jabbed it into Reuben's arm. "Yet. But when I do, Nobel Prize, here we come. You can be my plus one."

Buzz extracted another five milliliters of blood from Reuben and squirted it into the vial. Then he ran it through the machine.

He pulled out the vial and handed it to Reuben. "Now, what do you see?"

Reuben saw his blood in the damn thing. "What the fuck? My blood didn't disappear." He was both comforted and troubled by this. On the one hand, his blood hadn't disappeared into some unknown hell dimension. On the other, his blood being there meant he was a freak. "What does this mean?"

"I don't really know," Buzz said. "I need to run more tests."

Reuben rubbed the sore spots on his temples from Buzz's sensors. He thought back to everything that happened. It was all so strange, but then he remembered one odd event that had been lost in the shuffle of weirdness that was his life. He snapped his fingers, recalling the event. "What about the homeless guy and what he said? Can he time warp, too?"

Buzz shrugged. "Maybe. But there is a theory proposed by Dr. Patrick Ness that schizophrenia is really just the mind experiencing things that defy natural laws. While that's a bit on the extreme side, it is possible that the homeless guy's schizophrenia isn't schizophrenia at all, but rather him remembering the future. He doesn't actually warp back in time like you do, but he does retain some fuzzy memory of what had happened to him. You could see how that might mess with someone's mind."

Reuben dropped his hands. "Whoa."

Buzz nodded. "Yeah. If this is the case, then people like that homeless man don't have powers like you. When you die, you go back, and everything essentially resets. Also, you are able to come to terms with what the reset date and time is. But someone like him just remembers bits and pieces of the forgotten timeline like some terrible dream." Buzz considered this. "You must feel like a real shithead for resetting things and confusing the hell out of people like him."

Reuben still had issues with the idea. "But he was like this before my first time warp. Does that mean there are others like me?"

Again Buzz shrugged. "Maybe. But so far, my best theory is that this is a genetic anomaly. If I'm right, then you can't be the only one. But you might be one in a billion. Hell, ten-billion, even. A hundred billion. That would mean you are the only one in several generations."

"Like Buffy, 'there is one every generation.'"

Buzz shook his head. "No, you're one in several generations. Look, I don't have many answers yet. Like I said, I need to run more tests."

After another hour of experiments, tests, and numerous additional needles, Reuben's stomach growled. "Got any food?"

Buzz didn't look up from his microscope. He just yelled, "Rosa," so loud that Reuben jumped.

An older Hispanic woman appeared in a black-and-white maid uniform. "Yes, Mr. Buzz?"

"Really, Buzz?" Reuben tilted his head in judgment. "A maid?"

Buzz grinned from ear to ear. "When you're as rich as I am, it's a nice perk."

"Reuben would like something to eat," Buzz told Rosa.

"Yes, Mr. Buzz. Pizza, pasta, sushi, hotdogs?" She rattled off the menu at an almost inhuman rapid pace.

"Pizza," Reuben finally interjected, happy just to get anything.

Rosa nodded. "Margarita, pepperoni, pepperoni and mushroom, pepperoni and pineapple..."

"Pepperoni," Reuben interjected. "Just pepperoni is fine."

Another nod. "Soda?"

"No, thank you," Reuben said before she could start rattling off another list.

"That will be all," Buzz said, still not looking up. "Thank you, Rosa."

Rosa disappeared, and Reuben laid back on the couch and rubbed his face. "I can't believe you have a fucking maid. I don't even have my own place, and you have a goddamn maid. What is there even for her to do all day?"

Buzz didn't look up. "You know, I don't really know."

Reuben chortled, and Buzz clicked around on the computer. "How are things with Marshall?"

"Geez." Reuben snorted. "He's pissing the neighbors off again."

"Still running around in his underwear?" Buzz asked with amusement.

Reuben sighed. "No, he stopped that once we adjusted his meds. Now he's just stomping around yelling obscenities, and the management is fed up with him. They threatened to throw us out."

"Damn." Buzz went on clicking on his computer, not asking anything else. He was back in the zone.

Bored, Reuben got up to walk around the room. Up until now, he'd been so fixated on what was happening to him that he had been relatively quiet. But now, hours later, he was bored, bored, bored.

Buzz's lab was filled with seemingly random bits and bobs that more closely resembled garbage than actual scientific equipment. Reuben picked up what looked like a magnifying glass with a broken handle.

"Don't touch that," Buzz told him. "It's worth more than your car."

"I have a shitty car." Reuben examined the thing with interest. "What is it, anyway?"

Buzz sighed, unable to hide his aggravation at being disturbed. "What does it look like?"

"A magnifying glass," Reuben answered.

Looking up, Buzz narrowed his eyes in frustration. "A magnifying glass? That's a magnifying glass in the same way a bicycle is a jet engine."

Reuben put it down. "OK, but you just asked me what it looked like, and I—"

Buzz cut him off, "You know what, I'm coding a new test. But it's going to take some time. Why don't you have your pizza by the pool?"

Reuben raised his eyebrows. "Pool?"

"Yeah, had it installed a few weeks ago," Buzz muttered over the rapid clicking of his fingers on the keyboard. "Get Rosa to show you to the guest swimwear room."

"Guest swimwear room?" Reuben should have been surprised.

"Yeah." Buzz snapped his finger as if just remembering something. "And before you go, did you have your Apple Watch on when you, you know, blew up?"

Reuben nodded.

"Excellent. Give it to me." Buzz extended his hand.

Sighing, Reuben handed over his watch. "You're not going to destroy it, are you? I really like that thing."

Buzz didn't answer, transfixed by the laptop screen.

Watchless, Reuben wandered off through the mansion. He found Rosa easily enough. She sat in the kitchen with her feet up, watching a telenovela. A man lay in a hospital bed, surrounded by weeping women. He breathed deeply on a respirator. Then the hospital monitor beeped and the women burst into fresh tears.

"Dios mio," Rosa gasped at the screen as she clutched her heart. "Not Pedro!"

"Poor Pedro." Reuben shook his head. "Is that his wife?"

Rosa whipped around, startled. "Mr. Reuben. I have your pizza on the way."

"No worries." Reuben watched as the doctors flitted around Pedro's dead body.

"Pedro," Rosa shook her head, "he was a good man, but he accidentally impregnated his sister."

"How did he do that?"

"He didn't know she was his sister. He thought she was his business partner's daughter. So, then when they took a paternity test, he found out his partner was his father. So he admitted to sleeping with his sister, and his father chased him through the house with a gun and shot him. They thought he would survive, but no."

Reuben's eyes widened. "Damn."

Now the pregnant sister and father exchanged heated words in Spanish, and then it cut to commercial.

"Well." Rosa wiped her eyes. "What can I do for you, Mr. Reuben?"

There was something off about Rosa. She was your stereotypical maid. Too stereotypical. Like she had been copied from some 1960s sitcom or something.

In college, Buzz had once said that *when* he made millions, he was going to get a Latino maid just like the maid in *As Good As It Gets* or Consuela from *Family Guy*. Of course they had been high and just had a Family Guy marathon. Still, here was Rosa, fulfilling that wish. Reuben couldn't help but wonder if she was real. Maybe she was an actress Buzz paid to be like this or a robot that he made.

Reuben laughed at the thought, but when Rosa didn't move, just stared at him expectantly. As she waited for his request, he wondered if he might be right.

Unsure how to verify or disprove his suspicions, he stammered, "The, um, guest swimwear room?"

"Yes, yes." She showed him to a closet. Rows of swimsuits separated by gender filled the racks. "Mr. Buzz keeps these here for parties. When someone uses them, we throw them away."

"Parties, huh?" Reuben repeated as he browsed past rows of tiny bikinis. "Buzz has parties?"

"No." Rosa shook her head like a disapproving mother. "But Mr. Buzz likes to think he does."

Reuben nodded. "I see."

Rosa left, and Reuben picked a swimsuit and made his way to the pool. The pool was inside a two-story, domed room. One side of the dome was all windows looking out onto a large outdoor pool, which in early February would be too cold.

The bottom floor of the cream, marble-paneled dome held the indoor pool, a large, dark-blue saltwater circle. Colored track lights glinted off the water and dark wicker lounge chairs surrounded the pool, while a boulder fountain filled the room with the tranquil sound of rushing water.

The top story had metal railings overlooking the pool, and Reuben noticed a couple of telescopes up there. Buzz had his own observatory up here.

Reuben jumped into the pool and let the warm water relax his body. This whole experience had been confusing and upsetting. Maybe he really was having a mental breakdown.

What if I'm not? he wondered. *What if I really died? What if I could die again and again and always come back? I would have the power to save the world.*

What if I could save the world and get the girl?

Reuben couldn't help but feel like he was living in some sort of Marvel comic book reality.

"Maybe, but then again, what if I'm a real superhero?" Reuben said out loud as he propelled himself into laps through the pool.

He thought about Buzz and how the guy had probably had the shit bullied out of him as a kid. Now look at him, in his big mansion with a maid. Most of those kids were probably busting their asses in some entry-level job, kissing up to ten different bosses. Buzz practically had the president of the United States on speed dial.

If Reuben had all the time in the world, then what was to stop him from being Buzz in his next life? Or someone like him.

Maybe, just maybe, this was the best thing that had ever happened to him.

CHAPTER ELEVEN

Martha—Tuesday, February 14, 7:56 a.m.

Martha crept through the alley, trailing Alister. He was alone, and he had been since he'd left his condo that morning. His black trench coat blew in the February wind, and his dress shoes clicked against the concrete. There was an odd familiarity about the whole thing that she just couldn't shake.

She followed Pout into the parking garage, where he boarded the elevator bound for the fourth floor. She flew past the security guard, her gut telling her he was no threat. She entered the stairwell and ran up to the fourth floor.

It was locked.

She bounded down the stairs two at a time and reached the third floor. She ran up through the car ramp and tried to get up to the fourth floor that way.

"I'm sorry, ma'am," said a burly security guard roped off the entrance with a velvet rope. "Restricted access. You'll have to go back down."

Martha had that same sense of familiarity. "Thank you."

She rounded the corner outside of the guard's view and

peered over the railing to the fourth floor. She heard tires screeching and thought she could probably reach up there and jettison herself into the action.

But she had a bad feeling about it.

She pulled herself back from the railing and shuddered. That would have been a bad idea.

Instead, she darted back to the elevator. Pout would be off it by now, and she could sneak in undetected. Martha called the elevator down and pushed the button for the fourth floor. The light blinked, but the car didn't move.

"Damn," she whispered.

The fourth floor was locked.

She checked the ceiling. It was a flimsy plate of light tiles held together with aluminum bars. She climbed up on the support rails and, standing, could easily push the tiles out of the way. It was an empty hole staring into the dizzying shaft.

She hoisted her whole body up through the hole and stood on the top of the tiles. She was now in the elevator shaft. It looked like an upside-down hallway. It was a deep corridor with metal railings on both sides and orphan metal doorways rising in a line all the way up.

She grabbed onto the metal railing on the side of the shaft. These were the support rails that the elevator slid up and down on. She wrapped her legs around one, just like that rope-climbing exercise in high school gym class. Arm over arm, she slowly pulled herself up to the metal door directly above her.

She was now even with the door, but she was still about three feet away and had no extra hands to pry open the door. She noticed the tiny red light of a sensor. She flailed her legs toward the sensor, and poof, the door opened. She concentrated on carefully climbing over rails and bars to the open door. Then, she found herself stomach-down on the bare concrete of the fourth floor.

Success.

She crawled away from the elevator door, and now safely away from the shaft, she stood. She drew her gun and snuck quietly around until she heard voices.

This was it.

This was her moment.

She was going to catch Pout.

She pulled out her phone and called Jake.

"Talk to me," he answered.

"I've got him," she reported quietly.

"Who?"

"Pout," she said. "I've got him cornered in a parking garage." She gave him the location.

"What exactly have you got on him?" Jake asked.

"Just send backup." She ended the call and snuck around the corner. She hid behind a car and saw the white van with the weed leaf on it about thirty yards away.

"Ma'am?" The security guard had spotted her. "I already told you, you can't be up here."

She pointed her gun at him. "Yeah, well, I don't take orders. I just give them."

He raised his palms in surrender. "I'm just doing what the boss said."

"Who's the boss?"

"Pout." He chuckled. "What Pout says goes."

"Not anymore." She smirked, stuck the gun in his face, and grabbed him by the ear until he gasped. "Now you're going to tell me what's going on up here."

"The same thing you're doing," he told her.

"And what is that?"

"Making the world a better, safer place."

"Oh, is this the villain speech?" She chuckled. "You know, where the villain is busted, and so he tells the hero, 'We're not so different, you and I…'"

"I got news for you. You're no hero, lady."

She pressed the gun against his temple, and his face turned cold and silent. "Tell me what's going on."

He glared at her, dark eyes glinting with disdain. "The world order must be shaken to its core. Only then can greatness spout forth."

"What the hell is that supposed to mean? Jesus, is this what happens to all the world's English majors? They can't find work as writers, so they become poetry-spouting criminals?"

He said nothing else.

"Let's go, Keats." She rolled her eyes and led him by gunpoint toward the voices.

"Bloody hell," was Alister's response. "George, what have you gotten yourself into?"

The guard simply held up his palms and gestured back toward Martha and her gun.

"Well, well, well." Alister sauntered up to her with the slow, deliberate steps of the wealthy and self-assured. His cold blue eyes sized her up, and she could feel him visually undressing her. His wavy dark hair blew in the wind, and under his trench coat, he was impeccably dressed in sleek black that oozed sophistication.

Martha wilted and wondered how the hell she could have possibly thought she could take him down on her own. Maybe if she stalled him, Jake would get here with backup in time.

"What the hell are you up to, Pout?" She showily pressed the gun into George's side.

Alister raised an eyebrow, and the side of his lip rose in

slight amusement. "All right." He chuckled. "You want to play at the grownups' table, little lady? I'll play with you. But don't forget, I'm much better at this game than you."

He winked, and by now, a crowd of half a dozen guards had gathered behind him, laughing.

She moved the gun at an angle ever so slightly away from George's head, then fired into the garage.

"Shit," George yelled, and Alister and his entire crew hit the ground as the bullet ricocheted off the garage's wall.

"Tell me what you're up to, Pout," Martha demanded as the group rose.

Alister's face no longer held condescending mirth, only anger. "You've had your fun. But you're out of your depth."

"Stop, or I'll shoot," she warned.

He sighed as if bored. "No." Standing only three feet from her, Martha could smell the liquor on his breath.

Tall and young—but not too young—and clad in all black and swagger, she immediately knew why half of Manhattan's women ended up in his bedroom. If she didn't know what she knew about him, Martha wouldn't have minded the chance herself.

With a leather-gloved hand, he reached into his coat and pulled out a gun.

Martha came to her senses right at that moment. She swiveled her hand from George's stomach to Alister and pulled the trigger.

As if in slow motion, Alister fell back, a grimace on his face, but maintained his aim with his gun.

"You don't get it." He smirked as he lay on the bare concrete. "I've already died inside. So, to die now or to die later, it's all the same. You, on the other hand, still cling to the toxic notions of virtue and a life worth living. It's bondage, really. You live your life trying so hard to protect it that you never really live. You might think you have won here, but you haven't. You see, I've lived my life with a greater freedom than you will ever know in ten lifetimes."

Martha choked back the lump in her throat. This guy even died sexily. It was at that moment that he pulled the trigger, and she felt a fiery explosion hit her forehead and rip her skull apart.

CHAPTER TWELVE

Reuben—Tuesday February 14, 9:43 a.m.

Reuben sat at his desk and tried to work. Over the past couple of days, Reuben'd had more blood and other bodily fluids extracted from him than he'd had in his entire life. He'd even had to take off Monday from work.

At least Buzz gave him back his Apple Watch before he left. Buzz also injected him with something that he promised wouldn't cause any long-term effects like cancer, heart disease, or blood poisoning.

Reuben had stupidly agreed.

Now, he sat at work with Julian Schaeffer's photo taking up the entire screen on the main wall, and he was supposed to be working the angles on him. Was the kid connected with the bomb or not?

His stomach was in knots. Either he was going to die in blood-boiling pain in a few minutes, or he wasn't.

In other words, in one scenario, he was doomed to relive dying over and over again until he, the guy who failed to get his yellow belt three times, stopped a terrorist attack.

In the other scenario, he was crazy.

Reuben honestly wasn't sure which one he preferred.

Sven stopped by his desk. "How are you feeling? It's not like you to take sick days."

"Better." Reuben grabbed his stomach and smiled weakly.

Sven raised an eyebrow. "Glad to hear it."

Sven left, and Reuben sank into his chair. He remembered what Sven had said about being able to spot liars and knew he had not passed Sven's bullshit detector. Now he would be on Sven's shit list, and for what? A bunch of dumb tests by an egomaniacal scientist?

He broke into a cold sweat.

Whatever was going on with him, he needed to get ahold of himself, or he could ruin his whole life in one day. Well, really it had been three days, or maybe six days. Christ, he didn't even know what timeline he was on. If that was indeed the case at all. Buzz still hadn't been able to prove anything.

They didn't show this part in the comics. Man, being a superhero sucks.

Aki swished past him in black jeans, a turtleneck, and a midriff leather jacket. *Hmm. A different outfit than she was wearing on Valentine's Day the first time around.* Reuben couldn't take his eyes off her. She caught him staring and shot him a dirty look.

Right. He immediately averted his eyes toward the computer screen and tried to start working.

Then he heard Aki's laughter from across the room. It sounded so free and whimsical.

He had gotten the date last time, so maybe his whole fear of her was completely irrational. He had made her out to be this mythical goddess, completely unapproachable, when in reality she was funny and kind and super easy to talk to. She was at her desk reading printouts, and he knew this was his chance.

Crazy or about to die, talking to her was the best distraction he could think of.

He sauntered up to her. "Hey," he said, leaning against the desk.

She glanced up from the printout. "Hi." She shifted a little in her chair and then turned back to her work.

"You know, I've seen you around," he stated breezily.

She glanced up with just an eye movement.

"And I know you like that band, Je Ne Sais Pas," he told her.

"What?" She furrowed her brow.

"You know, that band from Montreal, Je Ne Sais Pas. You would go to May Fest every year…"

"What the hell?" She glared at him. "Have you been doing some kind of investigative file on me?"

An investigative file was the agency's term for a deep search on an individual. It was usually done when there was only speculative evidence on the subject and they wanted to uncover dirt.

"No, no." Reuben rubbed his forehead. "I had just heard that about you, and—"

"You heard things about me?" she cut in. "From who?"

Reuben cringed. "Look, can I just start over?"

Aki looked at him like he was insane. "I'm not even sure what your name is…"

"My name is Reuben, and I know you're going through a tough time—"

"A tough time?" she repeated. "What are you talking about?"

"After your breakup." This was going from bad to worse.

"Oh my God." She rose to her feet. "Look, I don't know who you are or who you've been talking to, or what you think you know, but my personal life is not your business."

"Right." He blushed and slunk back through the office to his desk. He glanced at his watch. It was 9:47. He really wanted to die. As in now, please.

As soon as he wished it, he heard the massive explosion. Turning, he saw a clear wave of energy rush toward him, and his blood started to boil. His skin dried up, and he felt himself evaporate.

And then nothing.

CHAPTER THIRTEEN

Reuben—Tuesday, February 14, 9:27 a.m.

Reuben stood in the middle of the crowded bullpen. Julian Schaeffer's senior photo innocently smiled at them from a screen, a problem rendered over global national security in MAX level capacity.

He checked his watch. What the fuck? He hadn't gone back three days like before. This was literally twenty minutes earlier.

I thought Groundhog Day meant always waking up at the same moment?

All around Reuben, hapless CIA agents scurried about trying to confirm if this college kid had a bomb or not.

Was it really that difficult? Reuben mused. Whoever was behind this had to be way more suave, sophisticated, and connected.

Smoking weed and posting on RedBook just didn't cut it.

Reuben glanced down at his watch. OK, it was 9:28, and this was the timeline where he'd skipped work yesterday.

Which meant Buzz knew and the bomb… Fuck, the bomb was going to go off in about twenty minutes.

Reuben really didn't want to die again.

He had nineteen minutes until he died again. Nineteen minutes until his blood started to boil again. There was no hope to stop the explosion on this timeline. He hadn't gone back far enough.

He had to figure out something.

Fuck, he hated this.

But what could he do? He didn't have to wait these moments out. If dying again and again taught him anything, it was that you made the most out of the moments you had.

But he didn't have the time. Maybe he could settle for figuring out a plan to deal with it the next time he…came back to life, or whatever it was called.

Aki was staring at a monitor, mulling over the same thing as everyone else. How to crack this case. Maybe that was his real *in* with Aki.

With butterflies in his stomach, he approached her. "Hi."

She smiled and barely looked up from her printout.

Reuben made himself continue. "Listen, I have a hypothetical I wanted to run by you. On how to catch Schaeffer."

She set the printout down and perused him up and down. "Don't you work in tech?"

"I do. I know I'm not an agent. In fact, the most action I see outside of the office is when I take the tech van out to a safe house or other asset to fix the security cameras or router, but we've got a real situation here. Maybe some out-of-the-box ideas might work."

She pursed her lips and leaned back in her chair. "Go ahead," she prodded. "I'm listening."

"He's a college guy," he told her. "What do college guys want?"

She cocked her head and considered his words. Her raven hair shone against the fluorescent lights, lustrous and dark, and her chocolate brown eyes flashed with a fiery intensity, as though in any given moment a library of thoughts all competed for her conscious mind.

And he had her undivided attention.

He choked back a lump in his throat and realized who he was really dealing with. This was her in her element. "That day," whenever it had been, in whatever lifetime, she had shared her goofy, playful side with him. But this was something different. She waited patiently for him to finish his thought.

"I just think... I mean, college guys are all about the parties and the girls, and let's face it, for a guy like Schaeffer, a little bit of weed."

She raised her eyebrows in slight agreement, so he kept going.

"We could put the word out in his social circle." He worked the idea out as it came out of his mouth. "A party, or free beer, free weed. Something that we could use to lure him in pretty quickly."

"We have an agent closing in on him already," she pointed out.

"In Albuquerque," he countered. "And we're worried he's going to run."

Aki regarded him with interest. "You've done your homework. It's an idea. But you're talking about staging a sting?"

Reuben shrugged. "I wouldn't call it a sting."

Sting operations were costly and bureaucratic. They didn't

have the time to put that together. What was he thinking? They didn't have time to put *anything* together.

But if he kept this going, maybe, just maybe, he'd get the chance to kiss those lips before the world ended again.

"It would be more like a trap. He meets a pretty woman there. You." He caught her gaze as he said it. She didn't react. She was just listening intently. "Gain his trust with a kiss." Did he really just say that? Her eyes faltered at the line, and a tiny, almost imperceptible smile crept across her lips. "Like a final descent into pleasure before the end of the world..."

Her lips parted slightly, and she shifted in her chair.

He corrected himself. "That's how Schaeffer would see it, I mean," he continued. "He knows that life as he knows it is over. Why not trap him into one last moment of debauchery before he detonates the bomb?"

She stared off for a moment, then held his gaze. "I like it."

His heart lurched. "You do?"

"I don't know if it will work, but given the ideas—or lack of ideas we have on how to catch this guy—I'd be willing to get behind it."

His heart leapt into his throat, and then he heard it. The blast. The god-awful but familiar pain of boiling and cracking and instant dehydration. Then disintegration.

CHAPTER FOURTEEN

Reuben—Saturday, February 11, 7:03 a.m.

The early morning light flooded through the apartment blinds, and 'ping,' like a microwave oven, Reuben woke.

He winced and rolled over in a silent argument, but it was no use. He wouldn't be getting any more sleep. He opened his eyes in surrender and sighed deeply at the unopened Amazon package on his dresser. How long would this purgatory of time travel last?

He sat up and raised his arms to the heavens. "Would it be too much to ask—God, Buddha, Einstein, Black Hole #2,546—to at least get my blackout curtains up at some point? I don't know how long we're going to do this, but it would be nice to get some good sleep every once in a while."

How long had it been?

He looked at his watch. He'd gone back seventy-four hours and forty-four minutes.

He wondered if that was the maximum amount of time he could go back. He'd have to ask Buzz.

First, he'd have to convince Buzz what was happening

again, but given that he'd already gone through it once before, this time around should be easier.

"I've died three times," he mumbled to himself, "Went back seventy-four hours twice now, and under thirty minutes once. So this really isn't Groundhog Day. I don't always go back to the same moment. Good to know."

He groaned. He hated this day. This one was worse than the others.

Before the bomb had gotten him this last time, he'd had the hasty idea that maybe he could persuade Aki to infiltrate Schaeffer's life days before the bomb went off to verify whether or not he was involved with the bomb.

Now he realized that he'd been crazy to think that might work. The success rates of his attempts at talking with Aki so far were mixed. Trying to get her cooperation before the agency even started cracking down on Schaeffer as a possible threat would be next to impossible.

Sure, Aki was a badass field agent. She'd probably killed bad guys in the line of duty and nearly been killed herself a few times out on missions. Why would she trust a tech guy like him?

Ugh.

He turned his attention back to today and why it was going to be so bad—aside from the looming threat of the bomb.

"Today..." Reuben squinted in thought, and then he grabbed the pencil and pad off the nightstand and scrawled down the events. Today, Marshall would be screaming at the police scanner, rambling about the pussyfoot cops, the robber at Peet's coffee with a pink baseball bat, and then he would complain about the old hash browns.

Stupid hash browns.

Two weeks ago, he'd made the mistake of making eye contact with a ruthless kiosk vendor at the grocery store who had suckered him into spending twenty minutes watching a demo for the Magic Skillet—a five-piece set of pans that sliced, diced, washed your car, and babysat your kids. Once he'd realized the Magic Skillet set cost about the same as his rent, he'd passed on the deal and ended up with a free paring knife and a coupon for half off a bag of frozen hash browns.

He hadn't realized until he got home they were made by a well-known Swedish furniture brand. Yeah, that one. Now, he was trapped for all eternity with frozen potatoes made by the same people who made abstract chairs and bookshelves out of cardboard. What more could he have expected?

Even the paring knife wasn't any good.

After Marshall complained about the hash browns, there was the whole scene with Patricia and the neighbors, and then he'd go see Buzz. He rose, tossed the memo pad on the desk, grabbed the last slice of day-old pizza, and prepared to face the day. Before that, though, he stopped, and with cold pizza hanging from his mouth, he rummaged through his drawers until he found his green shamrock t-shirt at the bottom of his drawer.

He had won it at a bar contest but didn't wear it much. He suspected the fierce-eyed leprechaun was supposed to be a Notre Dame mascot knockoff. He wasn't much for college football, but the non-mascot-mascot seemed the perfect symbol for his non-St. Patrick's Day-St. Patrick's Day.

"I may never see another holiday again," he muttered to himself as he slipped the shirt on. "Not if I can't live past Valentine's Day."

He actually felt a lilt of excitement when he thought about the possibility of no more holidays. Did that mean he didn't have to suffer through horrible family dinners and bad Christmas gifts and hearing endless renditions of that god-awful song about the kid that bought his dying mom shoes for Christmas?

For his own private St. Paddy's Day celebration, he planned to bury himself inside a nice cold ocean of frothing booze before this night was over. Maybe he'd die of alcohol poisoning and get to skip the hangover.

The scene in the living room wasn't at all what Reuben expected. Sure, Marshall was up and standing front and center on his soapbox, but...

"Can you believe these liberal imbeciles?" He gestured toward the TV screen.

A news anchor gravely babbled on about partisan gridlock on economic sanctions against a fascist regime in the Middle East that refused to give up their nuclear weapons.

Not that it would matter, Reuben thought.

But, the TV was on, and Marshall was complaining about Congress. It was usually the activities from the police scanner that set him off.

"Did..." Reuben pointed toward the silent scanner on the other side of the room.

"What?"

"Nothing."

"It's all going to hell!" Marshall tossed the remote onto the couch. "They're running this country into the ground. Liberal bastards! This isn't the America I was born in, and this isn't the America your mother and I raised you in. They're a cesspool of commies. That's what they are! Nanny government pussyfoot commie whiners."

"Uh-huh." Reuben let him ramble on and wandered into the kitchen.

What the hell? How had Marshall's monologue been able to change?

"Don't make those damn hash browns, Mr. Hash Brown." Marshall scoffed. "They're shit. And you always burn them."

At least that line was the same.

Reuben opened the freezer. The hash browns were still there, no matter how many times he'd thrown them out. Yet, the conversation was different? What was this?

He grabbed the eggs and started getting breakfast together.

Marshall scoffed. "All these criminals in Washington. They all need to be in jail. The whole lot of them. But just like the criminals on the street, they run free because of damn bleeding-heart liberals whining about how they had a 'disadvantaged childhood.' Bullshit. Cry me a river."

Reuben gripped the front of the stove and stared hard at the eggs sizzling in the pan. He tried to wrap his brain around what was going on. He had never been able to effect any change in the warp before. Everything reset as soon as he rebounded. This, of course, made his life pointless and trivial —not that it wasn't already, he thought with a smirk.

But how had this day been able to change? His watch clearly said the eleventh.

Everything else—the pizza box, the curtains, his notes in his notebook—all fell into that timeline. But Marshall was not following the script. He racked his brain for any clue as to what he might have done differently that could have affected a change. He stared so hard, he didn't notice the odor or tiny wafts of smoke rising from the pan.

"Damnit, Reuben!" Marshall ran into the kitchen and grabbed the burning skillet off the stove. "Are you just going to stand there or what?"

Shit. He had burned the eggs. "I…"

Marshall washed out the charred pan. "Computer science degree from Columbia and can't cook a damn egg!"

"Right." Reuben shook his head to clear his thoughts.

"You know, your mother used to burn eggs too. Not just eggs. Toast, pasta, broccoli. Once she even managed to burn a banana that was too close—" Marshall stopped mid-sentence, a deep sadness painting his face. Then, his face hardened and, looking over at Reuben, he said, "What's with the shamrock shirt? You look like you support Notre Dame. What, you Catholic now?"

Marshall opened the door to let the smoke outside, and they heard Midge and Sheera complaining down on the sidewalk. Disconnected words like "pacing around" and "should be in a home" drifted into their living room. Marshall heard it too; and his face hardened, and he stuck his head out onto the patio.

"Dad, don't please!" Reuben yelled. "Just leave it. What are you, trying to get us evicted?"

"Evicted?" Marshall whipped back into the living room. "Son, this is America, and last I checked, I'm not a doormat! I can't speak for you, but I sure as hell didn't raise you that way!"

Marshall stepped back out on the patio, and Reuben saw him lean over the railing to the sidewalk downstairs. He'd sure enjoy his St. Patrick's Day celebration tonight.

"You carpet munchers have something to say to me?" he yelled. "Come up here and say it!"

Reuben buried his head deep in his palms and cringed. Worse than he thought. He didn't hear their response, but he knew it wasn't "We're so sorry."

He had to get out of here. Why on earth these women insisted on messing with a man with guns, Reuben would never understand. Marshall Peet was by no means a violent man, but come on, ladies, have some common sense.

He ran to his room, finished getting dressed, and waited a few minutes to make sure the conflict had died down. The patio door slammed, and Marshall stomped around angrily in the living room for a couple of minutes.

When Reuben didn't hear any more noise from downstairs, he grabbed his keys, made sure to shove the memo pad into the pocket of his jacket, and raced toward the door.

He needed Buzz. Buzz had been a pretty easy sell on the warp the first time they'd gone through it, but the more complex this problem got, the harder it would be to catch him up from the beginning.

He wished Buzz could come with him on this warp.

Marshall cleaned up the kitchen from the aborted breakfast and noticed Reuben leaving.

"You just gonna leave this mess here?" Marshall snarled. "What? Did I bruise your little pussyfoot self-esteem?"

Reuben clasped his shaking hand around the doorknob. That was a scripted line. How did he stay in the script with some lines and not others without anything changing? He didn't reply to Marshall but simply drew a deep breath and walked out the door.

Out in the cool February air, Reuben wrapped himself deeper into his leather jacket and took the stairs two at a time.

His heart sank when he saw the scene downstairs had not changed.

Midge, Sheera, and Patricia still stood in a trio, scheming at the foot of the stairwell. They cast a frosty glance in his direction, and Reuben pretended not to see them. He reached the ground, hugged the corner, and hurried toward the parking lot.

But he wouldn't get off that easily.

Patricia yelled, "Reuben! *Reuben*!"

Shit. The regular conversation was hard enough as it was. He didn't want to deal with whatever fuel Marshall had just thrown on the fire.

"Reuben," she tried again. "A word with you, please?"

"Can't listen to anyone," Midge sneered. "It must run in the family."

Sheera scoffed. "Clearly."

"Reuben." Patricia's quick heels on the sidewalk closed in behind him. "Believe me, no one wants to get the law involved here, but when residents don't cooperate—"

Reuben stopped in his tracks. His patience gone, he whipped around with an uncharacteristically sharp and sarcastic reply on the tip of his tongue. That was one good thing about the warp. It was doing wonders for his confidence.

He stopped himself, though, as soon as he saw Patricia's face. She was still in her blue pantsuit and black pumps, and Reuben felt a twinge of pity for her. She was trying too hard.

Patricia halted mid-sentence, and she stammered as her face paled. From a few yards away, Midge and Sheera slunk back a few steps. Reuben raised an eyebrow at them, and he noticed them both bristle and then, miraculously, turn away.

Patricia's eyes narrowed, and she spoke slowly, "There's something...different about you."

Reuben's heart burst. He didn't know what he did to give that off but didn't trust himself to respond without killing whatever had happened. So he said nothing and pursed his lips, keeping his eyes locked on hers. She looked even more concerned.

"I don't like it," she finished.

Reuben scoffed and turned away from her toward the parking lot.

"Me neither," he whispered to no one. "Me neither."

CHAPTER FIFTEEN

Reuben—Saturday, February 11, 10:42 a.m.

Convincing Buzz about the time warps was easier than expected. He started by telling the story, giving him as much detail as possible.

As soon as he got to the part about Buzz's experiments with his blood, the mad scientist looked him over before asking, "Did I take your watch?"

Reuben cocked his head. "You did."

"And I injected you with something that, although not FDA-approved, won't cause cancer, heart disease, or blood poisoning."

"Argh…not FDA-approved," Reuben repeated. "I knew I shouldn't have let you do that."

Buzz's face lit up with excitement. "Give me your watch."

Handing it over, he followed Buzz as he hurried to his lab. Buzz put the watch on what looked like a wireless charging port and began to bang furiously on his keyboard, "Please, please, please."

Buzz punched the air. "Fuck me in a peach tree; it worked!"

"What worked?" Reuben asked.

"This," Buzz told him, pointing at the rows of green code that started pouring down from the top of the screen *Matrix*-style.

Reuben leaned in to get a better look. "What is that?"

"Data," Buzz informed him. "I injected you with a nanochip that perfectly imitates your body. It's a technology that no one has, something I've been working on for almost fifteen years."

Reuben was astounded. "Since you were a teenager?"

Buzz nodded. "Since before I had pubic hair. It operates with Bluetooth and is transferring data to your watch. Man, oh man. The mere fact you have this confirms everything. You are in a time warp, and this is the second time we're having this conversation."

"It's not exactly the same," Reuben explained.

"Indeed," Buzz agreed. "Time warps never are. Theories abound, but the leading one states that you can only have up to a 92% overlap with the last loop. Never 100%."

That made sense to Reuben. "How low does it go?"

"No one knows, but by best guess, no lower than 70%. Once you get lower than that, we start to get into parallel dimension shit."

Reuben took a deep breath. "OK, thanks for clarifying that. Why don't you speak to me like I'm not some kind of super-genius? What exactly are you looking at? And most importantly, what the fuck is going on?"

Buzz cracked his knuckles as he started to bang away at his keyboard. "So, your blood survived my wormhole replicator, but mine didn't, right?"

"Yep."

"I injected you with a chip that mimics your internal systems. It survived. Because it survived, I can get a sense of what you went through."

"Through Bluetooth."

"Through Bluetooth."

"OK, thanks. That makes perfect sense."

"Does it?"

"NO!" Reuben screamed.

Buzz clicked his keyboard twice. "Look, all you need to know is that because of that nanobot, I have access to any data your phone can pick up. Mostly sounds, but you'd be surprised by the kind of sensors your phone has. With some tweaks to the nanobot, we might even get visuals. Wait! Instead of using your phone's speakers and camera, I could sync the nanobot to your eyes and ears. Just think of the data we'd collect then. Give me a few secs here... Holy fuckatoos!"

Reuben hardly dared ask. "What?"

Buzz pushed back from his terminal and looked at his friend as he muttered, "I just witnessed your death."

Reuben—Saturday, February 11, 11:51 a.m.

Buzz looked at Reuben with genuine pain. "What?" Reuben said, feeling overwhelmed by his friend's expression. He'd known Buzz for years, and the scientist had never expressed heavy feeling, never showed genuine emotion.

But now... Now Buzz looked like he was going to cry.

"Listen," Buzz said, turning up the dial on one of his boards. "What do you hear?"

Reuben leaned forward. He couldn't hear much, only a

faint bubbling sound like something… "Boiling. I hear something boiling."

"What you're listening to is your blood bubbling." There was a splurting sound, followed by an intense hissing. Buzz winced. "That's your skin cracking, letting out steaming blood. Think old-school kettles."

"Jesus," Reuben said, running his hands through his hair. "Really? That's how I died. Three times."

Buzz nodded. "Judging by your, uh, side effects, I'm deducing that the bomb is using experimental microwave-based tech. Most of the research on that is currently centered in Canada. It's relatively new and, up until now, never used in actual warfare. It was designed to maintain infrastructure while wiping out all life in the area. Highly effective against water-based lifeforms like, well, like you." Buzz was rattling off facts like someone reading the features list on a website. It was something he did when he was really excited.

"Am I alive?" Reuben asked.

Again, Buzz nodded. "You have to be. Once you die, you reset. At least, that's my theory. You feel intense pain but only until your nervous system shuts down and you feel like you're disintegrating."

"And we're hearing this, how?"

"Your watch and the nanobot, which isn't affected by your warping."

"Fuck me…" Reuben was starting to panic. Before, when there was a real chance he was just crazy, Reuben had managed to keep the panic at bay. But now, he felt his throat tighten and his heart race. "I don't want to die like that again. I don't. There's got to be a way to stop this. Please."

For a moment, he thought he might just die here and now,

save the bomb the trouble. Of course, he'd just do the warp again and have to face the prospects of boiling to death again.

Buzz sat quietly, staring at his friend for a long time before he shook his head, a sly smile creeping along his face. "There is only one thing we can do to save you from dying like that again. Stop the bomb."

Buzz turned back to the watch, gleaning as much information from the nanobot as he could.

Reuben tried not to think about dying again.

After an hour of further analysis, Buzz snapped his fingers and said, "Follow me. We need more information." He was back to his old self, working the problem from every angle his genius mind could conjure.

Buzz turned toward the hallway, his slippers silently padded over the marble linoleum while his bathrobe swished around him like a cape.

Reuben followed, still trying not to think about dying again. "Buzz, why do you think this is happening to me?"

Buzz shrugged. "It might be genetic. Either that or you were bit by a radioactive clock."

Reuben was lost again. "Radioactive clock?"

"You know, like Spiderman, but your power is to manipulate time, so it's a clock."

"Oh," Reuben said.

Buzz rolled his eyes. "It's a joke."

"Yeah, I get that. I was just wondering if I was chosen or something?"

Buzz stopped, turning to Reuben. "What? Like an angel tapped you to save the world? If that were true, and just for the record, I do not think it is. Don't you think the angel would have tapped someone, I don't know, smarter?"

"Maybe, but—"

"Or stronger," Buzz interjected. "More coordinated. Hell, able to cook."

Reuben sighed. "Oh, ha-ha, I get it. I'm not exactly superhero material."

Buzz continued, "Since you'd probably remember being bit by a radioactive clock, I calculate that this is genetic at ninety-two percent probability."

A thought hit Reuben. "So, what? There's others like me?"

Buzz shook his head. "Unlikely. I suspect you have a genetic anomaly, think mutants from X-Men or something. It's most likely this genetic mishap gave you your abilities. But like I said, ninety-two percent probability on that one. There is an eight percent margin for error. That is not insignificant. Of course, there is the miniscule chance that this anomaly is the universe's version of cleaning up horrible events that should never have happened, like this microwave bomb in NYC. But let's consider one thing at a time."

They arrived at a door, and Buzz keyed in a quick code on a security pad, which opened the door to a cavernous room with high, vaulted ceilings. At first glance, it looked to be a server room.

"This," Buzz gestured, "is where the real science happens."

Reuben saw floor-to-ceiling computers and monitors. Cables ran everywhere, and just about every wall space had a screen on it. Built-in cabinets every which way held desktop computers and technology that didn't even exist yet in the field. It was only theorized in trade magazines.

Geez, Reuben thought. Buzz's lair made the CIA look like a basement hack operation. No wonder he had thought they were obsolete and irrelevant.

Standing in the center of the room, and with the authority

of Moses parting the Red Sea, Buzz spoke to the machines. "System book, level 7 dilemma protocols activate."

Several screens on the wall lit up with a calendar interface. Reuben considered himself on the brink of the technology curve, but this was beyond anything he knew was out there.

"We have two issues we need to work out. One, how to stop the bomb. And two, what's happening to you. I rank them in that order because stopping the bomb is the top priority. Once that's done, we'll have plenty of time to dissect you." From Buzz's tone, Reuben wasn't entirely sure Buzz was joking.

Buzz cleared his throat and spoke into the room. "The bomb explodes on February 14 at 9:47 a.m."

After a quick beep, the information appeared as a time note entry on the calendar. Buzz slowly lowered his arm toward Reuben, gesturing him toward the middle of the room.

Reuben came to tentatively stand in the center circle, where speakers and dial lights hung from every direction.

"Plot everything you remember," Buzz instructed. "The timetable system is designed to work with conversational data so that it processes the information in its format while you process it in yours."

More data collection. Reuben groaned. He was so sick of data collection and experiments. "I don't want any more tests. I want action. I want you to give me some sort of weird plutonium Doc Brown Libyan terrorist's potion that will magically cure all of this."

Buzz's face turned hard, his eyes cold. "Don't ever mention *Back to the Future* to me again. That film makes a mockery of the scientific profession and turns the legitimate work of serious researchers into Hollywood culture punchlines."

Then Buzz winked and slapped his friend on the shoulder. "I'll give you a hard copy of the data so you can study it and memorize as much as you can. This will fast-track us to recreating it if you lose this timeline. The code to access this room is Binnie, which no one else in the world knows. It will also serve as a memory key to fast-track us to this moment in other timelines."

"Binnie?" Reuben smirked. Binnie was the name of the robot in Buzz's erotic novel from college.

Buzz's eyes got a faraway look, and he stared off into the distance.

Reuben smiled and got his head in the game. "Right. On February 11 at 7:30, I woke up in my bed without the blackout curtains. I grabbed the pizza box dated February 10 and went into the living room with Dad."

Buzz sat at a computer monitor, and they both watched as the information appeared in calendar format on the screens. Encouraged, Reuben verbally vomited every event that had happened to him since the time warp started.

It took a few hours for Reuben to tell his whole story, taking into account the three deaths. He collapsed into a chair next to Buzz when he was done.

Buzz already had multiple graphs and charts with the information on over a dozen monitors. "OK. Much of that matches with the nanobot's records. Of course, we'll have to go on your memory for the first death since the nanobot wasn't in you then." Buzz generated an intimidating battery of graphs, pie charts, and stats pages that filled multiple monitors. "You're stuck in a timeline of three days. According to these calculations, it would appear that each rebound lasts anywhere from twenty minutes to seventy-four hours and forty-four minutes. In theory, you could travel back mere seconds if you knew how to control your power, but three days looks to be the maximum you can go back at one time."

It was good trivia, and if it wasn't so horrible to die, Reuben would have appreciated the numbers. But all he could think of now was how to get out of the constant repeats.

Death. Final death, he thought. *Is it really that bad?*

"This is good. This is good," Buzz said excitedly as he typed on his computer. "I've set up an automated process so that when you die, the nanobot syncs to your smartwatch, which then automatically sends the feedback through your phone to my computers. All my notes on your warps and the timeline are also reverse-synced back to your nanobot so that my computers stay up to date when you warp."

Reuben studied the graphs. "This is great, but how can I use this information to stop cycling?"

Buzz scratched his chin and clicked around on the screen, each click pulling up different elements of Reuben's experience. It was beyond impressive how intelligent the program was. Each entry was highly accurate, organizing all of the details and conversations into a cohesive timeline. It even had other information he hadn't given it, like a map of the addresses where the events occurred.

"Your problem is," Buzz clicked around as he spoke, "that the farthest you're going back is just over three days. We've got lots of research to do. And we've got to figure out a plan. That's not enough time to stop the bomb."

Reuben sighed. "Probably not, no."

Buzz's eyes twinkled. "What you need is more time."

"But I have no control over it," Reuben countered. "That's what I've been saying."

"Right." Buzz smiled. "But what if you did?"

Reuben tilted his head in confusion. "What do you mean?"

"You only go back to this morning because you don't control when you die. What if you did control when you died?"

"Like…" Reuben's face paled. "Suicide?"

"Don't think of it as suicide." Buzz rubbed his chin. "Think of it as controlling the cycle."

"You think if I killed myself," Reuben thought aloud, "it would give me more time?"

"Theoretically, yes. Because if you're going back up to seventy-two hours, you could potentially rebound at close to a week before the bomb explodes. That would certainly give you more time. If that works, you could experiment with other time ranges."

Reuben felt bile rise in his throat. "What if it's not just any death that causes the time warp? What if it's specifically linked to the bomb killing me?"

Buzz shook his head. "As a scientist, that doesn't make sense to me. It is most probable that you simply cannot die at this time. Old age is probably the only thing that can truly kill you."

Reuben had serious doubts. "But killing myself just feels wrong."

Buzz crossed his arms.

Reuben sighed. "Well, it's not the worst idea I've heard."

The time warp had done a lot for his confidence. He had told off his bosses and somehow scared the shit out of his landlady.

But, suicide?

That was an entirely different beast. Could he really conquer that? In the movies, the guy would always sweat during his moment of contemplation before he pulled the trigger. Could he do it in real life?

Buzz seemed to be tracking with his thoughts. "Think about it. If you get over your fear of death, then you would have conquered fear once and for all. You'd be unstoppable." Buzz pulled out a gun from his drawer and handed it to Reuben. "Now, temple or in the mouth?"

CHAPTER SIXTEEN

Reuben—Saturday, February 11, 2:32 p.m.

Reuben leaned against the side of the jacuzzi in Buzz's pool house.

Buzz sighed and closed his eyes, quiet as the jets massaged him.

"But that's the thing," Reuben told Buzz as Rosa brought them cold beers on a silver tray. "Dying is the worst possible pain you can imagine. After all, your body lives through any other pain. It can't survive death. Death, in essence, is your body waving a white flag to the injury because all of its built-in defenses have been maxed out and compromised."

"Thank you, Rosa." Buzz grabbed a drink and twisted off the top, and Reuben did the same.

They sipped their drinks, and Reuben let the alcohol numb his nerves.

"Well, you've only died one way, though. Death by explosion, yes. But the gun..." Buzz was still sour that he had refused to put a bullet in his head.

Reuben ignored him. "So what other ways could I die,

then?" Reuben contemplated, a little unnerved that this was indeed his real thought process.

Buzz grabbed his phone off the side of the pool and started searching for ways to die. "Poison, terrorist attack, car accident, plane crash, drowning, being crushed by a large object... The human body is alarmingly frail, and there are infinite ways to destroy it."

Buzz read the last item. "Gunshot."

"We've been through that one already," Reuben told him.

"Too messy and dark." Buzz sighed. "And it would be awful if Rosa couldn't get the bloodstains out of my rug. Terrible for the resale value."

"Your new house is ready, right?"

"How do you...oh," Buzz replied. "It won't be ready for another year."

"Right." Reuben thought about his apartment with his dad. It was just the way things were going to have to be for a while.

"Now, we could have a car wreck," Buzz suggested.

"The old car off a cliff, huh?" Reuben considered. "Seems a bit dramatic."

They sat in silence for a couple minutes.

Reuben looked up at the high ceiling. "What about jumping off a building? I saw a movie once where they said you don't die on impact on the ground, you die from wind impact."

"Plenty of high buildings around here. Empire State, Chrysler."

Reuben saw one issue with that. "Getting past security, though..."

Buzz nodded. "True, true."

"You could bribe security," Reuben suggested.

"I don't want to get involved." Buzz held up his hands, and

salty pool water dripped down his scrawny arms. "If this doesn't work and you are crazy after all, then I'd have to stay in this timeline. Murder, prison…" Buzz gestured toward his ultra-lanky frame in swim trunks. "*This* doesn't do that."

Reuben chuckled. "Yeah. It would be difficult to avoid being implicated."

Buzz sighed. "All right. This is getting us nowhere. Let's take a walk. We need new ideas."

They got out of the pool and started to dry off.

Buzz rattled off several ways one could stop the heart. "What you want is one that interrupts the vital systems. Those are fairly easy to find."

After several minutes of this, Reuben stopped him. "I think I'm going to be sick."

"Take a moment." Buzz slapped him on the back. "We don't have to decide right now. We'll get dressed and walk in the gardens. We have plenty of time to figure out exactly how to kill you."

CHAPTER SEVENTEEN

Reuben—Saturday, February 11, 2:40 p.m.

The crisp February wind in Buzz's garden stirred the trees, and there was an effervescent floral scent that Reuben could never hope to accurately place. He wished he knew flowers and plants. Knowledge like that may have proven helpful in his nonexistent love life. Birds flew overhead, and bright spots of red dotted the holly bushes and hedges while a fountain bubbled nearby. The tranquility of the garden put Reuben more at ease, and the surreal nature of what he was facing started to fade just a bit.

"Well?" Buzz fell into step with him as they strolled through the hedge mazes. "Have you come to any conclusions?"

"I don't know," Reuben admitted weakly.

Buzz nodded. "Let's head back to the lab. I'll show you what I'm working on inside Binnie."

The two men went back into the house and down the hall to the Binnie room. Buzz entered the code and took Reuben into the computer room.

As they walked, Buzz piped up again, "I was thinking about your questions earlier. How did you get this ability? Are you the only one? And what about others?" Buzz paused.

"And?" Reuben coaxed.

"I have no idea," Buzz admitted. "But, well, have I given you my theory on pseudo-schizophrenia in a previous time warp?"

Reuben nodded. "Yeah, but I don't know about that."

Buzz chuckled. "Hear me out. Not everyone suffering from schizophrenia, just a select few who are genetically predisposed to time warps. The .00001 percent of the population with a recessive time warp gene, if you will. But what if, on a more universal, common level, we all have a touch of access. No memories. Zero knowledge that anything happened, but we can sense a disturbance?"

"In the Force?" Reuben quipped.

"You are such a nerd." Buzz chuckled. "Yes, sort of like a disturbance in the force. That could potentially explain things like déjà vu, intuition, some dreams. They're really just the mind processing information that otherwise isn't accessible to the conscious mind."

Reuben gave him a blank look.

Buzz waved his hands. "OK, think of it this way. Someone has déjà vu, right? It's an odd feeling of familiarity. But because you've yet to experience it, the event just comes off as out of place. Odd. But what if that's a piece of their mind remembering the future? A future that was reset by a time warp? I'm not saying all déjà vu is that, but it is possible that can happen. The more important the memory, the stronger the feeling."

Reuben considered this but then shook his head.

"Wouldn't that mean time warps are happening all the time? Déjà vu isn't exactly a rare occurrence, and if my abilities are as rare as you've hypothesized, then time warps would be super rare."

Buzz nodded in agreement. "Maybe. It is possible there are more time warps happening that we don't know about. It is also possible that feelings like déjà vu have other sources outside of time warps, like us seeing events in parallel universes or—"

"Stop," Reuben stamped his foot on the ground, abruptly stopping. "This is already crazy enough without you introducing parallel universes into this."

Buzz laughed. "Yeah, you're right." Shaking his head, he gestured for them to keep moving. "Say, remember when we were in college, there was this one night we got really high and started talking about cool ways to die?" Buzz mused. "Do you remember what we said it would be?"

"We were horny kids, Buzz."

"True, but you did say it would be a great way to go."

"Sex is probably a good way to end it, but there are many problems with that scenario. One, I'm pretty sure I'd need some underlying condition for it to work. A bad heart, an aneurism, maybe. And two, there's no one around here to have sex with. Unless of course, you're volunteering."

Buzz and Reuben chuckled as the scientist led him into a concrete hallway off to the side of the room. They went down a long narrow stairwell into what could only be described as an underground bunker.

Reuben got a chill down his spine. "Buzz, you're creeping me out, man. What is this place?"

Buzz just smiled, and another shiver of fear went down

Reuben's spine. The bunker reminded him of the interrogation room at work. It was a large area with not much in it, only a metal folding chair and a lab panel with all kinds of weird switches, controls, and dials that looked like something like an audio sound board. Against one wall, a closet-sized opening was covered by a pink curtain with butterflies.

"What's back there?"

Buzz smiled. "Sit."

Reuben sat in the metal chair, and Buzz played with a bank of switches on the lab panel. The pink closet door opened, and out stepped the most beautiful woman Reuben had ever seen.

"Whoa," Reuben muttered.

The woman was in her mid-twenties, tall, with long, lustrous legs that flexed when she moved, huge brown eyes, and voluminous dark hair that hit her mid-back. With one manicured finger, she flicked her hair across her shoulder. She wore a pink-and-black negligee and thigh-high black boots. Every movement screamed sex.

"Hi, Reuben." She greeted him with a smile that seemed to say he was the only man she would ever have eyes for. "I'm Binnie. It's nice to finally meet you." Then, in a soft voice, "I've heard so much about you."

"I'm sorry." He did a back and forth between Buzz and the woman. There was something odd about her movements. Stilted, like a drunk trying to act sober. "Is she…"

He wanted to ask if she was real, but it seemed terribly impolite because he honestly couldn't tell if she was a normal human or one of Buzz's weird experiments.

He looked at Buzz for a clue, but he didn't say anything.

"Am I what?" Binnie asked. "Real?" She crossed her arms and gave him a stern look. But again, there was something off about the whole thing. It was like she was acting mad rather than actually angry. It reminded Reuben of cheesy 80s sitcoms where the mom or girlfriend would overact. It conveyed the emotion, but there was no doubt it wasn't real.

Still, if she was real, then Reuben was making a complete ass of himself. "No, it's just that, I don't... Do you live in that...closet?"

Buzz laughed. "Geez, dude. Play it cool, man."

"Right." Reuben still didn't quite know what to make of this woman.

She laughed, and with one quick movement, eased herself onto the lab table. "So tongue-tied. He's so cute." She grabbed a pack of cigarettes off the counter and lit one.

Could robots smoke? Surely not. They were machines. Now he felt like a real asshole. She was clearly a human, and this was just Buzz making fun of him. But at the back of his mind, part of him remembered how he suspected Buzz's maid of being a robot.

"You're..." Reuben stammered. "Of course you are... Sorry. It's just, my friend is a little eccentric. Of course, you would know that, right?"

Binnie took a long drag of her cigarette and blew a thin line of smoke into the air.

Something still lingered in the back of Reuben's mind. How did Buzz get with the most beautiful woman he'd ever met? Because he was loaded, but all the money in the world didn't make up for Buzz being Buzz.

And what was in that pink closet? Was there another bedroom back there? Was there a secret entrance to a whole new wing? If she was with him for his money, she wouldn't be content to live down in the basement. She would want to enjoy the money.

Reuben's eyes shifted around nervously.

Buzz nodded at Binnie, and she took a step forward. "Reuben. You're Buzz's friend."

Reuben nodded. "Um…yes."

"He is," Buzz said. "And we're looking to give him a Protocol One treatment."

"Oh." She touched her lips as her dark eyes met his. "Been a while since we did that." She took a seat next to Reuben.

"Protocol One? What's that?" Reuben shifted over to give her more room.

As he moved away, she slid over closer to him. "Buzz tells me that you're special."

Reuben looked at Buzz. "Buzz? What's going on?"

Buzz sighed. "It's just me being a good host. Go with it."

"But…but…"

"My Buzz is very generous." She wrapped her soft legs around his seated body and lowered herself onto his lap.

"I don't know if I'm comfortable with—" But before Reuben could finish, Binnie grabbed his hand and placed it on her breast.

Buzz put a hand on Reuben's shoulder. "Just relax. You know I'm into some top-secret shit. Stuff that the government would have no problem torturing, maiming, and killing for. Binnie and I have worked out a protocol to help with that."

Reuben tried to move, but Binnie wouldn't let him. She was surprisingly strong.

"Binnie is part of my home security…among other things. And before you ask again, yes, she is a robot."

"What?" Reuben tried to get out from under her weight.

Binnie traced a soft finger across his cheek, and she cupped his face in her palms.

"You said painless. This is as painless as it gets. Now, Binnie."

"No, Buzz, not like this—" But before Reuben could finish, electricity exploded through Binnie's body. It overtook Reuben, and he felt fire explode through his veins, killing him instantly.

CHAPTER EIGHTEEN

Reuben—Thursday, February 9, 7:51 a.m.

When Reuben came back to consciousness, he was alone in his cubicle in the CIA bullpen. No Binnie. No Buzz. No coworkers. No one.

He was alone at work. It would still be another hour before the morning shift started to trickle in. He looked at his watch. Thursday, 7:51 a.m. So he'd warped back two days and change.

Thursday was the day he went in early to work to get away from Marshall, who was in a mood that...well, *this* morning.

The high alert hadn't been issued yet, so they still held regular business hours. The wall screens were black, and no one at the agency had yet heard of Julian Schaeffer. It was the calm before the storm.

The first thing he did was step outside the office building and call Buzz.

"Whoa, whoa, whoa," Buzz said. "Time warps? Are you joshing—"

"The code to your secret server room is Binnie," Reuben

interjected. "You said to tell you that. That you're the only one who knows that."

Buzz gasped. "OK then. I believe you. I'll go and take a look at the nanobot data you say that your phone has already sent to my computers."

With that out of the way, Reuben sighed. He wasn't going to be driving out to Buzz's right now. Today was the day to do some much-needed research at the office.

Reuben sat in the silence and looked up Schaeffer's Facebook page on his phone. He didn't dare to use his work computer because once Schaeffer was named a suspect, he'd get dragged into the interrogation room for sure.

The kid seemed happy. It looked like he had a handful of goofy friends, miscreants for sure. There were lots of party pics, just teenagers having fun. In one of the pictures, a cute blonde wearing a tank top that read, *Tetris rocks*, was holding his hand. He was looking at her with the puppy-dog eyes of young love.

All harmless. All normal for someone his age. As Reuben browsed through the photos, it occurred to him that Julian's life was the life he'd never lived.

He had always been ambitious and smart, often sacrificing parties for study. He wanted his life to mean something. That was how he justified missing out on so much. Sure, he'd had a few girlfriends over the years. But nothing serious. Reuben liked to lie to himself and say it was because of his job. Working for the CIA, keeping the world safe for people like, well, Julian.

He flipped through a few more pics. Julian looked so

happy. So normal, and for a moment, Reuben wondered if he'd chosen the wrong path. Maybe, just maybe, he should have gone to a few more parties, tried a bit harder to be…normal.

The office started to fill up now, coffee-laden agents trudging in with jackets and briefcases. Desk phones started to ring, and computer monitors came to life all over the building. The day had begun. Reuben closed Julian's profile.

He had gone back far enough that maybe he could keep the other agents off Julian's ass for a bit. Get them to focus on the real threat, whatever that was.

Aki arrived, this time in a black wraparound dress with platform heels that showed off a small tattoo on her ankle. His heart skipped a beat. He had gotten so used to seeing her in the same outfit, he'd almost forgotten that she had other clothes.

From a distance, he heard her laugh, and he looked in her direction. Ugh.

Mike. Her boyfriend.

Reuben had almost forgotten about him. He was a field agent who hopped around the globe. By Valentine's Day, he would check into rehab for anger management, but today he was in the office.

Mike Fury was tall, with impeccably trimmed dark hair and striking blue eyes. He wore a black suit and a sultry expression that suggested he needed to correct any memory lapses that might have occurred during his exotic travel. No, his gaze reminded any amnesiac colleagues: she is NOT single.

That wouldn't happen until tomorrow, when he'd lose his shit and Aki in the process.

Aki floated back to her desk as Mike strolled down the hall toward the printer.

"Hey." Mike stopped at his desk. "Robert, right?"

"Reuben." He pointed to the nameplate on his cubicle wall.

"Right." Mike didn't hear him. "So, listen, can you run some reports for me? I owe a favor to the Canadian Secret Police. There's a maple syrup thing going on. Apparently Canadian gangsters are all about the syrup. You feel me?"

He put out his fist for Reuben to bump. Reuben wasn't a bumper, and it came off as an awkward, weak tap.

"Anyway," Mike continued, "Can you run a report for me? I'm looking for the identity of some gangster wannabe known as the Canadian."

"I'm sorry?" Reuben said.

"Yeah, yeah. I know. Suspect is known for being polite, saying 'sorry,' and is particularly known for being a 'nonviolent mobster.' Fucking Canadians. Can you just see what the databases call up? Like I said, I owe a few favors to a Mountie."

Mike burst into laughter. "I mean, 'the Canadian'? Whatever happened to 'Scarface' or 'Iceman'? Am I right?" He slapped Reuben on the shoulder. Hard.

He blinked slow and long, and then, in a patronizing tone, "Do you think you can handle this? I mean, we're not exactly looking for dirt on Al Capone."

Reuben pursed his lips in concession and took the papers. "Yeah. I think I can."

Reuben resented Mike's request, but it still gave him the cover he needed to run an investigation of his own. If he was going to save the city—and his own blood from boiling —he needed to do some investigating of his own. Looking for 'the Canadian' would be the perfect excuse.

For the next few hours, Reuben tried to think of everything and anything that would help him figure out where the bomb came from and how to stop it.

He was getting nowhere.

Aki swished by his cubicle in a breeze of perfume, and Reuben seized the moment. Mike was in the conference room, and he would be gone tomorrow.

"Aki," he called out.

She stopped and turned, glancing at him expectantly.

"Hi, I'm Reuben." He stood outside his cubicle. "I wanted to ask your advice on something."

"OK." Aki moved a little closer and stood near his cubicle.

"I have a hypothetical situation for you," he began.

She didn't say anything, so he continued.

"Hypothetically speaking, if a terrorist was going to do something terrible on Valentine's Day, and so far all activities are totally off our grid, how would you go about investigating it?"

"Well," she started slowly, "the first thing I would do is search the databases and cross-reference the names and numbers, build a suspect profile, and kick it up to Sven, who will assign it as a protocol."

"Yeah." Reuben scratched the back of his head. "But what if it's a new player? One we don't really have anything on?"

Aki shook her head. "New player or not, they'll have to use established pieces on the board to get the job done. They'll need grunts and local suppliers. No big move can be made in isolation. So, you'll need to see who on our watch lists is moving and start connecting dots until you get to something.

It's a lot of tedious work, but it's the only way to start from scratch."

Aki narrowed her eyes and leaned against his cubicle wall. "What are we dealing with here?"

Reuben shook his head dismissively and dug his hands into his pockets. "Nothing. I'm just running some simulations to help predict terrorist attacks before they happen."

"Smart one, huh?" Aki smiled, and Reuben swore he could hear the angels sing. "Remind me to come to you if I ever have computer problems."

If only she knew. "Will do."

She pointed to Mike's annotated paperwork on his desk. "Running Mike's reports?" she remarked. "You keep your act up, you'll have the tech team running your reports, too."

By mid-day, he had run a report on the Canadian, as well as filled a full legal pad and a half with notes on every sub-angle related to the bomb that he could think of.

CHAPTER NINETEEN

Reuben—Thursday, February 9, 3:12 p.m.

Reuben heard it in the faint whispers around him. The name popped up, like moles coming up from random holes in the earth.

Julian Schaeffer.

Shit. They were already onto him. However, it would still be a couple of days before he became the prime suspect.

Reuben had to come up with something before then. He knew Schaeffer didn't have the bomb and likely had nothing to do with it. But he had to find out who it was before they wasted all their time chasing him, and the real terrorists detonated the microwave bomb and killed everyone.

With a sigh, he turned his attention back to the info he'd pulled up on the Canadian for Mike.

He had to hand it to Mike; the maple syrup-smuggling ring was interesting. He started to read the report when, from the corner of his eye, he saw Aki and Mike talking.

No, not talking. Arguing. Their body language was tense,

and when Mike slammed his fist on the wall behind her, Reuben knew this was "the breakup."

The argument continued for a few minutes, with Mike getting increasingly aggravated before he finally broke off and headed right toward... Oh shit.

"Hey, Robert," Mike growled through gritted teeth.

"Hey, Mitchell," Reuben responded to his own surprise. *What the fuck am I doing poking the bear?* he thought. In the pre-time warp days, he would have never been so cheeky. But death does weird things to a person. It makes them unafraid of life. He was definitely unafraid of Mike Fury.

"My name's Mike," he corrected, his voice rising in a condescending tone. "Did you finish the search I ordered?"

"Partly." Reuben handed Mike's printout back to him. "It's not a long list, and I'm not sure how valid the intel is, but this should give your guys a lead."

Mike scoffed. "This isn't what I need. I need names, addresses. Results."

Reuben stared into Mike's haughty blue eyes with a lowkey smirk on his face. Mike would be gone later today.

Mike slammed the papers down on the desk. Then, to everyone's shock, Mike let out an ear-splitting scream. Everyone in the building stopped and stared. Reuben's stomach froze. Mike was burying his own career on the security camera. No one even had to do it for him.

Then, without warning, Mike punched the cubicle wall. Reuben backed away as Sven rushed through the building to the scene, but not fast enough. It was then that Mike completely and utterly lost it. With banshee yells, he overturned filing cabinets and knocked down whole cubicles. Office staff screamed and ran for cover. He grabbed a swivel chair, hoisted it over his head, and tossed it across the room, where it knocked over a computer and narrowly missed a tech agent before storming off.

Sven exited down the hall where Mike went, and people started to pick up the office equipment.

Reuben knew what was going to happen. Sven would confront him, and Mike would take a swing at him. Sven would hold his own before security intervened. Mike would be put on suspension and put into mandatory anger management.

Except the way it happened before, it was Sven who set him off. Not Reuben.

That was the first time he thought about the whole 'butterfly effect' conundrum. If he hadn't died so many times, he wouldn't have been so dismissive of Mike. If he hadn't been so dismissive of Mike, Mike would have blown up on Sven.

Whoa.

Then a thought hit him. While it had been entertaining—and a bit scary—to get first row seats to the Mike Fury Self-Destruction Show, Reuben wondered how this slight change of events might affect Aki.

Turning his head, Reuben noticed Aki standing by a wall with her hand over her heart, unmoving and pale.

Reuben went to the water cooler and filled a cup. He stood still a few yards away and tensed as he thought about approaching her. He still wasn't sure he should. He was, after all, the one who had set Mike off. But maybe it was one of those things. She should know who Mike was now rather than later. But, would she see it that way?

He still held the water cup, staring at Aki. It had to have been two or three minutes since the incident, but she hadn't moved. He had to say something. He couldn't just let her stand there, traumatized.

"Hey." He smiled gently as he spoke.

She didn't reply. With a sudden burst of confidence, he grabbed a swivel chair with one hand and wheeled it to her.

"Sit," he told her.

To his surprise, she did.

"Here." He handed her the water and knelt beside her. She took a tiny sip. Then she burst into tears. Oh shit. He hadn't expected that. What should he do? He glanced around for a tissue and settled for a clean lunch napkin on someone's desk.

"Hey, hey, it's OK." He handed it to her, and she wiped her eyes.

"No," she whispered. "It's not OK. But thank you for saying that. And I'm sorry. We got into a fight, and you were just the next person he dealt with. What an asshole."

Reuben shrugged. "Hey, I'm just glad it was me and not some random stranger on the street, you know what I mean."

"I do." She cocked her head in agreement, and then her tear-stained eyes looked into his. "You're such a nice guy, Reuben. Why can't I meet a nice guy like you? Thank you, truly."

She squeezed his hand, then got up and walked away. He knew he couldn't say anything more. He wanted her. He wanted her more now than ever. He wanted to show her that nice, good guys did exist and that she didn't have to put up with that asshole.

Reuben suddenly felt very anxious with the thought. He was starting to realize he was obsessing over Aki for the wrong reasons. He tried to put the thought away. To think about Aki and what she needed, but before he could think of anything, it was over.

Aki was gone, back to work, or at least pretending to work.

He went back to his desk, and a ping came through his work orders. Tech needed to replace the destroyed computer. The agent who worked on it had nowhere to work.

"Right," he muttered.

He did have real work to do. Chasing Aki wasn't going to stop the bomb. It took him a while to replace the computer, and by the time he was done, the office was back to normal operating order. He finally found a chance to read his maple syrup story.

The maple syrup story was odd. It had happened on Wednesday the eighth at the Detroit/Windsor border. Windsor, Ontario was the town on the other side of the US/Canadian border at the Detroit crossing point. Apparently, as three semis had been crossing the Detroit River bridge, customs on the US side had opened one of them up and found it was full of an illegal shipment of maple syrup.

"How could maple syrup be illegal?" Reuben wondered.

He read the supporting documents. It was apparently raw, unregulated syrup contained in regular mason jars with handmade labels. But all three semis, apparently, were full of this stuff, stacked top to bottom.

As customs had moved to seize the goods, however, one of the drivers had produced a semi-automatic weapon and fired warning shots at the border officials. The border officials, of course, emerged in full SWAT gear. But not before the semis made a break for it. Border police had chased the semis, shooting out their tires. The drivers of all three semis had pulled out guns and fired back.

Choppers had been called out, and a full police chase had ensued through the streets of Detroit for the better part of the morning. Finally, police had apprehended two of the semis, arrested the suspects, and confiscated the contraband. As of three days ago, the final suspect remained at large. His semi, when they'd found it abandoned in a warehouse district, was empty.

The suspects in custody had given very little information. But what they did know was that the shootout was related to a mobster known as "the Canadian." The same guy Mike was asking about.

Reuben printed out everything he could on this guy, threw his research into his bag, and headed home.

Reuben—Thursday, February 9, 6:27 p.m.

On the train ride through the city, Reuben texted Marshall to find out what he wanted to do for dinner. By the time he arrived at his stop, he still hadn't received a response. Most likely, Marshall was out drinking with his old cop buddies for the night and would leave him alone. As many problems as they had, he knew Marshall needed the camaraderie. Once upon a time, his dad had been someone who young cops looked up to. Some still did. It was good for him to be around people who remembered that.

Reuben had lost sight of it, that was for sure.

He stopped and picked up Chinese takeout and a case of beer and anticipated a long, restful night without Marshall. He wanted some time to really dig into this Schaeffer case, and without Marshall underfoot, it sure would be easier.

But outside the restaurant, he heard a grating voice say, "Mr. Hash Brown, everything's about to change."

He turned to see the same homeless guy from that first day

he'd died. "You!" he said, cautiously approaching him. "How do you know about my mom's nickname for me?"

"Nickname?" the homeless guy tilted his head in confusion. "That's not your name? Mr. Hash Brown? Or maybe it's, Brown, Hash Brown, 00-00."

"Dude," Reuben said, realizing that because he couldn't die, he didn't have anything to be afraid of. "Who the fuck are you?"

The homeless guy smiled, exposing two rows of yellow teeth, "I'm nobody except the guy who remembers just like you. I remember everything."

Reuben's eyes widened. "You can time warp, too?"

The homeless guy nodded, and leaning in close, whispered, "I can. I can also do the Funky Chicken."

He started flapping around doing what Reuben had to admit was the best rendition of the Funky Chicken he'd ever seen.

With a cackle and a howl, the homeless man danced away, leaving Reuben with his Chinese takeout.

He arrived at the apartment and stiffened when he saw Sheera outside. She calmly watered her plants on the stoop.

She smiled pleasantly. "Good evening."

"Good evening," he repeated.

She continued with her gardening, unannoyed. Today was the day *before* Marshall had royally pissed them off, and Reuben was relieved.

Given he was on a new timeline, maybe it was possible to keep the Saturday morning debacle at bay?

"That would be nice," Reuben muttered as he took the stairs to his apartment.

When he opened the door, he didn't expect what was waiting for him on the couch.

"Martha?" He tossed the Chinese food onto the counter. "Martha Dragone? What are you doing here?"

CHAPTER TWENTY

Martha—Thursday, February 9, 7:03 a.m.

Gigi's Breakfast Café was more crowded than Martha had expected. Hidden in a tiny strip center, it didn't appear to be much. But at just after seven a.m., business was booming. It was a good thing she didn't have to go into the precinct early this morning.

The café was trendy enough inside, appearing as if the design came from a mid-century ice cream shop merged with early aughts coffee culture. The room was brightly lit, all done in soft pastels with candy-colored high-backed barstools at laptop counters. Soft jazz played overhead, and at mid-morning, the clientele was primarily preschool moms, college students, and the occasional businessman puttering with a laptop while lingering over coffee.

Martha finished the last couple bites of her cinnamon apple crepe, washing it down with a couple sips from her cooling coffee.

All the while, she thought about how she was going to find the Canadian.

On a whim, she pulled out her phone, and with a quick search, downloaded an old issue of the society magazine, *The Scene,* searching for famous Canadians.

Who knew? Maybe her criminal mastermind would be hiding in plain sight? Outside of a few comedians and actors, only one hit came back, the venture capitalist Alister Pout.

Guess there aren't many Canadians investing in New York? she mused.

The first page was a stunning cover shot of his signature half-grin, piercing blue eyes, faint stubble, and wavy dark hair. He was one good-looking guy.

Alister Pout lounges on the deck chair of his Park Avenue penthouse and sips a glass of wine. The 32-year-old almost-billionaire is the whole picture. The penthouse, the wine, the scenic view of the city, and most of all, the women. A half-dressed Swedish model had to be safely stowed away on the yacht for the duration of the interview. He handed her the keys and promised to meet her in an hour.

"This shouldn't take too long," he'd promised her with a sensuous peck on the lips. She'd stared at him longingly and left with a coy smile.

Now, we're sitting on the deck to talk business. Or, at least try to. He's the most eligible bachelor in the city, and he laughs at the idea that he might be just a bit...cliché.

"Cliché?" he says. "Maybe a bit. But I think you've got to buy into the system before you can reform it."

Reforming the system is definitely an objective since he founded RedBook, a revolutionary online platform related to social media. According to its marketing campaign, RedBook isn't social media. It's a new platform that will redefine what is quickly becoming the bane of modern existence.

"I hate it when people call RedBook 'social media,'" he remarks

with disdain. "It's not. I think people hate the term and what it stands for. I don't blame them. I hate it myself."

Indeed, RedBook calls itself a "communications platform," whatever that means. Alister explains it with the gusto reserved for tech moguls in mansions.

"What we're doing with RedBook," he says, "is creating a platform that is as revolutionary to the world Facebook was in 2006. Facebook has lost its relevance and has been declining for a lot of years. Zuckerberg will likely take out a hit on me for that. Print that part, for security reasons, please."

He laughs, but it's not entirely clear if he's joking.

"But I don't care," he continues with a devil-may-care glint in his eyes. "I'll say it anyway. I predict we'll see the end of Facebook and the decline of social media in general within the next decade. RedBook is going to replace it by taking the essence of what social media can do and readapting it to meet the needs of the dawning decade."

Pout's plan for doing that is an unclear cacophony of buzzwords and hyperbolic testaments to the team at RedBook's parent company, S-wire Media.

The rest of the article was a straight-up advertisement for RedBook, complete with boilerplate paragraphs lifted from their marketing materials.

Lazy reporting, Martha thought. It sounded like the interview was a bust, and the writer was looking to fill space. That figured.

She did a quick online search for RedBook and S-wire Media. They had a strong media presence, carefully crafted posts, and slick web copy. Sifting through their social media accounts, she still didn't have any idea what RedBook actually did.

Maybe that was the thing. Maybe RedBook was a scam. A fake product used as a front for...what?

Her search on S-wire Media proved just as inconclusive. Their official website had a list of company officers, and she searched them all. At the outset, they all seemed legitimate. They were verifiable technology professionals and investors, all with the right credentials. Stanford, Duke, Yale, former board members of Dell, HP, Chase Bank. All respectable and all the right kind of people to invest in a company like this.

She sighed. Alister Pout was no more a criminal mastermind than that sheep bleating outside her window was a wolf.

But still, there was something nagging at the back of her mind. There was something about Alister Pout that intrigued her, but she couldn't put her finger on it.

He's good-looking, she thought. *Who knows, maybe I'm just yearning to move to Canada to find me a sexy Mountie and free healthcare.*

Martha chuckled at the thought as she tossed a five-dollar bill on the table and left. This was the day she had set aside to get answers on this case, and she wasn't any closer. She needed air.

She took the street slowly, mulling over what little she had on the Canadian. Maybe she should send it up the ladder. But she wouldn't. Her career depended on it. She would, instead, get more information.

A driver whizzed by. "Hey lady," he heckled, "get your head out of your ass."

She hadn't even realized she had wandered into the crosswalk. What was wrong with her? Car horns honked at her, and she waved apologetically and scurried to the other side.

That was when she noticed the van from Mr. Sudds Dry

Cleaning sitting at the red light. She stopped on the sidewalk and stared at it.

The logo was a big, meaty hand wrapped around a pink sponge, surrounded by lots of blue and white bubbles.

Why would you use that to advertise your dry cleaning? she thought. *No one wants to associate their expensive suits with bubbles and soap. They want to see their suit as pressed and put together with little to no effort on their part.*

But something about the whole van inexplicably bothered her. There was nothing wrong with having a dumb logo. So, what was it that made her suspicious of this van? Was it because the door hinges had little bits of rust on them? There was nothing wrong with having a little rust on an old van.

What is it about this van? No. It wasn't the van. It was that odd dry cleaner logo. Mr. Sudds. She felt like she knew it from somewhere, felt like she'd been there before, although she knew she hadn't. Had she?

Déjà vu. That was all she could blame it on.

Still, it was such an odd feeling that she felt compelled to follow the van and see where it led to.

Raising her hand, she hailed a taxi.

CHAPTER TWENTY-ONE

Martha—Thursday, February 9, 8:08 a.m.

She stared through the taxi's windshield at the white van they were following.

"This is what going insane must feel like," she muttered to herself.

"Excuse me?" said the taxi driver.

"Nothing." Martha grabbed the side of the seat until her knuckles hurt. "Can you go any faster?"

"Lady, we're in gridlock. Unless you want me to Chitty-Chitty-Bang-Bang this, we're stuck."

He was right. They were stuck in gridlock, and he really was going as fast as he could. But the van was several cars in front of them. If it turned and they got caught in a light, they'd lose it.

The light turned green, and the van moved forward.

"Go, go," she prodded, almost bouncing in her seat as they gained a few yards on the van. "Cut into the middle lane." She put out her hand and waved her badge at the car behind them. "Now."

"I'm going, I'm going." But there wasn't a traffic rule this guy was ignoring. All this playing it by the rules was really slowing them down.

When the cab finally caught up with the van parked against the curb in front of them, Martha took out her phone and snapped a photo of the plates. She texted it to Jake. *Can you run these plates?*

"All right." She turned toward the cab driver and pointed toward a curb opposite the van and the shop it was parked beside. "Right here."

"That's it?" The cab driver protested. "All that for a dry cleaner's? I thought we were going on a chase."

She didn't say anything. She just watched from the cab's window as the van pulled up in front of the dry cleaners, and a guy in a hoodie stepped out.

A moment later, a fancy car that looked like it had accidentally turned down the wrong street pulled up, and a man wearing a fedora stepped out.

The two of them spoke for a minute, with the hoodie-wearing man handing Fedora Man an old cell phone, presumably a burner.

Then they split up.

Martha didn't know who to follow. The fancy car or the van. She had already texted the plates to the van, so she went for Fedora Man.

The cabbie trailed the fancy car through the streets until they wound up in the financial district. The car stopped beside a skyscraper with one of those modern sculpture monstrosities out front and Fedora Man stepped out, sans fedora.

Martha's jaw dropped. Was that who she thought it was? Alister Pout, the Canadian venture capitalist and founder of RedBook?

What the fuck was he doing in front of Mr. Sudds?

CHAPTER TWENTY-TWO

Martha—Thursday, February 9, 11:42 a.m.

It was cold outside the precinct building. The air was clear and cloudless, and patches of ice dotted the sidewalk and melted into muddy puddles in the gutters below. Martha shivered as she pushed the glass doors open to join the freezing masses stepping outside to grab lunch.

As soon as she got outside, she passed a handful of officers shooting the breeze on a smoke break. They stood huddled in a group, smoke wafting around them like winter fog. It reminded her of some sort of animal pecking order, packing together for warmth and first-world social survival.

She rolled her eyes at the whole scene.

At the top of the pecking order would have been Tom. Tom was one of the senior officers and had been there longer than Captain Kenneth, a fact that made him think he owned Kenneth. While the current police chief could certainly hold his own in a power struggle, it was rare for anyone to get anywhere in the precinct without Tom's approval. This, she knew, was precisely why Jake kept his distance from her.

Martha had, by way of having a vagina, been excluded from Tom's list of favored players. Jake, by way of association, had to play both sides, working with Martha yet still being cool enough for the boys' club. Martha wondered how the dynamic between Jake and herself would have played out had Tom not been around.

Today, Tom was surrounded by a couple of his other douchebag buddies, neither of whose names she could recall. The loud, raucous laughter spoke of end-of-the-day comic relief, coupled with the strains of bottom-of-the-desk-drawer stress reliever.

"No, no." Tom held up his finger. "It was at the Detroit-Windsor border."

"How many semis?" asked a red-headed, baby-faced officer.

The kid didn't look more than twenty-three and had a rounded, well-fed physique that spoke of three square meals a day courtesy of mama's home cooking.

"Three," Tom explained. "So, the border patrol tried to confiscate the contraband—"

"Maple syrup?" the ginger-headed officer interjected. "Bootleg maple syrup? Really?"

The whole group burst out laughing, and even Martha raised an eyebrow.

"No, it's not cool, man." Tom's face turned sullen. "Three officers were shot at."

"Ah, fucking no!" the ginger officer swore.

The profanity rang heavy with unaccustomed vulgarity. He was trying too hard. He didn't talk like that over Mama's blueberry pancakes, and he overcompensated at work. At least Martha wasn't the only one trying to impress the boys' club.

"Two went into the hospital," Tom confirmed. "And the other… Well, they don't think he's going to make it."

Martha stood on the sidelines and listened to the gorillas beat their chests and curse up blue streaks.

"That's just bullshit." The dark-haired officer shook his head. "We oughta go down there and bust a cap right in their cop-killing skulls."

"Shit, yeah!" the ginger-haired cop agreed. "Did they take them down?"

Tom shook his head. "It was all part of some big operation, they think. Fucking Canadians, man."

"Fucking Canadians," the ginger officer echoed. "Fake Americans. I tell you, we fight all the wars for them, keep the whole continent safe. They just sit there freezing their asses off with their damn mooses and shit, thinking they can fly under the radar saying 'eh' and 'aboot.'"

Tom furrowed his brow at the ginger-headed officer. "Shit, Mark. Calm the fuck down. I served with Canadians in Afghanistan. They have their own military and were part of all major operations in the last hundred years. What the fuck did they teach you at school, man?"

Mark smiled sheepishly, studied the ground, and flicked his cigarette. "Are you kidding? I was too busy having sex in high school. I didn't have time for that shit."

Martha didn't believe that for a second. He said what was needed to fit in. Sadly, it worked.

The trio laughed and whistled, and Tom just shook his head. "Your generation scares me."

"Dude, we don't need a history class to go down there and bust some cop-killing, white trash bootleggers!" the dark-haired cop growled. "These colors don't run!"

Then he made a gun shooting motion toward the ground

and explosion noises with his mouth. "I'd like to see them go down. Anybody wanna road trip it?"

Martha shook her head. These guys called themselves cops? They did their job, but at times like this, they gave the precinct a bad name.

"I'd be down for that." Mark took a drag on the cigarette in his hand.

"Hey," Tom saw Martha standing on the sidewalk. "You should come with us."

"What?" Martha raised an eyebrow.

"Yeah," the dark-haired one jeered. "You can make some pancakes with all the maple syrup we're going to save."

The whole group dissolved into laughter.

"Yeah." Tom shook his head back and forth like a wet dog. "We'd stick her in the back with an apron. I'd bet she'd look totally fucking hot."

The others whistled and laughed, and Martha just groaned. "You guys are real classy, you know that?"

"Aww, come on," Mark jeered. "We're just having a little fun. Don't tell me you wouldn't be down for it?" He shimmied toward the ground, and the rest of the group laughed.

Martha grimaced. "Is that the best innuendo you've got, Mark? Is that what 'she said?'"

The other cops burst into laughter. "She got you, Mark. She got you." Tom even gave her a thumbs-up.

"Good one." Mark nodded. "We're grabbing an early lunch at the bar across the street. You in?"

So she'd gotten through, if only a bit. However, as much as Martha wished to fit in, she had bigger shit to deal with. Martha shook her head. "And embarrass your asses at pool? Nah. For a bunch of swinging dicks, you all suck at handling sticks and balls."

The trio burst out into laughter as Martha walked away. *Small steps,* she thought. *Small steps.*

When Martha arrived back at the police station it was bustling with sharp and put-together officers darting in and out. She entered the well-lit high rise, then took the elevator to the fifth floor where she worked.

It was a little quieter up here, with most of the officers out on patrol. With straight posture and a smug expression, she strolled through the blue-carpeted halls and half-empty cubicles, expecting to be congratulated any second.

She assumed Jake had done his homework with the photos and license plates and was ready to dive into whatever that had produced.

But Jake wasn't in, and before she could say anything, Captain Kenneth found her. "Hey, where have you been?" he asked. "That flasher case on Fifth was at it again. We got him."

Martha forced a smile. "Ah…wow. How?"

"Citizen's arrest." The captain cocked a thumb toward the holding cells. "I need you to take statements from those involved and get this guy booked. They're in the waiting room."

"But I have—"

"Now, rookie. Now." Captain Kenneth walked away before Martha could protest any further.

Martha—Thursday, February 9, 4:31 p.m.

Fuck, those witnesses could talk. Martha looked at her watch, lamenting how it had taken her almost five hours to interview the six witnesses, process the perp, and type up her reports. If someone had only warned her how much red tape there would be in police work, she would have donned a cape and cowl and taken the vigilante approach to crime.

Sighing in relief that it was over, she walked over to Jake. "Hey, did you get my texts?"

He looked up. "About the license plate?"

"Yeah." She placed her hands on her hips. "And the…never mind. What did you find on the plates?"

Jake pursed his lips and shrugged. "Nothing. That van's clean as a whistle."

"You mean you found nothing on that van?" Martha was surprised, to say the least.

Jake stared at her. "Should I have? I mean, what's going on?"

Martha told Jake about her unusual morning.

Jake pursed his lips. "So let me get this straight. You followed a random van on a hunch, saw a well-dressed man not doing anything illegal, and then followed him to his office? A well-dressed man who, might I add, is one of New York City's wealthiest members."

Fuck. Martha could see where this was going.

"Is there an official case on Pout?" Jake asked. "Is he a suspect in an ongoing investigation?"

"Well, no…"

Jake groaned. "The only law I see broken is the one you broke yourself."

Martha blushed red with frustration. "But don't you see?"

Jake chuckled with disbelief. "Look, you might be right that there's something shady going on there. But in police work, 'probably' and 'something shady' aren't going to cut it. I appreciate the effort and the dedication, but next time you want to take initiative, try not to do something that will get the precinct sued."

Jake reached out a hand to touch Martha's shoulder.

"Don't patronize me," Martha growled.

"I'm not; I'm trying to save you. Shit like this gets you on the—"

"The what?" she cut in. "I'm already on the tampon squad, aren't I?"

Jake didn't say anything.

"And now that I have an actual lead, you want me to, what? Bury it? Unsee what I saw?" She realized her voice was rising.

"There's protocols that must be followed," Jake told her.

"Got it." Martha was so frustrated that she knew she needed to leave before she said something to get her into more shit. She took a deep breath and said, "Look, I got to go."

He frowned. "Go where? You're still on duty."

"No," she answered coolly without even checking the clock. "I'm taking a personal day."

Martha—Thursday, February 9, 4:49 p.m.

Stepping outside the precinct, she fought the urge to scream. She knew Jake was right. But there was right, and then there was *right*.

"Fuck, that didn't go well," she muttered. Looking at her watch, she saw it was almost the end of the shift. She didn't need to take a personal day. She could have just stepped outside for a bit. "One less day off for me," she lamented.

She pulled out her phone and dialed an intern at the precinct who she'd worked with in the past. He'd been instrumental in helping her close an important case, and oddly enough, she felt like she'd worked with him on the Pout case too.

But she hadn't, had she? Déjà vu, much?

Sanctioned or not, she was going to follow this lead. Zach answered the phone.

"Hey, I know it's been a while, but can you do me a favor?"

There was a pause before he answered, "Will it get me in trouble?"

"Only if you tell anyone."

"I don't know about this."

"Look, it's a little thing," she promised. "If we get caught, I'll say that I lied to you. But we're not going to get caught. Promise."

Another long pause before Zach said, "OK, fine. What is it?"

Martha smiled. "I just want someone's schedule, that's all."

"Who?" There was a wariness in his voice.

"Alister Pout," she told him.

"Fuck."

"Yeah, fuck," she echoed. "Please?"

Zach groaned before letting out a long sigh. "Fine, I'll do it. But you owe me. Big time."

"You got it, Zach. Big time."

With that done, Martha took long, freezing strides to the train station. Right now, she needed to calm down. She needed a long, hot bath, hot chocolate, pizza, and a romcom to distract her.

This was one fucked-up day. She should have taken a sick day the second she found herself following some random white van.

What the fuck was she thinking? She wasn't. She was just following her gut, and it turned out to be right. There was some shady shit going down, not that she had any idea what it was.

There was the Canadian. Seven different crimes, including murder, attempted murder, robbery, assault, all tied together by this phantom. They all had similar patterns: burner phones, no real contact. But there was no real connection to explain any of it. Then there was this white van that seemed to be connected to something.

Then there was Alister Pout… A Canadian who had a burner phone.

She knew she had some of the answers rolling around in her subconscious. She just didn't know how to connect the dots and turn her intuition into something tangible.

Martha arrived at the train station and stood in line. While she waited, she pulled out her phone and looked up the maple syrup bust that the guys were talking about.

One of the hospitalized cops had died, which meant everyone would be on the case.

A case she knew she could crack. If only…

She needed to talk this out with someone who wasn't going to laugh at her or tell her to get back to the beat. Someone who would actually listen. Someone who knew a thing or two about following your instincts.

There was only one person she knew who could totally understand her—her old mentor. He had retired years ago, but he was good in a pinch.

She changed her train ticket and decided to pay him a little visit.

Martha—Thursday, February 9, 6:19 p.m.

Martha sat in the small living room, settled into the plush

orange couch, and attempted to ignore Bill O'Reilly miming politics on mute on the 52-inch plasma screen. Ignoring O'Reilly proved to be more difficult than she would have liked, which she figured was largely his goal in life. Mission accomplished, she mused, and Marshall Peet grabbed the remote and switched it off.

"Yeah, I'd heard about the Canadian syrup bust," he said as he grabbed a beer out of the fridge. He held up a chilled brown bottle. "You want one?"

Martha nodded. "Sure."

He grabbed two bottles, then opened the freezer door and gestured inside. "Don't ever buy these hash browns." He held up a small, shrink-wrapped box. "They're shitty, and Reuben always burns them."

"Duly noted."

He handed her the drink, and they both twisted off the tops and simultaneously threw the drinks back.

Marshall plopped down on the couch opposite her and leaned forward, elbows on his knees. "All right, so tell me what's going on."

CHAPTER TWENTY-THREE

Reuben—Thursday, February 9, 6:29 p.m.

Reuben hadn't seen Martha in years, and he certainly didn't expect her to be sitting in the living room that day. Not when the world was on a ticking time bomb.

She offered him a smile. "Hi, Reuben. Good to see you. How long has it been? Two, three years?"

He forced a smile. "Something like that."

He had still been with Rachel then. Rachel had never liked Martha because she wasn't "our kind of people." Reuben had interpreted that to mean gritty and mission obsessed.

Reuben wasn't like that back then. If it wasn't for the time warps, he wouldn't be like that now.

How things change when you die a bunch of times…

"You still with…" Martha's voice trailed off.

"No," he answered quickly. Too quickly.

"Like Reuben could hold onto a girl. She slipped through his fingers like that maple syrup crook slipped through those border cops," Marshall muttered as he shuffled to the bathroom.

"Ignore him." Martha walked over to Reuben. She gave him a quick hug. "I'm sorry to hear about the breakup. She was a nice girl."

Reuben grimaced. "No, she wasn't."

"You're right, she wasn't," Martha agreed, and they both laughed. "To tell you the truth, I never saw you with a girl like her."

"Yeah?" Reuben crossed into the kitchen and grabbed a beer out of the fridge. "What kind of girl did you see me with?"

He popped the top on the beer bottle, flicked it into the garbage, and joined her back on the couch. He didn't particularly want to rehash the old days, but he was interested in her analysis of his love life.

Or lack thereof.

She stared off for a moment, then back at him. "I always saw you ending up with someone random, who none of us in the old gang would have ever thought of."

"Random, huh?" Reuben smirked and sipped the beer bottle. "Like what?"

"Like…some Asian hottie over on Exchange. Someone sassy. You need sassy to keep you in line."

"Is that right?" He laughed. If only she knew.

"See, that's your problem," she continued. "We've got to get you out there. You're not going to find a girl like that at some tech job."

"He's not going to find a girl anywhere if he doesn't stop dressing like that." Marshall had emerged from the other room with his arms full of boxes. "You look like Bill Nye the Science Guy."

"Hello, Dad." Reuben eyed the boxes. "What's all this?"

"Evidence files." Marshall grinned from ear to ear and

dropped the files ceremoniously on the coffee table. They fell with a loud bang, accentuating their importance to the household.

"Is this what you were telling me about?" Martha tentatively opened one of the boxes.

"Evidence files?" Reuben furrowed his brow. "You've never let me see any of the evidence files."

"That's because you never work on anything worth investigating," Marshall said as he sorted the boxes. Some he put on the floor to be forgotten, and a couple he left on the table to be opened and sorted. "Martha here, she's got a big case she's working on. I wanted to show her all the loose ends I've got from Operation Old MacDonald."

"Operation Old MacDonald?" Reuben repeated. "The Canadian raw milk smugglers?"

The tall tale of his childhood. It got bigger and better every year.

The raw milk smuggling ring had originally supplied unregulated jugs to farmers' markets in upstate New York. The milk stayed under the radar for years, and they probably would have stayed that way. However, the milk became so popular that they got bigger and started taking in more farms. When both demand and supply rose, more distribution outlets had opened, and the suppliers got cocky. That was when the unpasteurized milk somehow wiggled its way into a local grocery chain. The details were all a little fuzzy, but it was worth noting that the owner of the grocery chain was married to the sheriff, whose uncle ran the farmers' co-op.

So the milk went public, and in the space of six months, thirty people died in one town. The only thing connecting them was that milk.

But when the police came in to investigate the deaths, no

one knew anything. Marshall spent years trying to get to the bottom of it and went around in circles. He never was able to solve it. It had all the elements of a great crime. A sick town with the dead and infirm piling up, and each week the papers printed the rising numbers.

Outraged mothers had been crying for justice over the corpses of the young, leading to a class-action suit battling through political gridlock. Meanwhile, farmers had protested against government overreach.

They launched whole milk education campaigns that stole the tired line from the drug war about making illegal products legal for the purpose of regulating them.

In the middle of it all were the small-town country folk who trusted no one in uniform. All the while, a stream of dirty money flowed through the whole mess like...well...bad milk. All in all, it was a juicy story, Reuben had to admit. If he hadn't heard it all his life.

It had become Marshall's enduring mission to find justice for the victims, but it had been over thirty years, and he was still no closer to an answer than he was when the case was finally closed.

"Yep, Canadian raw milk smugglers." Marshall unboxed files and pages.

"Dad, you will never solve that case." Reuben leaned back into the couch. "I don't know why you keep that old stuff around."

"Maybe I won't." Marshall grinned at Martha. "But Martha just may be able to. So, I'm going to let her in on all the old players. See if we can match up some notes."

Marshall moved about with the excitement of a child with a new toy as he set out his notes. He filled up the coffee table with photos and piles of documents. Reuben had vivid recollections of being a kid and being punished for even touching those photos.

"Now," Marshall handed Martha a carefully selected pile, "read that. Those are the basics of this case. We'll get into specifics as we get more into it."

Martha carefully read the papers while Marshall continued to lay out piles.

"You know, Dad, if you'd ask once in a while, you'd find I've got something big I'm working on, too," Reuben told him.

"Yeah, what's that?" Marshall asked around a pencil in his mouth. "A fried circuit board?"

"Forget it." Reuben turned to Martha. "So, what's this big case?"

"This past year," she set the pile on her lap, "we've had seven different deadly assaults or homicides all tied to a mysterious crime boss named 'the Canadian.'"

Reuben couldn't believe what he just heard. "Sorry, the Canadian?" That was the guy Mike Fury had asked him to research today.

Martha narrowed her eyes at Reuben. "Yeah, I know. Terrible alias. What ever happened to names like 'the Butcher' or 'the Finisher?'"

"I know, right?" Reuben agreed, his mind racing. How did she know about the Canadian? Could their two cases be linked? Could he tell her that he knew about this guy too without blowing his cover?

To that end, did his cover even matter, given what was at stake?

"An unassuming name for a dangerous criminal," Martha commented.

Reuben nodded, thinking back to his own case files. "Because he's super polite," he muttered.

Martha raised an eyebrow. "Yeah, that's right. How did you know that?"

"Ah...umm, because it's the typical Canadian schtick. To be super nice?" *Nice recovery,* Reuben thought.

"Still...that's a pretty big leap in logic for you to make." She was eyeing him that way she had when they were kids and he was hiding something like the last lollipop or piece of candy.

Not that great a recovery. "Lucky guess?" he offered.

"Or intuition, maybe?" Martha said.

"Intuition?" Marshall scoffed. "This guy has the intuition of a doormat. Where did you learn Canadians were polite? College?"

"Yep," Reuben shot back. "From that damn Columbia education, remember?"

"Smart ass." Marshall continued to sort papers. "Good for you. Four years and all that tuition money, and you learned how to stereotype Canadians and tinker around with circuit boards."

Reuben shook his head. "You have no idea what I do, do you?"

Marshall sighed. "Yeah, of course, I do. Some yada-yada with government pencil-pushing and bureaucratic bumbling. Look, it's all well and good if that's what gets ya paid. But nothing compares to being out there in the nitty-gritty, wrestling criminals to the ground, getting feces thrown at you, getting shot at."

Marshall lifted up his shirt, and Reuben groaned. He knew where this was going.

"See?" Marshall pointed to a couple of tiny red scars on his chest and back. "I've been shot twelve times."

"I know, Dad," Reuben told him as he lowered his shirt. "You've shown me. Probably both of us."

Marshall wagged his finger at Martha. "That's what's in a good day's work. Don't you forget that. When you can come home and know you helped make the world a better place."

"Please ignore our dysfunctional family politics," Reuben apologized to Martha.

"I have for twenty years." She laughed graciously. "I find them endearing now."

"Endearing?" Reuben leaned back on the couch with a long chuckle. "Well, that's a new one. We should tell that one to the neighbors. What do you think, Dad? Are we endearing?"

"The neighbors." Marshall slapped a sticky note on a pile of papers. "Couple of lesbo dykes with sticks up their asses. That's what happens to women when they don't get regular meat injections—"

"OK, Dad. Let's cut this rant short before you say something really insensitive," Reuben interjected as Martha stifled a laugh.

"Sorry, excuse my French." Marshall placed his hand over his heart and cleared his throat.

She laughed and rolled her eyes. "Please, I'm a fucking cop. Or don't you remember?"

"A damned good one at that. Tell Reuben what you've been telling me. Listen." He pointed at Reuben. "Just listen to this story. You gotta hear this."

Reuben cleared his throat, not particularly interested in whatever Marshall might think he "had" to hear.

"OK, so I've had this sense about this Canadian character," she started.

Reuben raised an eyebrow. "Yeah?"

"I knew he was part of something big, but I couldn't figure it out. So I followed this dry cleaning van, really for no reason other than intuition."

Marshall grinned at her. "Intuition is the backbone of a good cop. That's why this guy over here will never make it. No instincts. No intuition."

"Fuck," Reuben whispered and started to his room.

"Where ya goin'?" Marshall's voice chased him. "Did I say something that hurt sissy pants' feelings?"

Reuben wasn't sure what had snapped. Maybe it was dying a few times and always getting a reset and repeat to try again. But repeats wouldn't work here. He could repeat it a million times, and his dad would feel exactly the same about him.

But dying gave one a new perspective, and the perspective Reuben had was a simple one. His dad was a grade-A asshole. For the first time in Reuben's life, he decided to fight asshole with asshole. "Tell me, where was your 'intuition' when mom left?"

Dead, tense silence took over the small living room and sucked the life out of it.

Marshall faced Reuben, staring at him with a burning intensity.

Reuben, perhaps for the first time in his life, held his dad's eyes. Locked them in, refusing to waver.

After what felt like a lifetime, Marshall slammed his fist on the table. "You don't know shit about what happened between your mother and me."

"I know she left and never looked back." Too far. Reuben was beyond giving a fuck. "Why was that? What would make a wife run off and leave her husband and ten-year-old kid without so much as a whisper? Huh? What might have happened?"

Martha set the investigation documents gently down on the coffee table. "I'm going to—"

"You snot-nosed little prick," Marshall yelled at Reuben. "I seem to remember your mom packing while I was saving your ass. Both your asses," he pointed at Martha, "from that psycho. And what was your saint of a mother doing? Fucking sneaking out the back door."

"Taking the best chance she had to get away from you," Reuben shot back.

"Reuben, that's not fair," Martha said, but both Reuben and Marshall glared at her. Martha raised her hands in surrender.

Marshall turned his hate back on Reuben. "You don't know what you're talking about. Yeah, she left because raising a family was hard. Raising you was hard."

"And yet millions of families manage, but not the great Marshall." Reuben was filled with rage at this point. "He couldn't muster what it takes."

"You think you know what it takes?" Marshall shot back. "You think you know what it's like to have kids? To do what's best for them day in, day out? Earning a steady paycheck so your kid can take karate, and piano and God only knows what else? No, you don't know shit about the day in, day out of being a parent or, God knows, being a husband. You think you're an expert now? Is that what you think? 'Cause you went off and played house with what's her name…Rebecca?"

"Rachel." Reuben narrowed his eyes at Marshall while he thought back to Rachel and their short-lived romance. They'd bonded over their love of ballroom dancing. Had even competed together in some local competitions. And what had she done? Left him for a better dancer.

Needless to say, Reuben had never told his dad that part of the story.

Marshall muttered something under his breath. "Yeah, whatever. Your mother and I lived together for thirteen years. You couldn't even make it to the altar. You shacked up with her for what, six months? Then when it got hard, guess what? Oh, where's Reuben? He ran like hell."

Reuben clenched his hands into fists. "That was not what happened, you old fuck."

"Wasn't it, though?" Marshall yelled. "Marriage isn't easy, son. It takes work and dedication, and it takes sacrifice. Don't you dare say you knew what went on in ours because I guarantee you, you didn't."

Martha was backing away from the two of them, seriously considering calling in backup.

"Whatever," Reuben mumbled as he headed to his room. "I'm going to find some maple syrup."

"Wait." Martha's eyes widened. "What did you say?" she muttered as Reuben slammed his bedroom door.

CHAPTER TWENTY-FOUR

Reuben—Thursday, February 9, 8:01 p.m.

Reuben paced in his bedroom and replayed his fight with Marshall. God. What the fuck was wrong with him? He knew better than to engage his dad.

But the whole cop thing with Martha just annoyed him. He worked for the goddamned CIA. He wasn't flipping burgers or cleaning toilets. Of course, according to CIA protocol, his dad thought Marshall worked at the "State Department." So did Martha. The only person who knew was Buzz, and technically he wasn't supposed to know.

But Marshall... He couldn't know. At least his father knew he had a good job and was a decent, law-abiding citizen.

Whatever was changing in Reuben made Marshall's constant bullshit wear on his nerves. It was funny when it was Red Foreman on *That 70s Show*. But in real life, Marshall was getting to be unbearable.

He hadn't meant to push his buttons about his mom. Carolyn had left when he was ten, and he knew it was a sore topic with Marshall. He didn't even know why he did it. Maybe it was all Marshall's holier than thou, nitty-gritty criminal crap. Maybe it was the time warp thing. Maybe it was the Mike-Fury-freaking-out-on-everyone thing. Whatever the reason, Marshall had really gotten under his skin.

But it was more than that. Martha knew about the Canadian. She might have a lead. Something that would help him crack the case. He'd have to call her later and figure out a way to subtly pick her brain on what she knew and—

There was a knock on his bedroom door.

"Go the fuck away," Reuben yelled.

"OK, sorry," Martha answered from the other side.

Shit. It wasn't her fault.

"Hey." He opened the door. "Sorry, I thought it was Marshall."

"Yeah." She entered the room. "You two sure can go at it."

"That was a mild one." He chuckled, shutting the door behind her.

Martha pensively walked into the room and fingered the old lamps and dusty desk. "This room hasn't changed much since we were kids."

Reuben scoffed. "Yeah, well, excuse me. I'll have to add 'call a decorator' to my list right after 'get over failed engagement.' You of all people should know about that."

"Sorry, I just meant we have a lot of history together, you and me."

Reuben cocked his head but didn't respond. He leaned against the desk and drummed his fingertips against it. "Martha, if you're here to make peace, I'm not really in the mood."

She looked a little hurt, and he felt a twinge of guilt. She wasn't Marshall. "No, nothing like that. I'm just..." she started but shook her head before finishing. "Do you ever think about her?"

"Who? Rachel?"

She shook her head. "No, your mom."

Reuben pursed his lips. "Sometimes."

"I remember her." Martha got a faraway look in her eyes. "She was so pretty. Way out of Marshall's league, even back then. I remember this one time we were playing in the street, and I fell and skinned my knee. She rushed out to help me. I tried so hard not to cry in front of her because I didn't want to distort my face in front of someone so pretty, if that makes any sense?"

Reuben cracked a smile. "Little-kid logic. And yeah, she was pretty. What the hell she wanted with Marshall, I'll never know."

Martha chuckled. "You think that's why she left? Because Marshall was too hard to live with?"

"I don't know. He only changed after she left."

"What happened?" she prodded softly.

"Well, it was all tied up with the whole…incident."

"Right." She nodded slowly. "God, that changed everything."

"Yeah."

The incident. Reuben was in fifth grade. The day had started innocently enough. He'd woken up and dressed for school. He remembered his mom fussing over his homework. He was supposed to write an essay on George Washington, but he had waited until the last minute. Mom hadn't been happy with the rushed and finished product.

"This is not the quality of work that gets you into places like NYU or Columbia," she'd chided as she peered over the two pages of pencil-smudged, wide-ruled paper. "If you want to be a computer engineer, you've got to have good grades. This is not how you do it. You've got to start planning your homework better."

"The bus is going to be here any minute, Mom. I have to go."

"Have a great day, sweetie." She'd pecked him on the cheek and held him just a little too long. "And remember, whatever happens, I love you more than anything in the world."

"OK, Mom," he'd mumbled through the fabric of her shirt.

"You know that, right?" She'd seemed desperate.

"Yeah." The school bus horn honked outside.

"Bye, honey." She'd given him one last squeeze before he broke away and ran toward the school bus.

He remembered thinking that moms were weird sometimes—little-kid thoughts.

He also remembered thinking that if he had known this would be the last time he would ever see her, he would have held on a little bit longer.

It was 8:32 when he boarded the bus that morning. He knew that because that's what the psycho had said when he attacked.

Reuben had sat with his usual group of neighborhood boys near the front of the bus behind the driver. At the stop on the next street over, they picked up Martha and her sister. When Martha saw that her usual seat was taken, she sat next to Reuben. All in all, it was an unremarkable Tuesday morning. A forgettable day of fifth grade.

Until it wasn't.

The last stop on the bus route was out of the way. They had to pick up Bobby Grenshaw. On this day, as Bobby stepped onto the bus, suddenly standing behind him was... someone else.

"Get down!" yelled the tall, wild-eyed man with tattered clothes. The bus driver tried to shut the door around him, but he pushed his way in. He waved a gun around the bus. "Everybody get down on the ground."

Reuben remembered the hysteria, especially among the little kids. Some of the younger ones began to wail for their mothers, and the wild man fired his gun out the window.

"I said shut up! All of you, not a word! 8:32. 8:32, that's when you got on. That's when it starts. That's when it ends."

Reuben and the others crouched low on the school bus floor, pressing their faces against the ridged rubber walkway. Reuben remembered the smell of dirt from the collective shoes and tried to concentrate on a piece of gum under the seat.

The wild man continued to yell, ranting about how if anyone moved, he would kill them all.

"What do you want?" the bus driver had stammered from the floor.

"I want you to get off the floor and drive this bus," he'd told him. "It's all about time. I need time."

The wild man squealed with laughter, and Reuben remembered thinking it was not at all like the powerful villains on television. His laugh had a disturbing, grating quality to it. The only thing he could compare it to was his childish idea of a mental patient, but not the maniacal ones. At least those were intriguing. He was like the creepy ones who ate plastic grapes and rambled nonsensical rhymes to no one.

This guy was more like that. But with a gun.

The next couple of hours were a blur to him. The bus driver had been ordered to drive the bus into a certain building about an hour outside of the city. The kidnapper had given the police instructions that they were to get Hopper, whoever the fuck that was, to Grand Central Station before the bus got to the building.

"I need her. Otherwise, everyone dies!" the wild man had squealed into the CB.

What was this about? A girlfriend? A breakup? Some fucked-up stalker?

Reuben remembered Martha crouched next to him, looking terrified. He'd remembered what his dad had told him, that a good man always protects others even when they're scared themselves. Protecting others, he always said, was not being afraid even when you were. Reuben had seen her little trembling hand with glittery pink nail polish lying next to him, and he'd reached over and grabbed it. She'd looked up, and they had locked gazes. He'd never forgotten the mixture of fear and relief that passed between them.

He'd squeezed her hand and hadn't let go.

Meanwhile, NYPD, including Marshall Peet, had gone on full alert. Years later, Reuben would hear from Marshall's partners that his dad had realized very quickly from the dispatch that it was Reuben's school bus and hadn't even asked permission to take the call.

He'd just jumped in a car and rushed full throttle, lights flashing. There was even a report that he had said, "Protocol be damned. I'm saving my kid."

Of course, Marshall himself never admitted as much to Reuben. He always said he was assigned the call and did his duty for all the kids on the bus. *Just once, Dad,* Reuben had thought. *Could you say you loved me?*

Whatever the reason, Marshall Peet had been on the scene, along with half a dozen other cops and a chopper. Reuben remembered the bus racing down the highway with police sirens following them.

A police car had come up alongside the bus, and Reuben had heard the unmistakable blare of a megaphone.

"Mr. Thorne," it blared, "there's no escape. You got a dozen squad cars following you and even more on their way to cut you off. Surrender now."

So the guy's name was Thorne?

"You know my name?" Thorne yelled out the window. "Good. That means you've spoken to Hopper. Bring her to me, and this will all be over. Don't bring her to me, and they all die."

The statement, even in rhetorical form, had made Reuben shiver with fear. Martha had squeezed his hand tighter, and he'd tried to push away the fear. *Protecting others is not being afraid even when you are,* he'd told himself.

"It's going to be OK," he'd whispered to her, and everyone who could hear him. "There are policemen everywhere. They're going to help us."

"It's going to be OK," Martha had whispered to her younger sister, who was curled beside her. "There's policemen everywhere."

Reuben's heart had swelled with pride. That must be how his dad felt all the time when he helped people. The bus was largely silent as it wound through the streets.

"Sir," the bus driver had pointed ahead, "there are spikes in the road ahead. What would you like me to do?"

"Drive over them, of course!" Thorne had demanded, doing a jig that reminded Reuben of Willy Wonka.

But there were other plans. Before they got to the spikes, a squad car barricade had blocked them off.

"Keep driving," Thorne had said.

The driver's eyes had widened as he frantically shook his head. "No way. I can't. It would flip the bus."

"Goddamn it, I said keep driving." Thorne had stepped on the accelerator, forcing the bus to lurch forward.

The bus driver had pushed back. "It'll flip. The kids don't have seatbelts."

At the exact moment Thorne had turned to the driver, the back door to the bus swung open. Reuben remembered a lot of yelling and cursing and curling up tighter on the floor.

But, the voice was unmistakable. Marshall Peet was on the bus.

Later, Reuben would be told that Marshall had been on the hood of a squad car that got up close to the back. It was some Keanu Reeves in *Speed* acrobatics, but he had managed to get in. There was helicopter footage of him doing it, and reporters all over the world asked how a cop who'd never had any SWAT or acrobatic training was able to do it. His response: "Your body does some crazy shit when your kid's in trouble." But something hadn't been right about it. There was something Marshall wasn't saying. To the media, to his cop buddies, and definitely not to Reuben.

"Thorne." Marshall's hands had been out as if he was trying to calm a rabid dog. "We're working on getting you this Hopper gal. But you've got to end this."

"I'll end it when I see Hopper."

Marshall had taken a cautious step forward. "This isn't like the movies. There are only two ways out of here. Death or jail."

"Nah, there's a third. I get Hopper, and she gets me what I want."

"OK. We'll get you, Hopper," Marshall had agreed, but Reuben recognized that tone. That was the tone Reuben was treated to when he was so far out of line, he had no idea how much trouble he was in. The fallout was always less than agreeable.

The bus had started to slow down, and Thorne had immediately turned to the driver. "Keep going."

Marshall had taken another step forward.

"Don't come near me," Thorne had growled. "I'll shoot."

"We're working on getting you, Hopper," Marshall continued to edge slowly toward him. "But—"

Marshall's voice dropped right as his boot fell next to Reuben's curled frame near the front of the bus.

"But what?"

"But you're going down, motherfucker." With one swift kick, Marshall had wrestled him against the side of the bus. "You want to do this the hard way or the easy way?" Marshall breathed into Thorne's face.

Reuben grimaced. He'd had enough of the hard ways when he'd misbehaved as a kid to know this guy was fucked.

"Get off me," Thorne had yelled, and Reuben could see him trying to turn his gun on his dad.

But Marshall was ready. As soon as Thorne moved his hand, Marshall had pushed his arm out the window. Thorne had pulled the trigger twice, the bullets flying outside, harmlessly striking the asphalt below.

Everyone on the bus had screamed and curled tighter on the floor. Reuben pulled Martha in closer.

Thorne had screamed like a wild banshee and attacked Marshall, and the two wrestled on the bus's floor, with Thorne keeping a tight grip on his gun. As they wrestled, the bus came to a stop. Later, Reuben would see that it had stopped just feet before the spikes.

As soon as they'd stopped, another officer had boarded the bus.

"Get the kids off here," Marshall had yelled. "Get them out of here."

Thorne was cursing and yelling, but Marshall had him pinned to the floor of the bus. However, the wild assailant was still waving the gun around, and the kids whimpered.

Reuben then remembered the odd line he'd never quite understood. In one solitary moment of weakness under Marshall's grip, the gunman had cried, "All I wanted was to end the whole thing."

If he had kept going that route, things might have turned out differently for the gunman. But instead, he'd fired off his gun into the side of the seat. There was complete chaos, and Reuben only remembered the fear. Marshall had kept a tight but precarious grip on the desperate Thorne while the officers swiftly evacuated the bus.

A few minutes later, Reuben had stood on the side of the highway with all the other kids while Marshall and Thorne continued to wrestle inside the vehicle. The vehicle shook as other officers boarded, and then Thorne had somehow slipped from Marshall's grasp, jumped out of the bus, and started running for his life down the side of the highway.

Marshall and all the other officers had taken off after him.

Thorne had jumped into the bushes alongside the road, and Reuben had watched his dad disappear into the woods after him.

Ambulance workers had handed out blankets to the kids, who had begun to cry from the shock of the ordeal. Reuben had just watched for his dad through the trees. It seemed like hours, but eventually, another bus had come to pick up the kids.

Reuben never saw the body, but the reports were clear. Marshall had shot Thorne, and he'd died from a bullet wound to the back. In later years, when Reuben had talked to Marshall's partners, they said it was a lot more gruesome than that.

"We can't tell you anything," one of them had said. "But it was personal back in those woods. Your dad loves you, kid."

"But there's one thing I never understood," he told his dad's friends. "Was she really there?"

"Who? You mean your mom?"

"Yeah."

"No, they weren't letting parents anywhere near the scene, so she wouldn't have been there. They had the roads blocked off and everything. The parents were all watching the newscast back at the school."

"But I swore I saw..." Reuben had never finished telling them what he saw.

But he was certain he'd seen her in the EMS crowd, walking away when he disembarked from the bus. He'd tried to run after her, but the officers were so strict about keeping order that he couldn't get to her. By the time he got off the bus and away from the officers, she was gone.

Martha now listened to him tell the story how he remembered it.

"I never saw her again after that. She wasn't with the other parents waiting at the school." Reuben's voice was distant, empty.

Martha nodded. Her mom and dad had been there to hug her and hold her tight the first chance they got.

Reuben shook his head like he was chasing away a bad memory. "Marshall was still at the scene, my mom was gone. I came home to an empty house."

"What did Marshall say?" Her eyes narrowed with empathy. "About where she went?"

Reuben shrugged. "Not much. He was a different person after that. Cold and bitter. The city heaped all kinds of awards on him. TV appearances."

"Right. He was everywhere for a little bit. There was the whole script fiasco."

"Oh God, the movie." They both laughed.

Reuben sighed. "Marshall hated the idea. Said he didn't want everyone gawking at his life. 'Nothing to see here, folks.' He didn't want to have anything to do with it and believe you me, I watched him do everything in his power to make sure that thing never saw the light of day. You think he's an asshole to me, you should have seen what he was like with that scriptwriter."

She laughed. "Sounds like Marshall."

"Yeah." Reuben's voice was soft. "The new Marshall. He wasn't like that before."

Martha patted his arm. "I'm sorry it's been hard for you. If you want to know, he's why I decided to become a cop."

"Yeah, he was a good dad once upon a time. Now?" Reuben just shrugged.

"And you're a good son," she said. "I see how you take care of him."

"Not that he notices," Reuben complained.

"He does. He just can't tell you. He's a proud man, but he loves you."

Reuben raised an eyebrow. He knew Marshall loved him somewhere deep inside. But he didn't know where.

Reuben listened for noise in the house. "I think he's asleep." When he was convinced it was silent, he peeked out. Marshall typically forgot arguments once he had slept. But if he encountered him without sleep or significant booze after an argument, then any interaction would turn into round two or three or four.

The living room was empty, and Reuben tiptoed down the hall. Through his cracked door, he could see his dad asleep.

"Yep, he's out." Reuben laughed. "You can sneak out now."

Martha shook her head. "I wanted to check on you and get away from Marshall, true. But what I really wanted was to pick your brain. You know, one cop to another."

"I'm not a cop."

Martha gave him that look again. "Well, you were raised by a good one. I figure you inherited some of those instincts Marshall's always on about."

Reuben chuckled. "Maybe. What's up?"

"Well, earlier you mentioned something about maple syrup and the Canadian..."

CHAPTER TWENTY-FIVE

Reuben—Thursday, February 9, 8:25 p.m.

Reuben and Martha grabbed a box of half-eaten pizza from the fridge and headed back to his room. Now it was just the two of them, very much like when they were teenagers.

Reuben took a bite of the cold pizza. "So, what's up?"

"I'm working this case. Looking for a guy with the alias, the Canadian."

Reuben forced a chuckle. "The Canadian? Guy sounds douche-y."

"You have no idea. I have been obsessing about this for days now." She pinched the bridge of her nose.

Reuben totally understood the feeling. He'd been obsessing, too. Not about maple syrup—about the bomb. He scratched his chin. He was beginning to think both of their cases were related. If so, maybe she would know something that would help him.

He'd have to ease into the conversation, though. "Canada and maple syrup. Doesn't sound like obsession material."

She laughed. "It's funny how easy it comes, being obsessed with one case."

He related more than she knew.

"Anyway," she tossed the empty beer bottle into the bin, "I keep running across weird links. Do you know about this maple syrup bust at the Detroit border?"

Reuben tried to keep up his poker face. "I've read about it. There was a bust of illegal maple syrup at the border. Then there was a shootout with the cops."

Martha nodded. "Yeah, two were wounded, and one died earlier tonight," she explained. "I can't help but think these two are connected. And then, you know that Canadian investor, Alister Pout? I think he's connected. But it's just a feeling. I don't have any evidence. Just what I saw this morning at that dodgy dry cleaners, and the fact that Pout is Canadian."

Reuben raised an eyebrow, and he wondered if this was the lead he needed. Still, Reuben didn't know anything about Pout other than the occasional tidbit he caught on the news. "Who is he?" Reuben asked, opening his laptop and doing a search. RedBook was the first thing that popped up.

Martha pointed to a picture of him. "Wealthy RedBook creator, and he wears a douche fedora. Mastermind criminal for sure." She tried to chuckle at her own joke, but the problem was, she believed it to be true. "I just have this weird feeling that he's either the Canadian, or he's connected to him. And that this Mr. Sudds Dry Cleaning and the shit at the border are somehow connected. I just can't see how."

"RedBook, huh?" Reuben remembered reading the maple syrup bust report. "Well, you know the deal with the platform, right?"

"It's just another social media thingie, right? Like Facebook or the other things where people send each other dick pics and nudes."

"Snapchat," Reuben said, shaking his head. "Not exactly. It's designed to record the events in real-time so that people can stay safe. People who sign up agree to data transfers if they are in a Red Zone."

Martha lifted an eyebrow. "Red Zone? I don't understand."

"OK, let's say you're at the bank and an armed robber comes in. If someone on RedBook notifies the system that there's a crime or disaster in progress, then RedBook will automatically turn on the cameras, mics, whatever on the phones and devices of anyone else signed up in the area. Then you get a multi-sourced breakdown of what's happening in real-time. Robberies, traffic jams, tsunamis, bombs." Reuben paused at this last thought.

A microwave bomb would only kill humans and other biological beings. It wouldn't damage buildings or infrastructure or...computers and cell phones. Which meant that devices with the RedBook app would keep running and would transmit images and videos of the event in real-time all over the globe to anyone on the platform.

"Fuck me," Reuben muttered. Could Alister Pout be planning to skip town and then set off the bomb to, what? Drive up his stock?

Technology in the guise of a social media platform that could be used in times of crisis was beyond valuable. It wasn't difficult to think of the government applications for it: Search and Rescue, manhunts...*spying*.

Pout would become one of the most powerful men on the planet when everyone bought his tech. The cost: all the thousands—maybe millions—of human lives wiped out in the bomb's radius when it took out part of New York.

"Ah, Martha," Reuben stammered.

"Yeah?" she said, looking up from her screen.

Here we go. Reuben rubbed his hands together. "I'm going to tell you something. You're not going to believe it at first, but I swear to you two things. One, I'm not crazy, and two, we need to stop this Canadian dude before he kills a lot of people."

CHAPTER TWENTY-SIX

Reuben—Thursday, February 9, 9:39 p.m.

Reuben pulled his Mazda through the circular drive of Buzz's mansion.

On the drive over, Martha wanted to know what was up, but Reuben knew better than to try and explain this without Buzz's help. Not that it stopped her from asking a million questions.

But now she was silent, her mouth agape as they rolled up to Buzz's mansion.

Buzz was already standing outside in a bathrobe that would have made Hugh Hefner jealous. All he was missing was his pipe.

"This is your college roommate's house?" Martha asked.

Reuben rolled his eyes. "That's him in the driveway. Ahh, before we get out, just know that he's a…character."

"Reuben." Buzz spread his arms. "Does she know everything?"

Reuben gave Buzz a look that said now wasn't the time to tell her about his warping ability.

Buzz nodded. Then he turned to Martha. "To what do I owe the pleasure of this visit with such a lovely lady?" He took Martha's hand and kissed it in a manner far suaver than Reuben thought him capable of. For a moment, he wondered if Buzz had made a playboy robot version of himself.

"My, my." Martha laughed. "Aren't you the gentleman?"

"I try to be." He gestured magnanimously toward the house. "Come, we shall drink."

Reuben tried not to die laughing. Buzz around women was quite a different creature than Buzz the pot-smoking mad scientist.

Buzz clapped his hands as they entered his marble foyer. "Rosa."

The maid appeared with the same smile she always wore. Reuben couldn't help but wonder if she was just another of Buzz's robots, like Binnie. He thought about asking but knew he wouldn't get a straight answer, so he decided not to. *Some mysteries are best left alone.*

"Please, get some drinks for our guests," Buzz requested.

"Yes, Mr. Buzz," she replied, sighing. "Will there be a party tonight? Because if there is, I get overtime."

"Six and a half-times pay. Absolutely." Buzz turned to his guests. "Make it seven times because tonight, we dance."

They walked into Buzz's pool room, and Reuben wanted to jump into the talk. Buzz gave him a look that said, *patience.*

Fuck patience. The end of the world was at stake. But he knew Buzz was right. They needed to find the right opening to let Martha into the loop.

Martha turned to Reuben and mouthed a hearty, "Damn."

Reuben nodded and mouthed back, "I know."

The trio reclined on the cream couches under dimmer lighting than usual. Reuben felt a twinge of jealousy. He and Martha were by no means together. But, really? Was Buzz trying to set the stage to get with Martha? *It isn't going to happen, dude,* he felt like telling him. Reuben smirked at the very idea. Yeah, he didn't know who would die first, but he'd pay good money to watch that on reality TV.

"So, what brings you to my abode?" Buzz said once the small talk had commenced.

"Uh, Buzz." Reuben cleared his throat. "Can I talk to you?"

"Of course, of course." He gestured around the room. "Ms. Martha, bask in the relaxing glow of strategic lighting and imbibe."

Reuben took Buzz to the foyer.

"First of all, dude, she's so far from your type. You can lay off the charm."

"Whatever do you mean?" Buzz sipped his margarita. "I'm simply being kind and gracious to a member of the fairer sex."

"Uh-huh." Reuben nodded. "Dude, I'm serious. She's not going to go for it."

"You don't know what the future holds for any of us," Buzz countered.

"Yeah, why don't we, uh, put a cap on comments like that?" Reuben said. "Considering that I can warp back from the future."

Buzz sighed. "OK, yes, yes. So what is our business here today, then?"

Reuben was glad Buzz had already checked the nanobot data and had gotten up to date on the timeline so that he was fully aware of all their previous discussions.

"I think Martha might be one of the déjà vu people,"

Reuben told him. "You know, the ones who remember parts of the past but in a scrambled up kind of way?"

Buzz's interest grew. "Really?"

"Yeah," Reuben said. "I need to find a way to explain everything to her. But I don't know how to in a way that she'll believe."

"What does she know so far?" Buzz asked.

"Nothing. She's a police officer who's experiencing a lot of 'intuition' that feels familiar to her. Something with a van. I told her I wanted her to meet you because you've studied this kind of thing. It goes directly in line with the déjà vu theory you were telling me about. So, here we are. I need your help to help me figure out how to explain it to her."

Buzz stroked his chin. "Well, our calculations show that you tend to travel between twenty minutes to three days."

Reuben waved his hands impatiently. "Right, we've covered this."

"We can use that information to replicate the experience," Buzz suggested. "We get her to tell you all about her last three days. Then you kill yourself and come back to this time and tell her what you know."

"Not a half-bad idea." Reuben grimaced. "I don't want to kill myself again, though. Dying sucks. That said, Binnie was a nice way to die."

Buzz's eyes went hard. "Binnie is a treat for special occasions and certainly not for untested observants."

"All right, all right," Reuben reluctantly agreed. "We'll do it."

They arrived back in the living room, where Martha lay with her eyes closed, having found the massage feature on Buzz's couch.

"I didn't know that couch was a massager," Reuben told Buzz.

"I don't use it," he said. "It's just for show."

Martha turned off the massager and sat up now that the guys had returned. "Did you boys have a nice meeting?" She sipped her drink.

"Yes." Buzz cleared his throat, and Reuben sat next to him. "Ms. Martha, we have something we'd like to explain to you."

"OK." Martha looked skeptical.

Reuben started slowly. "I am in a time warp."

"What?" Martha's expression was one of confusion. Like she didn't know if she should laugh or call the psych ward.

"You see, I can die and come back to life at a different time," he said. "I've done it multiple times."

Martha just sat there as if waiting for the punch line.

"Valentine's Day, this year," he said. "I've already lived it. Three times."

Martha peered into her drink. "What's in these things?"

"See, I told you. She doesn't believe me," Reuben told Buzz.

"Allow me," Buzz said. "I have a way with the ladies."

Reuben rose from the couch and paced the room. Why had he tried to tell her? Maybe she didn't have the gift. Maybe this whole thing was a mistake.

"Miss Martha," Buzz tried, "what Reuben tells you is true. I've verified it by scientific method."

"Scientific method?" She raised an eyebrow. "You can't scientifically prove that someone is in a— time warps don't exist. That's crazy. I don't know what you guys are on, or what you think I'm on, or how stupid you think I am. Is this a way for you guys to make fun of me? I get enough of that shit at work."

"No, no, no, Martha." Reuben rushed to her side on the

couch. "No one is making fun of you. Look, maybe this is all a mistake. I thought maybe you might have it, too."

"Have what?"

"Maybe your déjà vu isn't as déjà vu as you think," Reuben told her.

"No." She rose from the couch. "This is what happens when I let too many cop egos get to me. I got too eager to kiss ass and get promoted. I listened to way too many old cops drone on about intuition, and then I ended up following vans and connecting non-connecting pieces, and let my imagination go crazy. *This* is where that leads."

She set the drink on the table so forcefully it splashed. "From now on, no more drinking. No more intuition. No more. I don't even know what this place is, some sort of Peter Pan fantasyland. I don't know."

"OK, OK, OK." Buzz rubbed his hands together. "This isn't working."

"No, it clearly is not," Martha said. "And this room smells like weed. Do you have a permit for that?"

"Shit." Buzz turned to Reuben. "Why did you bring a cop in here?"

"She's an old friend. She's cool. Right, Martha?" Reuben made eye contact with her and nodded in expectation. "Give us a chance, Martha. Please?"

"Fine." Martha sighed and collapsed on the couch. "But you guys better start making sense."

"Fair enough," Buzz said. "What we'd like to do is conduct a scientific experiment to prove that what Reuben says is true."

"A scientific experiment to prove a time warp?" Martha laughed.

"Yes," Buzz and Reuben said in unison.

"Is this guy for real?" Martha asked Reuben.

Reuben nodded. "Just go with it."

"I thought you said you'd start making sense?" she protested.

"Of course," Buzz said. "What makes more sense than science?"

Martha cocked her head. "Bring it on."

Buzz sat on the coffee table right in front of her. "What we need you to do is tell Reuben things that have happened to you in the last three days. Highly specific details. Conversations you've had, places you've eaten. Events that have happened. Once he's compiled enough data, then he'll kill himself—"

The color drained from Martha's face. "I'm sorry, *what?*"

"He'll kill himself and then come back to you in this timeline and tell you what you told him."

Buzz and Reuben both stared at her, waiting for her agreement.

After a brief silence, Martha burst into uncontrollable laughter. "What the fuck? You're going to kill yourself and then come back to life? What are you, Jesus Christ?"

"No, just immortal," Reuben said.

Martha's smile faded. "Oh my God. You guys are freaking serious."

Reuben nodded in emphatic agreement. As he did, he realized he probably wasn't helping Martha take this in. He slowed down his nods and said in as even a tone as he could muster, "Yeah, he's totally serious."

"OK, no." Martha shook her head vehemently. "This is wrong on *so* many levels. I don't even know where to start."

"It's not wrong," Reuben told her. "I killed myself on Saturday and warped back to today." Fuck, time warps were complicated. You needed several graphs, spreadsheets, and a supercomputer to keep it all straight.

"What?" Martha was shocked. "OK, first of all, as a member of law enforcement, I can't condone suicide. Secondly, if this is the way you're seeing things, you… You're not OK. You need to see a counselor at least, a psychiatrist at best. I don't know what you guys have been doing in here, but you can't keep doing it."

Buzz shook his head at Reuben and left the room.

Martha took out her phone.

Reuben tilted his head. "What are you doing?"

"I'm calling Marshall," she announced.

"Jesus." Reuben jumped up and grabbed the phone out of her hand. "Martha, you cannot do that. You don't know what you're getting into."

"I do." Martha tried to grab her phone, and he kept it from her. "His son just told me he's going to kill himself. I think he needs to know."

"He'll have me committed. Look, I take it all back. I'm just high. I'm saying weird things, OK? Don't pay any attention to me."

"No, don't try to play this off," Martha insisted. "You and your friend are into some dark stuff, which is one thing. But talking about killing yourself like that, that's a whole different level. I cannot in good conscience—"

"Martha, stop being a fucking narc for once," Reuben cut in, surprising himself with his forcefulness. "Listen, I'm opening up to you about a very personal experience, and I think you owe it to me to at least try to take me seriously."

At that moment, Buzz came up behind them. With a loud buzz, Martha fell to the floor, unconscious.

Reuben's mouth dropped. "Is that…"

"Taser." Buzz tossed it up into the air, then caught it with flair.

Reuben looked down at Martha's unconscious body. There would be hell to pay when she woke up. He just hoped they could talk fast enough. "I can't believe you have a taser."

Buzz grinned. "It comes in handy."

"When?" Reuben exclaimed.

"There's a lot you don't know about me," Buzz told him.

"*That* I am definitely aware of," Reuben said. "What else do you have hidden in this place?"

"You have no idea."

"Yeah. And something tells me I don't want to know."

CHAPTER TWENTY-SEVEN

Martha—Friday, February 10, 12:06 a.m.

When Martha came to, the first thing she felt was the rope around her wrists. It took a minute for her vision to clear. She was in a concrete room. The nape of her neck felt like it had been burned. She tried to move, but she couldn't.

She looked down. She was tied to a wooden chair. Her wrists were bound behind her, and her feet were bound to the legs of the chair.

"What the hell?" she gasped. Then she screamed for help.

Reuben and Buzz quickly appeared.

"What the fuck?" Martha demanded. "Let me go!"

"I'm sorry it had to be this way," Buzz told her. "Really. But we just couldn't risk you not completing the experiment."

"You're a fucking psycho!" She yelled and wriggled in her chair, then turned to Reuben. "And you! I don't even know what to make of *you*."

Angry, hot tears hit the surface, and she hated that she was crying. She choked them back and stared at her captors with cold, steely eyes. She had taken a course in her police training about being held captive. She tried to remember anything from that course.

"Martha, I know this is nuts." Reuben knelt in front of her. "But it's not what you think."

"To think, I was just starting to think that—" She stopped herself, and tears of hurt welled up in her eyes again.

"Starting to think what?" Reuben asked.

"Never mind, it doesn't matter," she said. "Why am I here?"

Reuben grabbed a gun off the counter and pointed it at his head.

She screamed louder than she knew her voice could go. The sound went nowhere in the concrete bunker. "What the hell, Reuben? You're fucking crazy!"

"Calm down, Martha," Buzz said softly. "It's not as crazy as you think."

"I don't know why you guys keep saying that," she cried. "But all evidence points to the contrary. Please, just let me go."

Buzz nodded. "After Reuben kills himself, then you can go."

Martha's eyes widened in horror. "Oh my God. You have completely lost it. Both of you. You're going to prison, you know that, right Buzz?"

A shadow crossed Buzz's face, then he regained his composure. "Not when you see what we're trying to do. Now, are you willing to cooperate?"

Martha struggled against her restraints. "Like I have a fucking choice."

"Not really," Buzz stated.

Reuben lowered the gun and pulled a chair in front of Martha. "Look, I know what you're thinking. We're crazy. But all this intuition stuff, the déjà vu. It's your brain holding onto pieces of the time warps. For some reason, I can remember the warps. You can't, not entirely. Buzz theorizes that things like you're experiencing are happening because this case, this *obsession,* is so important to you that you're holding onto glimpses of what you learned in those warps."

"Reuben, we can get you help," Martha said.

He shook his head. "We need to stop the bomb, and I believe that we can only do this if we work together. You want to stop him, right?"

Martha pursed her lips. Her childhood friend was having a psychotic break. She'd need to play along to help him. She nodded.

"Tell Reuben everything you can about the last three days of your life," Buzz said. "Be specific. Dates, times, anything there's no way he could possibly know."

Reuben sat patiently in the chair with the gun on his lap.

"OK." She didn't seem to have a choice in playing their little psycho Russian roulette game. "Three days ago, let's see… Oh, I was late for work because I went to do my morning workout and my gym was closed for renovations. It threw my whole schedule off. That meant I missed the morning meeting and didn't know there would be a film crew in the station that morning. One of the officers, Sergeant Bramley, was being featured on some stupid reality show."

Buzz and Reuben laughed.

"I mean, everyone knew he was doing it one day, but we all thought it was going to be like, months from now. But they just showed up that day. So, when I came in and the cameras were everywhere, I yelled at them for getting in my way." She shook her head. "I made a total ass out of myself. But they didn't stop me. All these film crew guys gathered around me like paparazzi, and they were all like, about to wet their pants with excitement. They kept egging me on to get me to say more stuff. It was horribly embarrassing. Now, I'm going to be on national TV acting like an ass."

"This is good." Buzz nodded. "Good stuff."

"Yeah, you're not the only person to say that to me this week. So then, after that, let's see..." Martha recounted her meals and a couple of work things. "Then there's this intern, Zach. He's a real ass-kisser, but he does a good job. My boss will probably hire him after he graduates. I appreciate him; he's been a real help to me. But I'm also a little jealous that he's doing so much better at his job than I was at that stage."

The rope cut into her wrists, and she wiggled her hands to try to massage them. They tied ropes well for a couple of computer nerds. "He does all the computer modules, which everyone thinks are about as interesting as watching paint dry," she said. "I wonder if he can make it out in the field, though."

She rambled on about following the white van in the cab, about going home that night, trying to buy herself some time. "I was going to go to a concert with Jenna, but it's hard to talk to Jenna. We went to UVA together, and we were both from the city. Once we graduated, it was fun to keep up with each other and have drinks now and then, but now our lives are just drifting apart. She's married and is on her second pregnancy. I mean, I can usually follow a woman going through her first pregnancy. I can talk to her about all the cliché topics like morning sickness and choosing a Lamaze instructor. I've had so many girlfriends go through it that I've actually got a few helpful tips. But once you get past the first-timers, then I don't know what to talk about. I can't talk about sleep training and GERD, whatever that is. What is the obsession with pregnancy and babies? How did I not get that gene?"

Buzz and Reuben just stared at her, dumbfounded. They both scratched the backs of their heads.

"Yeah, that's uh…good," Buzz said.

She sighed and moved on to relatively safer topics. She talked about going to Gigi's Breakfast Café that morning and ordering the cinnamon apple crepe while researching Alister Pout and reading the article on him in *The Scene*.

"He's a real womanizer," she said. "That kind of guy makes me sick. I have this feeling about Alister Pout. Remember Thorne? I hated him for trying to hurt us. I hate Pout the same way. Like he was trying to hurt me. I don't know why."

Reuben nodded. "It may be that in one of the warps, he did hurt you. That's why you have this visceral feeling about him."

Martha didn't know about that. But she couldn't deny the particular brand of disgust she had for Pout mirrored her feelings for Thorne.

She went on rambling, and she looked for an escape route. It appeared the only way out of the room was through a metal door with a sensor on it. It didn't appear to need a code to get out. She thought about staging some kind of emergency to find out if they needed a code to get out, but she couldn't think of one and kept the rambling going at the same time.

"So, Reuben pulls up to the house," Martha continued. She wasn't even paying attention to what she was saying anymore. "I remember seeing the purple lilacs and wondering if they have those at the garden center near my house. I go to Frank's Nursery and try to keep a garden going on my patio. I also noticed that the fountain outside is not well maintained. It all makes me think that this Buzz guy is rather pretentious."

She knew she was being a jerk, but they deserved it. Besides, they weren't going to hurt her. They needed her for their little game. But she was scared. She rambled when she was scared.

"He wants to look a certain way," she kept going, "but he can't keep it up. It's all an act. When I got inside, I didn't like the frescoes on the ceiling. The modern art design clashed with the rest of the house. Plus, I thought the artist's technique was lacking a bit of soul. The fresco had no soul. It was like it was painted as a hollow tribute to something."

Buzz cleared his throat and shifted in his seat.

"Sorry, Buzz." She wiggled in her ropes. "You had to put the brutal in honesty."

"That's fine," Buzz said. "It's all for science. We need the most accurate data possible."

"Absolutely," she said. "So, as we rang the bell and we waited there, I thought, 'Reuben is really turning into a handsome man.'"

Reuben pursed his lips in shock, and Buzz whistled. "You hear that? She's into you, dude."

Reuben and Martha both blushed, and Martha realized what she had just said. She knew it was true. It had been true for a while. Maybe since that day on the bus when he had grabbed her hand. But she was only aware of it now.

"Well," she stammered, "I mean, you know, we knew each other when we were kids, and we're both grown adults, and you know for some other woman..."

"I want to know more about this." Buzz rubbed his hands together. "Tell me, have you ever done anything together?"

"Christ, Buzz." Reuben smacked Buzz, and Martha cleared her throat.

"How long do we have to do this, just so we're clear?" Martha asked, squirming in her chair.

"All right, you think you have enough?" Buzz asked Reuben.

Reuben pursed his lips, and Martha noticed he appeared tenser than she'd ever seen him.

"Are you really going to do this…suicide thing?" she asked.

Both men nodded, and Martha scrambled to think of something, anything to stop this from happening. "Can I make a request?"

"Shoot," Reuben said. *Yeah...probably not the right word to use.*

"I don't want to watch," she told them.

"OK." Reuben and Buzz nodded to each other. "We'll move the supplies."

Buzz and Reuben grabbed a bunch of gear and took it to the adjoining room. Martha wasn't even sure what they had. Now that Martha was alone, she wiggled and squirmed to get her hands free, feeling around the rope knots. She'd been working them for an hour now. They were tight.

What the fuck? she thought. *How did they get this tied so well? A couple of computer nerds would know how to tie a rope because?*

"Boy Scouts," she whispered.

But she had one up on that. She had taken a course in Afghanistan on how to handle an abduction scenario. It was taught by Marines, and they had gone over the basic knots and how to dismantle them.

She glanced down at the bindings on her feet. Yep, that was definitely a Boy Scout knot. She racked her memory as she felt around her wrists. She replayed the video in her head. There should be a loop to pull right…about…here.

Yep, there it was. If this loop was pulled, the ropes should come right off.

Buzz and Reuben's voices grew a little louder, and she

stopped. It sounded like they were coming back. She waited a couple of minutes, and they didn't return.

Then, with one quick pull, she loosened the knots on her wrists and broke her arms free. She didn't take long to bask in the freedom. She immediately moved to her feet and unbound them just as easily.

She was free. She ran to the entrance, a metal door with a sensor on it.

"Fuck it." She shrugged and slammed it open. The sensor sounded, and Buzz and Reuben came running. But by then, Martha was already out into the hallway of the mansion.

"Shit," Reuben yelled. "Martha, wait."

She grabbed her phone as they chased her through the hallway. She dialed the precinct, and it rang endlessly.

"Damn switchboard operator," she mumbled. "Stop watching Netflix and pick up the damn phone."

She gave up and called Jake directly.

"Yo, Jake here, talk to me." He yawned, and Martha realized it was after midnight.

"Yeah, Jake, I'm going to need backup."

No sooner had she finished giving the address than Buzz and Reuben both screamed simultaneous curses. Then they ran out the front door and through the gardens.

Martha began chasing them. As soon as Jake got there, she would have backup to arrest them.

When Martha finally caught them, she found them in the garden house. They sat peacefully on benches, poring over papers.

"You assholes are under arrest." Martha leaned over and panted as she caught her breath.

They ignored her, which confused and concerned her.

"This would work much better," Buzz was saying to

Reuben, "if you came back an hour earlier than now. Think you can do it?"

Reuben shook his head. "Well, I have no control over—"

Buzz pulled out a gun and aimed it point-blank at Reuben's face.

Martha screamed when he pulled the trigger.

CHAPTER TWENTY-EIGHT

Reuben—Thursday, February 9, 9:44 p.m.

Reuben and Martha stood in the doorway of Buzz's mansion, the chime of the doorbell still ringing against the tranquil drive.

OK, Reuben thought. *We're here. Only went back a few hours.*

For a brief moment, he wondered how. He had wanted to come to this point. It would have been the easiest place to start over. But was it dumb luck or because he'd controlled it? He had no idea.

He glanced at Martha and felt a calm sense of relief from her being here. It felt good being able to have friends he could trust and relax around, even when shit was going crazy in his life.

Maybe Buzz's nanobot would have some insight into how to control how far he warped back. But for now, he needed to focus on convincing Martha.

Buzz met them in the foyer, padding through the halls in his red silk pajamas.

"Do you have anything to say to her?" Buzz asked.

Reuben shook his head. "Not yet. But very soon."

"You do?" Martha frowned at Reuben.

Buzz bowed to Martha. "Come in. You'll need a stiff drink for this."

Martha stared at Reuben. "What's going on?"

Reuben grimaced. This was the moment they had gambled on with the suicide plot, but now he had no idea how to explain this to her. A guy could get slapped, committed, or both for spouting what he had to say. He spotted a basket on a foyer table full of solved Rubik's Cubes. He rolled his eyes. Of course, Buzz would have that. He sauntered up to the table, grabbed one, and tossed it in the air.

He caught it with flair and then caught Martha's eye. "Back there, as we were walking in, you were thinking about the lilacs."

"Oh." She shrugged with a smile. "Yeah, you saw me looking at them. What about them?"

"No," Reuben continued with another toss of the cube in the air. He caught it with finality. "No, I didn't see you look at them all. But you weren't just noticing them. You were really thinking about them. You wondered if they had those at Frank's Nursery near your house. You try to keep a flower garden going on your patio, but you don't have the time."

"Did I tell you that?" Martha furrowed her brow.

Reuben shook his head. "Not in the way you think."

"What way is that?" Her lips rose in confusion. "Was I drunk or something?"

He didn't answer but continued reading her mind as they walked. "You thought the fountain outside was not maintained well, and it made you think Buzz is pretentious."

At this point, Buzz brought her a drink, and she laughed weakly.

"I never said that." She clasped her hand over her heart in apology to Buzz.

Buzz winked at her. "Oh, I take no offense. I am pretentious. In fact, some would say it's my defining characteristic."

Martha faked a high and uncomfortable laugh.

Reuben paced the foyer, taking over the space as he talked. "You think the state of the fountain is a reflection of Buzz's character. According to you, you think he wants things to look a certain way, but he can't keep it up."

She downed the entire glass down in one gulp. "I don't know what he's talking about. I'm so sorry, I would never."

"You hate the frescoes on the ceiling," Reuben interrupted. "And you think the design clashes with the rest of the house."

"How do you… I was an art history major," she stammered, casting apologetic eyes at Buzz. "I have an eye for these things. Don't take it personally."

"You find that the artist's technique lacks soul," Reuben continued, "and you feel it was painted as a hollow tribute."

Martha stopped protesting and watched Reuben with her mouth agape.

"But I won't stop there." He smiled. "Let's go back further than Buzz's lilacs. Let's talk about your work life."

"What the hell are you doing, Reuben?" Martha asked.

"Three days ago, you were late for work because you messed up your whole schedule when your gym was closed for renovations."

"Do you go to CardioMax?" Martha gasped. "And how would you—"

"Just listen," Reuben cut her off. "You missed the morning meeting, and you didn't know that that was the day Sergeant Bramley would finally be filmed for the reality show. You yelled at the film crew and made a total ass out of yourself."

"I know I didn't tell anyone *that*," she stated.

"And now you're concerned about it being aired on national TV," Reuben said. "You're also jealous of the intern Zach."

Martha frowned. "The intern? No. Who have you been talking to?"

"Just you." Reuben winked and tossed the Rubik's Cube to Buzz, who caught it. "You're not ready to admit it, but Zach's a major suck-up. You're worried he'll show you up, or already is. He's doing way better at your job than you were at that stage. He does all the computer modules and gets content out of them. While you admire the help he's been to you, you wonder if he can do the work out in the field."

She was quiet now.

Reuben rushed on. "Then the day after the reality show fiasco, you went to Gigi's Breakfast Café. You ordered a cinnamon apple crepe and researched Alister Pout in *The Scene*."

She blinked in disbelief.

"You think he's a jerk, a real womanizer, but he's involved in something and you know it. But you can't prove it. It makes you crazy. Later that night, you were supposed to go to a concert with your friend from UVA, Jenna. You've had a hard time connecting with her because she's started her family, and you just don't have that much in common anymore. In fact, you feel that way about most of your girlfriends because they've all started pairing up and having kids, and you're still single."

She gulped at that part, and he could tell he'd hit a nerve.

"You wonder if you've missed out on some 'gene of womanhood' because none of those things interest you."

A tear welled up in her eye. "Stop," she whispered. "Stop."

Reuben's heart sank. He had gone too far, and now he felt like a real asshole.

"How are you doing this?" she whispered.

"Martha." Reuben gestured toward the living room. "I think you'd better sit down."

Reuben—Thursday, February 9, 10:31 p.m.

Reuben, Martha, and Buzz had gone down to Buzz's computer lair. The two guys were busy updating the timelines and yelling voice commands into the machines.

Amidst the commotion, Martha silently grabbed a folding chair and sat down. They had told her what they were up to. Not that any of it made any sense.

A time warp? That kind of thing only happened in dime-store novels and sci-fi movies, or that one where Bill Murray was a newscaster and the alarm clock played that Cher song every morning. What was that movie? Had these guys seen that movie one too many times?

But, how could he have known all that stuff? Like what she was thinking about the lilacs? Or about the reality show thing at work? She hadn't told anyone about that. Even if she had, which she was almost certain she hadn't, she wouldn't have told them Sergeant Bramley's name. Plus, while she did have some kind of latent feelings about Zach the intern, he wasn't on her mind enough that she would have told Reuben that.

The whole thing with Jenna? While there was the remote possibility that she might have, in a drunken state, mentioned Zach or the reality show, she knew Reuben knew nothing about Jenna or that they had plans to go to a concert together. The whole thing about her feeling left behind as her peers became mothers and not understanding the need to fulfill that biological imperative; those were all deeply personal thoughts. Reuben was a good friend, an old friend. But they didn't have that kind of relationship.

Even *that* she might have chalked up to perception if he hadn't known all about the specific details of her breakfast that day. How had he known she went to Gigi's Breakfast Café, of all places? It was a tiny, hole-in-the-wall restaurant that no one who wasn't looking for it could find. Not only that, he specifically knew what she had ordered. There was no way for him to know that. Then, he knew she'd looked up Alister while she ate.

It was all too weird.

Just weird enough to warrant the insane explanation. A time warp? Suicide?

"This one is different," Buzz explained as they made notes on the calendar software. "How you controlled the timing of the repeat."

Overcome by curiosity, Martha walked to the calendar on the screen and glanced at it. Seeing all the times Reuben had had the same breakfast with Marshall, she frowned as she read about the hash browns. Were those the same ones that Marshall had warned her about?

Martha kept scanning through the calendar, seeing several references to Reuben's differing interactions with a CIA special agent named Aki.

"I don't know that I controlled it." Reuben rubbed his chin. "I'd like to find out what patterns it's taking to decide."

Martha's eyes narrowed. "What's this?" She pointed to a recurring event that on each timeline occurred at the same time on Valentine's Day. "Endgame? What does that mean?"

Buzz and Reuben glanced at each other.

"Microwave bomb," they said in unison.

"Wait." Her face paled. "You mean you guys know about a bomb threat?"

"On Valentine's Day at 9:47, a lot of people in NYC are going to die," Reuben informed her.

Martha's heart leapt. "What? That's, like, four and a half days away!"

"Yup," both of the guys said at the same time.

Martha looked from Reuben to Buzz. "Well, why don't you tell someone? Like the government or the CIA, or something?"

Reuben cocked a half-smile. She didn't know he actually worked for the CIA. "What do you think is going to happen when we go to the CIA? We tell them I have some kind of special power to predict the future and that I know there's going to be an attack? What do you think they'll do if they don't dismiss me as a crackpot? I know exactly what they'll do, and it's not pretty."

Martha groaned. "Well, there has to be *something*. You can't just sit on knowledge like that."

"Welcome to my world." Reuben laughed bitterly. "What we have to do is figure out how to stop it."

"On our own?" She looked at him like he'd gone insane.

"Who else is there?" he answered. "Are you in, or are you out?"

Buzz and Reuben stared her down, waiting for an answer.

She took in the whole lab and the men before her. This whole thing was ridiculous. A microwave bomb? A time warp? All in the hands of a scientist and a computer tech guy who did God only knew what for the government.

A part of her wanted to believe they were crazy. But then again, the intuition that had led her to chase down harmless dry cleaning vans wasn't any less cockeyed.

"We'd have almost four and a half days," she repeated.

Reuben smiled. "The future of the human race depends on it."

"OK," she said. "For the future of the human race."

"For the future of the human race," Buzz and Reuben said in unison.

"Let's map out a plan," Buzz said.

CHAPTER TWENTY-NINE

Reuben—Friday, February 10, 9:17 a.m.

"We have a zero-tolerance policy for workplace violence," Sven droned on in the emergency meeting the next morning.

An emergency briefing had been called after the dismissal of Mike Fury. It had something to do with him leaving the agency the way he did. When an agent left that way, there had to be an investigation as to whether security had been breached.

By law, there was a manhour quota that had to be filled for the investigation and security debrief. Sven had so far filled part of it with a long and completely unnecessary lecture on violence in the workplace. Reuben scanned the crowd, looking for Aki.

"What Mike Fury did was inappropriate and inexcusable," Sven continued, and Watson nodded gravely. "We'd like to remind everyone that your insurance does cover counseling if any of you need it after Thursday's events."

Reuben didn't see her in the room full of bored agents. These guys were some of the sharpest minds the government could find. An agent having a straight-up meltdown wasn't going to rattle them too badly, and it probably wasn't the worst thing they'd encountered so far that week.

As a matter of fact, many of them probably empathized with Mike, in as much as the stress of the job could make a person completely lose their mind.

Still, Sven had to cover his legal bases, although even he seemed uninspired by his speech.

"Any questions?" Sven perfunctorily asked in closing. No one responded, and so he nodded. "Back to work, people."

The crowd dispersed, and Reuben went back to his desk. He passed another operative's computer and caught the picture of Julian Schaeffer being edited on photo software.

"Classified," the agent barked and turned the screen away from the hallway.

"Sorry." Reuben smirked at the subtle ego trip.

Security clearances in this hallway were generally low, so the agent was taking the opportunity to let everyone know about being assigned a high-priority project. Reuben took the opportunity, however, to note that Schaeffer had made it down to lower security levels and would soon become general knowledge in the agency.

Reuben arrived at his desk and pulled up Schaeffer's social media pages on his phone so as not to get flagged. There he was that morning with the cute blonde tagged as Stephanie Dwyer at a shopping mall.

Me and My Boo, the status read.

"Hold on, Julian," Reuben muttered. "I got ya."

He remembered what Martha had said about Alister Pout.

"Where are you, you Canadian scumbag?" Reuben pulled up the traffic cams and tried to remember what Alister's company was called. Everyone knew who he was, but no one really knew too much about exactly what he did. He did a quick online search on Pout and realized it was going to be more work than he'd thought.

Blah, blah, blah, Canadian investor... Blah, blah, blah, RedBook.

"The New York office," Reuben groaned. "That's all I want."

Blah, blah, blah, grew up in both Montreal and Manchester and went to boarding school in Paris. Blah, blah, blah, a whole lot of fancy degrees and schools, knows a lot of Canadian MPs, photo op with Justin Trudeau…

"I just want to know where this guy works!" Reuben slammed the keyboard. "How hard is it?"

After more online searching, he kept running across the Trillium Group. The Trillium Group, it appeared, were a bunch of Canadian hotshot investors that funded a lot of New York projects. On the board of the Trillium Group was none other than Alister Pout. Alister had bought in to the Trillium Group by way of his own group, BTI—Better Tomorrows Incorporated.

Reuben searched for BTI and came up with a long list of investment projects. The latest one was owned by one Tom Dwyer. He searched Tom Dwyer on Facebook and quickly came across a familiar photo.

"Stephanie Dwyer," Reuben said. "Julian Schaeffer's girlfriend."

Tom Dwyer was Stephanie's older brother, a software engineer for a company called S-Wire Media. Reuben scrolled through his photos and thought he could have been friends with Tom in a different life if their paths had crossed. Tom frequented a lot of the same bars he did, as a matter of fact.

"Shit," Reuben muttered as he clicked on Tom's information. Tom had graduated from Columbia during Reuben's freshman year. "I might have known this guy."

Reuben searched through the Columbia alum databases and didn't find much more information other than an email address. He drafted up a quick email with a cover story of networking for a computer tech job at S-Wire but then thought better of it. If Sven saw that email, Reuben might not have to lie about looking for a job. He deleted the draft email and searched for S-Wire Media. It appeared that their primary output was an online portal called RedBook.

"What?" Reuben protested aloud.

It made no sense, and reading the marketing material made less sense. Reuben grabbed a pen and notepad and jotted down what he was finding. Stephanie Dwyer was Julian's "Boo," and Tom was her older brother. Tom wasn't just a software engineer. He actually owned S-Wire Media, which was invested in by BTI, Alister Pout's investment group. Now these people were starting to connect.

Reuben searched for BTI and couldn't find an office, but the Trillium Group had a twenty-story building downtown. That was what he needed. He pulled up the traffic cam software and entered the Trillium Group's address. Just as he did, an Interpol alert popped up on his computer.

"Interpol has indicated a status of 'unknown or missing' on a weapon of mass destruction in Canada, possibly headed toward the US border. Type: Experimental. Please be alerted for further details as the situation unfolds. Assigned Case #U95643E-1."

These sorts of alerts happened often. Usually it was the Department of Defense, but sometimes Interpol sent alerts as well.

They usually went away without any notice, but it meant that the agency had opened a case, and if anyone had any information, they could reference it to that case number. He vaguely remembered the alert popping up the first time. Countries, unfortunately, miscounted weapons and nuclear material from time to time. The different holding bases had to count it all daily and submit the counts on a deadline. If the counts were off at the deadline, an alert would be generated, and a protocol had to be followed. The weapons and material were usually found, and within hours the case would be closed. Reuben knew this one was no miscount.

This was for real, and if not stopped, that experimental microwave weapon would be detonated on Valentine's Day.

Reuben zoomed in on the traffic cams outside of the Trillium Group. It was a wet and cold February morning, and the streets buzzed with gridlocked downtown traffic and pedestrians with umbrellas. He zoomed in farther and couldn't find Pout in the crowd. It was mid-morning, so Pout was most likely inside working. He had to get into the building security camera.

After a little bit of hacking, he found that the building was secured by the company 952 Grey, which was, of course, owned by S-Wire Media.

"Geez." Reuben shook his head. How deep did S-Wire and Pout go?

Hacking into the S-Wire feed wasn't difficult. In fact, it was surprisingly easy, and Reuben began to doubt the effectiveness of their pet project, RedBook, especially because of all the data sharing RedBook was designed to do. If a foreign agent were to get into these databases, it would change the landscape of everything.

He patched into their feed, and he had almost located the signal for the Trillium building when the power went out.

"Shit," Reuben said as the lights dimmed all around him.

A titter passed through the office, even though laptop screens remained on. It would take up to two minutes for the backup generator to power up all the technology, and it might take a couple minutes longer for the Internet to come back on.

The agent who had been on the power trip now navigated through the hallway lit by cell phone flashlights and laptop screens. He blinked like a groundhog coming up out of the dirt. “Say, it’s pretty dark in here,” he told Reuben.

“I didn’t notice.”

“Power went out.”

“That explains it.” Reuben smirked in the dark.

“Storm coming in,” the agent said. “Can’t control the weather.”

“Indeed.” Then Reuben took advantage of the situation. “You got any notes on that Schaeffer? I lost what I was working on. It’s not in the system. Damn.”

“Oh, yeah.” The agent stretched. Without proper lighting and proper brain functioning, the agent didn’t register that Reuben didn’t have the clearance he should have. After all, how else would a low-level security agent know about Schaeffer? “The top brass has known about a breach at a Canadian experimental weapons testing facility for a few days now. Can you believe it! They're trying to keep it under wraps because no one knows if it was nuclear material that was stolen or some high-tech weapon."

Damn, Reuben thought. The microwave bomb had been stolen on the seventh or the eighth? "But how is this connected to Schaeffer?"

"They're convinced that Schaeffer is connected to the breach. Especially since he arrived in New York three days ago.”

"He came to New York three days ago?" Reuben frowned. That was definitely not in the reports on Valentine's Day.

"We think so." The agent popped his back. "It's the weirdest thing. I swore I saw that name on a plane roster from Delta. He went from Des Moines to New York. But then, just as I went to pull it back up to submit it as evidence, his name was gone from the roster."

"Just like that, huh?" Reuben scratched his chin. "Disappeared?"

"Yeah, oddest thing. I don't know, I think I might have imagined it, but just between you and me..." The agent glanced around, and in the semi-dark powered by battery-operated devices, the agent made a drinking motion. "You know, I was into the tequila a little bit, so who knows what I saw?" He laughed a bit too loud for Reuben's comfort.

"Indeed." Reuben forced a chuckle.

"You want a shot?" He pointed in the general direction of his desk.

"No. I've got my own stash. Everyone does." Reuben didn't know if that was true or not, but it seemed like something this guy would believe.

Reuben didn't have any alcohol at his desk but wanted to keep the guy talking. What this guy wouldn't remember three days from now could alter the course of Western civilization.

"I was going to look into it more, but then the power went out," the agent continued. "We've got flight records for him going to Albuquerque on Valentine's Day. Aunt's place."

That was old information to Reuben. "Got it. Thanks."

"Yup." Suddenly, the power hummed back to life in the building and the lights came back on. The agent blinked. "Time to go back to my desk. Catch you later."

Reuben nodded. "See ya."

The agent stumbled back toward his desk in the bright fluorescent light and clumsily tripped and fell on a computer wire. Reuben saw Sven standing at the window of his office, watching the whole thing. The director frowned and picked up the phone.

So that was what happened to the guy, Reuben thought. He had never seen him before. Now, thanks to his stash of tequila, he would never see him again. But he had his information.

The agent said that Julian had come to New York three days ago, and apparently the flight records had been erased from Delta's system. But, Reuben reasoned, if Schaeffer was still in New York, there would be all sorts of records of his visit. He would have swiped credit cards, made hotel reservations, paid for transportation.

Once the Internet was back on, Reuben used the agency database to cross-reference Schaeffer's name on credit and debit cards. Why was he going to New York, anyway? He had checking and savings accounts at Chase Bank and a student Discover card. With a little bit of hacking, he tapped into Schaeffer's online banking.

The kid ate a lot of fast food, shopped at PacSun, and spent $164 at...Victoria's Secret?

Damn, Reuben thought. *Go, Schaeffer.* Especially considering, according to the direct deposit information, the guy only made about $200 a week. He pulled the cocky-looking photo of Julian back up and rolled his eyes.

Yeah, this guy could get that kind of action.

He scanned back through the banking information up until the beginning of the year and didn't find anything out of the ordinary. Regular paychecks, gas... But there was nothing indicating any kind of travel or travel plans or even any recent swipes in New York. He did a keyword search for Delta, and nothing came up. He switched over to the savings account; he had a few thousand in there but no recent withdrawals. This guy checked out on all bank records.

It took a lot longer for him to hack into the Discover card records, and he couldn't do it. He had to call his contact at the Discover office. He just hoped that she would help him.

"Angela, I just need to look into an account," he told her.

"I'm sorry, Reuben, I need a warrant this time," she said. "You almost got me fired last time."

"Come on," he told her. "Julian Schaeffer, he's a nineteen-year-old student account holder from Des Moines. Just send it to me."

"No, Reuben. You can't just call up here and demand account information. That's not the way it works. You have to go through the proper channels."

"It takes months to go through the proper channels."

She was silent.

"Don't make me do it," he said. "Come on, Angela, do me a solid."

"Reuben," she said. "I can't do it for you this time. I'm serious. I'll get in big trouble. Get a warrant, and I'll give you whatever you want."

"Angela…don't make me say it."

There was a long silence on the other line before Angela said, "Then don't say it."

"I need this. I will play the card."

"Please don't."

Reuben sighed. He didn't have time for this. Besides, he would most likely die a few dozen times before this was over. Angela wouldn't remember him being an asshole. "Your ex-husband. The very illegal cyber-stalking I did for you, proving he was cheating. Cyber-stalking and the untraceable proof you needed to get a very, very healthy divorce settlement and the beach house in Malibu."

"I bought you a nice bottle of whisky. Oban 18, remember?"

"I do, and it was delicious." Another silence. "Listen, Angela, I really need this. This will be the last favor I ask for like this. Ever. I promise."

Unless I die and don't have this conversation next time round, he mused.

"OK. I'll print something out for you. No digital records."

"Great, I'm coming over," he said and hung up before she could finish.

Reuben—Friday, February 10, 11:23 a.m.

Reuben grabbed his keys and coat and walked the two blocks through the freezing winter weather. He arrived at the tall glass building and took the elevator to the fourth floor. The elevator opened to a large marble lobby with the Discover card logo emblazoned on the wall.

A tall brunette receptionist greeted him. Other than her, office workers filled in the desks and cubicles lining the floor. Most of them wore headsets or Bluetooth earpieces and paid no attention to him.

"Can I help you?" the receptionist asked.

"I'm here to see Angela Steele," Reuben told her.

"Absolutely." She directed him to sign in.

He scrawled Jim Lewandowski on the sign-in sheet. Jim was one of the alter egos he often used when out in public on agency business—usually just short rides in the tech van to fix a computer or router in one of the CIA's other buildings it owned. It made him harder to trace if anyone outside of the CIA caught on to him. It also helped if he had to get around privacy laws like he was about to now.

He pointed down the hall toward Angela's office, although he knew exactly where it was. "It's back that way, right?"

She shrugged and pointed through the empty hallway. "Yeah, you can just go back there."

"Thanks." He smiled and took the carpeted hallway down to Angela's office.

Angela sighed when she saw him. She was a heavyset woman in her early thirties with wavy dark hair, probably of Hawaiian descent. Right now she was eating a candy bar and washing it down with a Sonic slushie. When he arrived, she surreptitiously glanced through the hall, and satisfied that no one was there, she nodded toward the office door.

He shut it behind him.

She reached into a desk drawer and pulled out a file folder. She silently handed it to him, and he stuck it in his jacket.

He turned to walk out of the office but paused near the side of her desk. Then he closed his eyes and waited for it. There it was.

She planted her hand square on his butt, and he grimaced as she gave it a nice, hard, luscious squeeze.

"That's enough," he told her. Man, he could write a book on the awkward situations he found himself in when he went on "tech calls" outside the office. Oh well, the fate of the world depended on her information. Letting her grab his ass was the least he could do.

She let go.

"Pleasure doing business with you," he said.

"Likewise."

They both nodded at each other, and he left the office.

Back out in the street, he skimmed the file while he walked. The personal details all checked out. Julian Schaeffer, proper date of birth, and he vaguely recognized the social security number and the address in Des Moines, Iowa. He read the account details—a couple of payments and some late fees. There was a six-hundred-dollar charge to a community college in early February.

"Good for you, Julian." Reuben nodded. "Go back to school."

He'd check the school's records once he got back to the office to see if he'd enrolled for the next term. This wasn't completely relevant to the time period, but it would help to build a case that this was a frame job and that Julian was just an average college guy. It also showed that he had plans to stay in town and helped to anchor him to Des Moines, even though the agency had him jet-setting to New Mexico. Although it could be argued that a criminal might have staged the college enrollment for that very reason. But the more he got to know this guy, the more he was starting to like Schaeffer.

He wanted to save him from the fate the agency had for him.

The rest was the usual. It looked like he'd had his car repaired, and there were charges to a tire shop and a $200 payment to Nintendo and a takeout pizza.

Then Reuben laughed.

He could tell where Stephanie had hijacked his card. More Victoria's Secret. Bath and Body Works. A nail salon. A spa. The next page was upside-down, and there was a $100 charge to Mr. Sudds? The dry cleaner Martha told him about?

Damn. This case was getting juicier and juicier.

This also meant that Julian had been in New York three days ago. Unless only Stephanie had come. This was starting to become an interesting frame job, indeed.

He read the rest of the statement. Nothing else indicated a trip to New York. The only other charge that day was an Uber ride for $29.62. He assumed that must have been the ride from the airport to Mr. Sudds, and if he could find the time of day that had happened, he could use the traffic cam to see what happened.

With a little bit of hacking, Reuben ran a report detailing all of the Uber charges on that day. It was New York City; there were thousands of them. He narrowed it down to rides costing $29.62. Only about a hundred charges popped up.

He clicked on the fields, and the names on the charges appeared. He searched for Schaeffer in the name field, but nothing came up. He searched for Julian and nothing came up. He tried Stephanie, but no luck. What about Tom Dwyer? Still nothing.

Martha texted him. **Did you find anything?**

The truth was, he was finding quite a lot. But, damn that CIA security clearance. He couldn't tell her much of anything. The security cameras were so advanced in that room, they could even read a text. He knew if he told her anything that wasn't publicly accessible, he'd be fired on the spot. He wasn't due to take a break anytime soon where he could step outside and call her. To cover his bases, he set his phone on the desk in clear view of the camera and texted her, **No, we'll keep looking.**

He hated that he couldn't help her. She was helping him,

but so much of what he knew was classified. Outside of work, he could violate some clearances without getting caught. But he was trying to play it safe by giving her hints and knowledgeably directing her toward publicly available sources. Right now he was mainly following Julian, and she could never know about him.

Whose Uber account would Schaeffer have put his Discover card on? Suddenly, he had an idea. It was a long shot, but it might pay off. Reuben pulled up Julian's Facebook page and generated his friends list. Great, he had over a thousand friends. He printed off the list, and one by one, ran the names through the Uber report. After about thirty tries, he found it.

"*Ha-lle-lujah.*" With an operatic flair, Reuben burst into a rendition of Handel's *Messiah*.

"Sorry." He cleared his throat at the dirty looks his coworkers were giving him.

Gina Dwyer. Stephanie's sister-in-law, married to Tom.

Reuben laughed. "These people get more and more interesting."

Had Julian used Gina's Uber account to book a ride to Mr. Sudds? Or did Stephanie go with him and book it from her sister's account? Or did Tom use his wife's account? Maybe Julian wasn't even actually in New York. The possibilities were endless.

Regardless, the Uber charge had someone arriving at Mr. Sudds at 3:14 p.m. three days ago. Reuben pulled up the traffic cam on Mr. Sudds at 3:10 p.m. that day. He wanted to make sure he saw as much of the vehicle arriving as possible. He waited for three minutes and then saw a red Camry pull up to the dry cleaners.

After a minute, the door opened, and Julian Schaeffer stepped out. Stephanie wasn't with him.

Reuben's heart leapt at the sight. Regardless of the method of his investigation, this was the kind of hard evidence that even Sven would jump all over.

Schaeffer had spiky blond hair, wore a blue flannel shirt and torn jeans, and carried a red backpack over his left shoulder. Reuben couldn't tell much more about him from the traffic cam. He enhanced the image and noticed that he seemed shifty and kept looking over his shoulder. The Camry waited for a couple more minutes and then left.

Schaeffer stood on the sidewalk of Mr. Sudds and waited. He kept biting his fingernails and looked nervous. He glanced around, looking for something, someone. He reached into his backpack and pulled out something. Reuben squinted. A pack of cigarettes. Julian lit one and stood outside smoking for a minute. The door to Mr. Sudds opened, but Reuben couldn't see who was on the other side. Julian turned and said something, and then the door closed again. Julian tossed the cigarette on the ground and went inside. He stayed inside for several minutes.

Reuben stayed glued to the screen, watching the empty sidewalk.

"Reuben." Sven's voice through the speakerphone made Reuben jump so hard he hit his leg on the underside of the desk.

"Yes, sir?"

"Can you come in here for a moment?"

"Absolutely."

Reuben paused the footage and scrawled down the time stamp just in case. Then he minimized the window on his screen, locked his computer, and went into Sven's office.

Sven leaned back when he saw Reuben and toyed with a gold pen. He motioned to a chair in front of his desk. "Do you know why I called you in here?"

Reuben gingerly eased into the chair and answered honestly, "I don't."

Life with Sven was a confusing mess of mind games, and Reuben never quite knew how to navigate them. He figured he'd probably failed at all of them, and Sven mostly considered him an affable moron, too harmless to fire.

Sven tossed the pen on the desk and met Reuben's gaze. He knew enough of Sven's games to know he was supposed to win at a staring contest with his boss. It showed something like accountability or honesty, or soul vulnerability, or something like that. But damn, was it unnerving.

He sat listening to the clock tick on the wall.

Tick, tock. Tick, tock.

Reuben tried not to squirm, but now all of this stuff with Schaeffer was burning just under the surface, and it started to bubble up like hot lava in his chest. He couldn't tell Sven about Schaeffer without telling him how he knew.

He also knew he wasn't in trouble, exactly. If Sven were upset about something, he wouldn't confront him this way. This method of confrontation was simply to do exactly what it was doing to Reuben. To make him spill any kind of secret beans that the agency didn't know about.

"What can you tell me about the incident with Mike Fury?" Sven finally asked.

"Oh, that." Reuben was relieved it would be about that. "He asked for me to run a report, and I couldn't do it along with my own work, and he responded."

Sven listened and pursed his lips. "You're not telling me everything."

"No, sir." Reuben surprised himself with his own response. "I'm still figuring out the details. I wouldn't want to waste the agency's time, money, and other resources."

Sven's lip rose in shocked approval. "Agent Peet, how long have you been here?"

"About two years, sir," Reuben answered.

"Two years," Sven considered. "I'm not sure if you are aware, but Agent Nick Perry has been removed from case *#U95643E-1*."

"I'm not familiar with him. That case number has to do with the Interpol alert, right?"

"You spoke with Agent Perry during the power outage," Sven explained with a gesture toward the security screen on his desk. "Correct on the case number. As for Perry, we're diverting his attention to another case." Sven spoke with a tone that told Reuben *not* to ask any questions.

"Right," Reuben said. "I wasn't aware of his name."

"In any case," Sven continued, "I need someone who can replace him on that project. I can't divert my higher-level agents from their duties at this time, but this alert has persisted past the four-hour mark, so I have to put someone on it. If you can resolve that case with efficiency, we'll see about putting you on some higher cases."

Reuben's eyes widened. Had he just been put on the Schaeffer case? "Sir, I'd be honored."

Sven's lips twisted in disgust. "Don't bullshit me, kid. Get your work done, and get it done right."

"Yes, sir." Reuben rose from the chair and left the office. He practically breezed back down the hallway, almost missing Aki. Almost.

He crashed into her with a loud thud in the hall. "I'm sorry."

She smiled and rubbed her head. "You're fine. Robert, right?"

"Reuben."

"Yeah." She nodded slowly. "Thanks for talking to me yesterday, after the... You know..." she trailed off, embarrassed.

"Yeah." He ran his hands through his hair. "I'm sorry about what happened."

Aki shook her head. "Don't be. It was an accident waiting to happen. You just got caught in the crossfire."

He stood in the hallway with her and had so much to say. He opened his mouth, but no sound would come out. She smiled kindly, and with a quick squeeze on the arm, she swished away, leaving a trail of perfume in his memory.

After she was gone, he leaned against the wall and grimaced. Why couldn't he say anything? He knew her; he knew her so well. Right then was the moment he had been waiting for, hand-delivered to him. But he couldn't so much as utter a peep. What was wrong with him?

He went back to his desk and pulled up the traffic cam at Mr. Sudds again. He tried to put Aki out of his mind. Now that he was officially on the Schaeffer angle, he could devote all his energy to it.

An alert popped up from Sven. He had been added to the case file.

He opened the link in the directory. The angle he was supposed to be working on this case was whether Schaeffer stole the bomb. Perfect. This was exactly what he wanted to work on.

The agency already had his basic profile, and that he was connected to a looming bomb controversy by way of his connections with a handful of conspiracy theorist groups.

Reuben snorted. Julian wasn't a conspiracy theorist, at least not openly enough to warrant government surveillance on that account. He may have had some friends who were, but his posts were about his girlfriend, his skateboarding, and hanging out in bars with friends.

Besides, the bomb wasn't nuclear. It was an experimental microwave weapon. The radioactive material in the dumpster near Julian's house that had initially gotten the kid on the CIA's radar was probably planted.

Unfortunately, Reuben shouldn't officially know any of this. He was days ahead of the CIA in terms of what he knew and they knew. He had to be careful about how he proceeded.

Reuben clicked back over to the traffic cam to watch the interaction with Schaeffer at the dry cleaners. Schaeffer was still inside, and there was no action. Reuben tapped his pen against the desk and started to wonder if they had murdered Schaeffer in the dry cleaners. This would explain why no one could catch him on Valentine's Day.

More minutes ticked by, and still no action. What the hell?

Reuben moved the security cam to the side of the screen and pulled up the case file on his directory. He started filling in everything he knew about the Schaeffer case, keeping the security screen in his periphery. He wanted the CIA to know what they needed to know and when to stop the threat on Valentine's Day. Now that he'd put in the work to hopefully clear Julian's name, the agency could focus on finding who was really behind the threat.

He linked the credit card documents and the bank statements. He explained what Nick had said about the missing Delta flight. He also scanned in the credit card documents. He knew Angela would burn if that ever went to court. It was illegally obtained evidence. The agency was fine with illegally obtained substantiated evidence, so long as you could use it to get legally obtained evidence before it went to court. With the street cam evidence, they were covered.

Julian still hadn't come out of Mr. Sudds.

Reuben moved the time bar back just to see if he had missed anything. Nope, Julian had gone in and still hadn't come out. If this went on much longer, he would check police records to see if there was anyone matching his description who showed up in the murder cases. He went back to filling in all of the information he had into the agency files. Hopefully, this would be enough information that when Valentine's Day came around, Julian wouldn't be the prime suspect. Reuben included a note about Stephanie Dwyer and her connection to Tom Dwyer, and yes, he connected them to S-Wire and then threw in the reference to BTI and Alister Pout.

It was dark by the time he finished, and the office was thinning out. Julian was still inside the dry cleaners. It had been three hours. What was he doing inside there for three hours? Finally, Reuben fast-forwarded through to the end of the day. Two workers came out of the dry cleaners, locked up, and disappeared down the sidewalk.

No Julian. Had they seriously killed the guy?

Reuben again tracked back to when Julian went in. He watched again to see if there was any clue he was missing. He enhanced the view to find anything moving in the windows. He saw the tiniest glimpse of Julian's shirt sleeve move in the window, and then it went away. He enhanced the view as high as it would go, not working with much more than pixels. He stared into the window, and then he noticed it again. The blue pixels jumped in the same way, and at such a high enhancement, it became obvious that the blue color on the screen disappeared and reappeared randomly.

"Are you kidding me?" Reuben gasped.

The security tape had been looped. What the hell? How had Schaeffer and whomever he had working with been able to doctor the security footage? This stank of Dwyer, or Pout. Or the S-Wire folks.

With a little bit of hacking, he was able to tap into the signal for the ATM across the street security footage. He scrolled through it—nothing of note.

Reuben checked to see what was next door to Mr. Sudds. There was a fast food place called Hurley's Chicken. He clicked a few more times and got into the restaurant's cameras. There were views of the lobby, the alley, and then finally he found the sidewalk view, with a perfect shot of Mr. Sudds.

On the Hurley camera, he didn't see Julian arrive in the red Camry but saw him go inside Mr. Sudds. This view of Julian's face was a little bit clearer, and he noticed a chin ring. Then, Julian came out minutes later.

"Shit." Reuben laughed. This wasn't in the city footage.

Julian stood on the sidewalk for a moment, pacing back and forth, biting his lip. He moved in and out of frame several times, and Reuben kept thinking he might have lost him. Finally, a black Mercedes pulled up next to Hurley's Chicken. The window rolled down, and Julian talked to someone from the sidewalk.

Reuben couldn't see who it was, but it wasn't going so well. Finally, the door opened, and two figures stepped out. One was a man wearing a white hoodie with stripes on the shoulders and the hood pulled up. He turned away from the camera and disappeared down an alley. The other man was—

"Holy *shit*!" Reuben exclaimed.

It was Alister Pout.

Julian and Alister chatted tersely for about a minute on the street, and Julian looked uncomfortable. Finally, he reached into his backpack and pulled out something. Reuben couldn't make it out.

Alister reached out and grabbed it and stuck it in his coat. He shook the kid's hand and got back in his Mercedes. Alister left, and Julian walked out of frame.

Reuben backtracked through the footage to look at what had been exchanged. He enhanced the view to see a plastic bag with a Canadian maple leaf on it. That was all he could tell.

He tried to follow Julian through the streets but couldn't switch the cameras fast enough. Now that Pout had no doubt compromised the footage, he couldn't trust it anyway.

Reuben was stumped. He didn't know how to follow Julian past leaving Mr. Sudds that day. But he knew someone with the fieldwork and experience that might.

Aki.

CHAPTER THIRTY

Martha—Friday, February 10, 9:17 a.m.

Martha sank into the chair at her desk and rubbed her temples. It had been the week to end all weeks. Or at least, so she had been told. The whole experience with Reuben and his weird friend Buzz was the strangest thing she had ever been through in her life. She still didn't know what to make of it.

"Can I get you anything?" Zach's perky face popped up over her cubicle wall and made her headache worse. "Coffee? Red Bull?" He held up a silver can toward her.

Martha grimaced. "Oh, God, no. That's the last thing either of us needs."

"You want to do some talk-throughs?" Zach used the proper police force terminology for the technique of talking through a case, hoping to figure it out. It worked sometimes, but with all the career politics that went on around here, the last thing anyone wanted to do was show all their cards.

She shot Zach a look, and he sat back down. "Any word on Alister Pout's schedule?" she asked.

"Yeah, I mean, you didn't exactly give me much time, and I still don't know why we're looking into him."

Martha shot him another look, and Zach backed down. "Well," he produced a stack of papers two inches thick, "this is what I found."

She frowned and grabbed the stack. He had appointments and engagements back from the beginning of the year.

"This is good work, Zach," she said. "Where did you get this? And in one night, too."

He smiled, cleared his throat, and glanced around the office. "Pout's assistant."

Martha narrowed her eyes. "You just walked up there and asked for it?"

"Well, no." He grinned. "I did a bit of research on his staff. Trying to get results as quickly as possible, you know."

"Research?"

"Yeah, Twitter," he clarified. "It's like voluntary surveillance. Anyway, I found out some of his staff were having a big birthday party at a bar near their office building. They even tweeted what booth they were in. One of them just recently broke up with her boyfriend and said she needed to find some artsy guy like a painter or writer she could be all sensitive with."

"She tweeted that?" Martha raised an eyebrow. She was young, practically a rookie herself. But this Twitter stuff was making her feel old.

Zach blushed. "Actually, it was on Tinder."

Martha held up a hand. "Hold on. You stalking this girl?"

"No!" Zach denied hotly. "I was researching. I went to the bar with my laptop because I was working on my cop novel."

Martha resisted the urge to laugh. "You're writing a cop novel?"

Zach shrugged. "Well, my dream is to be James Patterson, but you got to start small. So I just tinker with it. I've been working on it for about four years."

"OK..." She pondered that image. It actually worked better than Zach as a cop.

"So, I'm in the bar, pretending to write, but I'm really watching her. After a while she's had, like, six drinks, and I introduce myself. I tell her I'm a cop working on my thriller novel and need a femme fatale. I ask if she would be my femme fatale."

"And that worked?"

"Oh yeah." His voice lowered, and his smile got goofier. "Let me tell you, she's cute. Long brown hair, huge breasts—"

"OK, Zach," Martha cut in. "Spare me the details. Save it for the novel."

"Fair enough," he answered. "We start talking. I'm asking her questions about herself for, you know, the novel. I'm looking for inspiration. At least, that's what I say. I'm already on chapter thirty-six, and let me tell you, my femme fatale is one—"

"Zach!" Martha chastised. "Focus!"

"Yeah, sorry. Anyway, she starts telling me all about how she's Alister Pout's assistant. Bingo. She's working the billionaire assistant angle for my book. That might be the sequel," he muttered to himself. "She talks about her job, Pout, and then she starts complaining about her boss and how he's an asshole and he sleeps with everyone and doesn't even notice her. How she feels so invisible because how could he sleep with half of Manhattan and not even at least want to sleep with her. So, he's the reason for posting about the artsy type on Tinder. A writer is just about as different as possible from a billionaire..."

"That's odd logic," Martha countered.

Zach nodded. "Totally agree. James Patterson made close to a hundred million last year."

"No," Martha clarified. "The sleeping around part."

"Oh, yeah. I thought so, too. Like I told her that she's beautiful and sexy and that he's just an asshole, and then I invited her back to my place, and you know..." He cleared his throat.

"Right."

"But here's the thing." He glanced around the office and then back at Martha. "When she left my place this morning, she grabbed her purse. But, she forgot to take this." He reached backward toward his desk and produced an iPad.

Martha gave him a stern look. "Forgot?"

Zach shrugged.

She pursed her lips. "This is some gray area you're working in here."

"It fell out of her bag," he explained.

"She'll want that back."

Zach blushed again. "We've got a lunch date today. I'll give it back then, but not before we find everything on it."

Martha's eyes widened. "You know, none of what we find holds up in court."

"Of course not." He shrugged. "Illegally obtained evidence. But it can give us some leads on how to find legally obtained evidence."

Martha grinned and grabbed the iPad. "No password."

"There is," he said. "But I figured it out."

"What is it?"

He made a face. "Carrie Bradshaw."

Martha made the same expression. "Ugh. How did you figure that out, by the way?"

He cleared his throat. “Let’s just say there are some things a man learns when he’s with a lady.”

Martha jumped up from her chair and gagged with disgust, and Zach dissolved into laughter. The image of Zach … Ugh. She couldn’t even complete the thought.

“OK.” She composed herself. “Let’s check this baby out.”

“Yeah, let’s.” He leaned over her shoulder, and they pored over the screen.

“This is the appointment book,” he explained as he opened an app. “It’s synced to her work computer. It’s where I got the printouts. I came in here early this morning and printed it all out so that we have it after I give it back.”

“Good thinking.” She clicked on the contacts tab in the app, and a screen of names and numbers popped up. “Everyone Alister Pout knows.”

“It gets better.” He tapped on another tab. “He’s one of those fancy dudes who doesn’t make his own phone calls.”

Of course. “Right.”

“So he has her make them for him.” He scrolled down a call log. “This is a list of calls from his office.”

Martha couldn’t believe it. “Oh my God. How could she be so careless?”

“I don’t think she’s the only assistant,” he said. “I think she’s like the junior one, and so this isn’t everything.”

“But it sure as hell is enough,” Martha said.

They snooped through it a while longer.

“Her emails,” she whispered as she tapped on the mail button. “This is so illegal.”

“Yes, it is,” he said. “But it’s like Jake told me: sometimes you got to bend the rules to follow the rules.”

“Right.” Martha felt a surge of guilt in her stomach like falling rocks. She couldn’t keep looking through this stuff.

This was wrong on so many levels. They didn't have any hard evidence against Pout, and she couldn't go snooping through a private device.

She shut the cover on the tablet. "We can't do this," she said. "This is wrong. You have to give this back to her. Now."

He stammered. "But I thought you wanted evidence?"

She handed the iPad back to him. "We have to do this the right way."

"This," he held up the tablet, "is a gift from the gods. You can't just refuse a gift."

"Yes, we can, and we will." She dropped the report on his desk. "Shred that."

Zach's face fell. "Martha."

She shook her head and walked away, then bumped right into Captain Kenneth. "Sorry." She blinked with embarrassment.

"No biggie." the captain winked. "How are you doing on the Canadian case? You getting anything?"

She gave him a thumbs-up. "We're working on it."

"Tell you what I want you to do." He turned toward her. "I want you to partner with Sergeant Bramley on this."

Martha frowned, recalling the embarrassment his stint on camera had landed her in. "Bramley? From the investigative unit?"

"Yeah, let him get his hands in the pot, find out where your holes are." He sipped his coffee. "It will make the whole process go a lot smoother."

"A lot smoother?" Pride swelled up in her chest. "Sir, I'm on this project. I can handle it. I just need a little more time."

Captain Kenneth pursed his lips. "I appreciate your enthusiasm; I do. But I think your investigation might benefit from a little more experience."

"Sir, I don't think this case needs the kind of media attention that Sergeant Bramley is in the middle of," she said. "If this case goes like I think it will, it will draw its own media scandal. We don't need to jeopardize an ongoing investigation or perhaps drag an innocent suspect through the mud on reality television."

The captain raised his eyebrows in agreement. "All right, I'll give you till after the weekend. If you can't get this Canadian character solved by Monday, I want it kicked upstairs."

She sighed. "Yes, sir."

Captain Kenneth walked away, and she went back to her desk. As she passed Zach's desk, she grabbed the iPad.

"If we're going down, we're going down fighting," she said.

Zach smiled. "We've got three hours before we have to give this back."

Martha nodded. "Let's make it good."

They spent the next two hours going through everything. Appointment confirmations. Morning meetings. Flight reservations for people who weren't Alister. There was so much there, she couldn't begin to sort through it. And it was still synced to the woman's work computer, so new emails were popping up.

One in particular caught her eye. It popped up in a blue box on the side of the screen. *Re: Alister Traffic Ticket.*

She clicked on it and laughed. It appeared that Alister didn't even so much as manage to pay his own traffic tickets. He had his assistants do it. She scrolled through the email, snickering as his assistants discussed the logistics of paying the citation. They needed his driver's license number and had to decide which of his cards to charge it to.

Man, she thought, *one day I'll be so rich, I can have someone else pay my traffic tickets.* It didn't say what the ticket was for, and so Martha logged into the police database and looked up his name. She found the record easily enough. But her face paled when she saw it. It was with the Detroit police department. He was speeding, right at the Detroit-Windsor border.

Three hours before the maple syrup shootout.

Reuben—Friday, February 10, 1:22 p.m.

Reuben finished telling Aki the situation. "I need your help."

He leaned against her desk and let his story sink in. Well, certainly not all of it. He knew damn well better than that. But what he did tell her was enough.

"OK." She narrowed her eyes. "Let me get this straight. Sven wants you to find this kid Julian Schaeffer because he thinks he's behind the alert from this morning."

Reuben nodded. "Right."

"He's from Des Moines, and he was an erased passenger on a Delta flight to New York three days ago, but you tracked him down on the security footage doing a shady business deal with...*Alister Pout?*"

He nodded again. "Correct."

"OK." She furrowed her brow in disbelief. "I think Alister Pout has better things to do than hang out on street corners with nineteen-year-olds."

"You would think, but I've got the footage," he said. *"And* it was erased from the CCTV reel. Only somebody with some serious connections could do that."

"Same with erasing a passenger off a commercial flight manifest," she thought aloud. "How does he even know this guy?"

"Julian is dating Stephanie Dwyer, whose brother is Tom Dwyer, who owns S-Wire Media."

Aki frowned. "S-Wire Media? They manage that weird RedBook thing that no one can figure out the point of, right?"

"Actually, it's a social media platform designed to aggregate information during a crisis event like a… You know what? Never mind. It's not important. What matters is that Alister Pout is invested in it."

"I read an article where he was talking about it," Aki told him. "He came off like a real asshole, with this Swedish model hanging around on his boat or something." Her phone pinged with a text, and a shadow passed across her face. She read it, and her mood darkened.

"Mike?" Reuben asked.

She didn't reply, but he could see it on her face. "You know, you'd have to find some harder evidence than what you've got. You're just chasing mirages, and it's not going to get you anywhere."

Reuben pursed his lips. "That's why I'm asking for help. This kid is suspected of experimenting with homemade bombs back home. Due to materials found in a dumpster." Reuben was hesitant to mention the microwave bomb at this point for two reasons. One, she might not know what one was —he certainly hadn't until he was killed by one. Two, she might ask questions as to how he knew such specific information.

Aki eyed him conspiratorially. "From what you tell me, this kid can't write a five-paragraph essay. I highly doubt he can hijack a VW van, let alone steal the experimental weapon from that Interpol alert."

"That's my point," Reuben insisted. "He's on our suspect list and only rising higher. We need to clear his name and find out who did."

"You know, I'm so swamped with high-security cases." She gestured toward her computer, flickering with dozens of open windows, and the printouts on her desk. "I'm not saying it's not a compelling case. It's a good one to start out with if you're trying to rise as an agent."

Reuben's hopes fell. "But you won't help me."

Aki shook her head, smiling. "Thank you for thinking of me. Let me know if the alert level rises, and I'll see what I can do."

"Yeah." He turned and walked away, his legs feeling like lead.

She had been so easy to talk to that one day, but she was sickly-sweet aloof the rest of the time. Where was the easygoing, free-spirited, intelligent, driven agent he had met in the previous timeline?

"Reuben," she called after him.

He whipped around. "Yes?"

"All the same, link me in on your case," she told him. "I may not have time to pursue it, but I could give you a pointer or two."

"Sure, thanks." He could feel the smile on his face expand exponentially. "Will do."

He went back to his desk and immediately added her permission in the access pane. He updated all his notes, adding in the new information about the looped CCTV footage. He also copied the relevant Hurley's Chicken footage and linked it to the case file. He was almost done with his notes when he glanced up and saw her.

Aki stood at his desk, wild-eyed. "You're serious about finding out what this guy knows?"

"I am," he answered earnestly.

She gave him a big smile. "Then let's go get him."

"We'd have to fly to Des Moines," he stated.

She laughed. "No, silly. He's still in New York."

"What do you mean?"

"You didn't catch that update I just added?"

"No." He clicked on his screen and refreshed it.

She leaned over his keyboard, and the scent of her perfume made his head cloud and his heart race. He was acutely aware of how close she was and tried not to stare at the reflection of her cleavage on the computer screen.

"See?" With a few clicks, she brought up a hospital document. "There was a Julian Schaeffer from Des Moines, Iowa, who showed up in the emergency room last night with alcohol poisoning. He was released this morning, and the bill was paid by Tom Dwyer at this address."

With the mouse, she highlighted the Long Island address on the form.

"He's staying with Tom Dwyer," he said.

"Yep," she said. "That's why there's no hotel bill and very little digital footprint. The Dwyers are taking care of his food, probably lent him a car, too."

"That's why the Uber was in Gina's name," he figured out. "Tom's wife Ubered him from the airport, and instead, he added his own card to make his own stop." Reuben reflected again on his quick thinking and how he'd found Gina among Julian's Facebook friends and connected her with the Uber charge.

Aki's smile was infectious. "Let's go pay him a visit."

"It's that easy." He laughed. "I've been chasing this guy for all this time, and the answer is right there."

"Let's go, silly," she said. "He won't be there forever, you know."

He smirked. Little did she know.

"How did you get this bill?" he asked as they headed toward the door. Medical records were practically impossible to get, even with security clearance. Even if an agent with high clearance like Aki could get them, why didn't they get them before?

"Oh." She shrugged. "Based on what you wrote about him, I figured the chances that he added the New York nightlife scene to his agenda were an absolute certainty. I used to know those kinds of people, so I sent out a mass text asking if anyone had seen or heard from a Julian Schaeffer. I put out a picture. Someone said that they thought they saw someone who looked like that leave the Exit Room in an ambulance. So, I called an old boyfriend who works at the ER and asked him to look him up, and he found him. Sent me the records."

Reuben laughed. People do what they have to do to get the job done. They left the building and stepped into the cold February air.

Aki pulled her keys out of her pocket. "We'll take my car."

CHAPTER THIRTY-ONE

Reuben—Friday, February 10, 1:45 p.m.

Reuben couldn't stop thinking about how improbable it would have been before the warp that he would be alone with Aki, going out to her car. What the hell was happening to him? He wished Buzz were here to see this. Or even Marshall. Although, he was sure Marshall would figure out how to use it to insult him.

They arrived in the parking garage, and Aki clicked the remote in her hand. A sleek black Porsche sprang to life, and Reuben tried not to be intimidated.

"Nice car," he said breezily.

"Thanks," she said as she got in the car.

He opened the door, and the thick smell of new leather greeted him as he folded his frame into the tiny vehicle.

"You ever been inside a Porsche?" She smiled coyly as she slipped on her shades. He noticed the Versace label on the side. Of course she would have Versace shades.

"Ah, not to question you or anything, but how many pay

grades above me are you?" he stammered as he buckled his seatbelt.

She threw her head back and laughed. "A lot. But most of this stuff belongs to the CIA. I, um, signed it out."

Reuben laughed. "Got it. For a moment, I thought you were a part-time model."

She gave him a pointed look. "Model?"

Reuben blushed. "Yeah. They're paid a lot, and you're pretty."

Aki's hands tightened on the wheel. "Is that all I am to you? Tits and ass?"

Reuben was lost for words. "No...no! You're...you're—"

"What am I, Reuben?"

Flustered, Reuben said the first thing that came to mind. "Smart, strong, sexy. You've got all the Ss. Not to mention special agent. So all the Ss and an A."

Did I really just say that?

Aki burst out into laughter. "First off, I'm just messing with you. Secondly, that was the best response I've ever gotten from a guy when putting him on the spot." She gave him a long hard look. "As in ever. Good under pressure. Witty. There may be more to *you*, Reuben, than meets the eye."

"Thanks." He wasn't quite sure if he liked the compliment. He didn't know how he'd made her laugh. He wasn't even trying to be funny.

She lurched the car into gear, and with a squeal of tires, they burned rubber through the streets of New York.

Reuben—Friday, February 10, 2:06 p.m.

Reuben and Aki arrived at Tom Dwyer's address on Long

Island. It was a small cottage, a one-story gray brick building with a white door and modest porch. She pulled into the drive, where two young girls in winter hats and coats ran around outside.

She unbuckled her seatbelt. "Dwyer's a family man."

He didn't know what to say to that. He couldn't tell by her inflection whether she approved or didn't approve of being a family man. Should he say he wanted to raise a family? Should he scoff at Tom Dwyer for being domesticated and tied down? He didn't care what he had to say, as long as he said the right thing in front of Aki. She drove a Porsche and had an all-consuming job. It wasn't like she wanted to be June Cleaver or anything. But a man who didn't want kids sounded like a selfish asshole. His mind screamed for an answer. What should he say?

"All right." She slipped the glasses off. "Here's our cover story."

Phew. The family man moment had passed.

"We're government agents, and we're investigating Alister Pout. We know he had something to do with Dwyer, and we want to know what."

Reuben was taken aback. "How is that a cover story? That's just the truth."

"Exactly," she said. "Minus a few details."

They exited the vehicle and walked up the garden path to the front door. A wooden birdhouse hung from the porch, and potted plants filled the entryway with greenery. It reminded him of when he was little and his mom was still around. He had forgotten what a difference those subtle feminine touches made to a home.

She knocked on the door, and it opened quickly enough.

There in the flesh, standing before them, was Julian Schaeffer. Reuben just about had a heart attack. He wore an oversized t-shirt and dark jeans and had a silver stud on his chin.

Julian glanced back and forth at the two agents. "Hi."

"Hi." Aki let loose a thousand-watt smile, and Julian grinned and rubbed the back of his neck. "Julian Schaeffer?"

He eyed them skeptically. "Yeah…"

"My name is Agent Yamashiro, and this is my partner Agent Peet," she introduced them perkily. "We're with a government agency, and we have a few questions to ask."

"I…uh…" Julian's eyes widened.

"You're not in trouble," she said softly. "We're investigating a case and think you might be able to help us. Can we come in?"

Justin looked unsure. "Uh, this is my friend Tom's house. He's not here right now. I'm just babysitting."

"That's fine." She batted her eyelashes. "We're not on official business. We just want to talk."

She used a sultry tone, and even Reuben felt his heart beat a little faster. But without a warrant, they were limited in what they could and couldn't do.

Aki played it well.

"Uh, sure." Julian grinned from ear to ear.

They entered the house, which was modestly furnished with soft brown velour couches, and toys everywhere.

"Sit down." Julian rubbed his hands together and gestured toward the couches. "Can I get you anything?"

Aki smiled. "Like I said, we're not on official business, and to prove it, I'd love a glass of wine."

"Yeah." Julian looked like he was about to burst with excitement. "I, uh, yeah, we got beer."

"Beer's even better." She ran her tongue over her lips.

"Sure." Julian turned toward the kitchen and almost tripped over a stuffed bear on the floor. "Dammit. You know kids..."

She laughed, and he blushed and tossed the bear on the couch.

"So, this is Tom Dwyer's place?" Reuben asked when Julian returned with the beers. "From S-Wire?"

"Yeah." Julian sipped from his bottle. "You know S-Wire?"

"RedBook is supposed to be a new revolution." Reuben nodded with forced enthusiasm. "Can't wait."

"Yeah." Julian frowned and scratched his head. "It's supposed to be something huge."

"Oh my God," Aki suddenly gushed. "I totally know you."

Julian furrowed his brow. "What?"

"Yes." She snapped her fingers. "At that club. The Exit Room. You were there last night. Totally. I saw you."

"Oh, yeah." Julian scratched his head. "I was there. I didn't see you."

Aki feigned disappointment. "Are you kidding me? You don't remember me?"

Julian's mouth dropped, and he stammered for words.

"You bought me drinks..." She tried to jog his memory. She also touched her neckline, revealing a bit more skin.

He snapped his fingers. "Yeah."

She pouted. "We were going to leave together, and then I lost you in the crowd, and I thought you ditched me."

"Oh, my God, no." Julian's face dropped, and he leaned in. "Totally no. You see, I got sick, and I don't know what happened. Can we...start over, maybe?"

She laughed too loud. "Oh my God, you are so cute. Do you have a girlfriend?"

"Um," he stammered. "No."

Reuben thought he would throw up. "Do you mind if I use your bathroom?"

"Yeah." Julian pointed down the hall. "Second door to the left."

"So tell me." Aki leaned forward, exposing even more cleavage than before. Julian noticed too, and from his expression, that was about all Julian noticed. "Are you staying here, in this house?"

"Yeah." He sat across from her and spoke to her chest. "I'm in New York for a little bit, and I just thought I'd stay here. What is it you guys are investigating?"

"I need to know…" Aki batted her eyes. "Well, my boss needs to know, and maybe you can help me out a little bit. Everything about Alister Pout."

"Alister Pout?" Julian's eyes got bigger. "Yeah, I know him."

Aki batted her eyelashes. "Like, Omigod, you like, *know* know him?"

Reuben slowly ambled down the hall, taking in the view. Family pictures of Tom, Gina, the kids, and there was one of Stephanie. Then he found what was clearly a guest room. A meticulously decorated room with a suitcase and clothes strewn all about. With Aki occupying Julian in airheaded conversation, he had a few minutes. He stepped into the room and peered around.

The room looked like it was out of a home-decorating magazine, with rustic farmhouse furniture, carefully placed jars of seashells, and a starfish hanging on the wall. A stack of art books sat perfectly angled on a corner shelf topped with a rubber succulent in a geometrically shaped terrarium.

He stepped over Julian's clothes, jeans, and t-shirts and rapidly pawed through the open suitcase on the floor. At the bottom was where he found it. The same plastic bags he had given Alister. They had a Canadian maple leaf label with a serial number, and they were full of weed.

CHAPTER THIRTY-TWO

Martha—Friday, February 10, 11:42 a.m.

"This is the citation issued by Detroit-Windsor police." Martha set the printouts on Captain Kenneth's desk. "This is the story here about the maple syrup bust. As you can see, I highlighted major points of the story."

"Right." The captain scanned the printed news article.

As he did so, Martha worried her next part might lose him. She had this déjà vu sense going on in her head. Something about wire mesh at a dry cleaner's named Mr. Sudds. Crates and crates of the stuff being transported by van. But she couldn't tell him that.

Kenneth glanced up at her. "You said you had something else?"

Martha nodded and took a deep breath. "I've uh, got a source that can link Pout to a dry cleaner's where he's been transporting a bunch of metal mesh. Odd for a dry cleaner's, right?"

Captain Kenneth tapped a pen against the desk top, its cap chewed into a crumpled witch's hat. "Wait. Metal mesh. I think I read somewhere about terrorists in Europe using it to wrap around a homemade EMP bomb of some type. A gamma bomb, maybe?" He bit down on the pen's cap. "No. Wasn't a gamma bomb. Something like that, though."

Martha's breath caught in her lungs. Homemade experimental bombs? This was a new low for Pout and proved yet again how dangerous the man was.

He set the pen down and picked back up the printouts Martha had brought in. "I'm not so sure about the mesh thing right now, but this syrup bust." His face grew serious. "A cop died during the ensuing shootout."

A few moments later, he nodded grimly when he saw Pout's traffic citation on the page in his hands. "I feel sorry for the bastard that had to issue that ticket. I mean, how do you issue a ticket in the name of Alister Pout? Geez."

"Well, sir, when we're done with this case, we won't be issuing a ticket," she said. "We'll be issuing a warrant."

He sighed and tossed the papers on his desk. "Maybe. Look, I think you might be onto something, but this isn't enough."

"He was clearly part of the maple syrup operation," she said. "There was an officer who died. He was partly responsible."

"You've got to be a certain brand of crazy to label Alister Pout a cop killer." He blinked in disbelief and leaned back in his chair. He cupped his hands over his head. "But, I don't think we should drop it."

Martha's heart raced. "So you want me to move on it?"

"I'm not sure yet." Captain Kenneth studied the ceiling. "I mean, what would he want with maple syrup bootlegging? He owns half the rich people in Manhattan. I just think it's not his style."

He looked at the article again. "The syrup was supposed to be owned by a company called White Mountain Natural Foods. I've never heard of them."

He turned to his computer, Martha whipped out her phone, and they both looked up White Mountain Natural Foods. He found it first. "It's in Montreal, and it's a natural food production chain. Like a co-op."

Martha thought about Marshall's co-op with the milk producers.

"The thing about food co-ops," she knew she sounded knowledgeable, "is they get big and they get sloppy. Then they start messing up."

Captain Kenneth laughed. "You're right about that. When I was a rookie, there was this unsolvable case…"

"Raw milk?" Martha asked.

"Yeah." He laughed. "Politics and family connections. Who knows who, and the next thing you know—"

"Someone's getting poisoned," Martha finished.

The captain chuckled and had a faraway look. "It was already considered unsolvable when I came around. But the veterans like to ramble on about it. It was an interesting case. No one ever got to the bottom of it."

Martha knew all about it, thanks to Marshall. "But this one we can solve. I know Pout's at the bottom of this."

Kenneth clicked around on his computer some more. "White Mountain Natural Foods is owned by a company called Manchester Enterprises. They own a bunch of software companies. These guys are all over the map."

"Manchester Enterprises?" She searched on her phone and found it quickly enough. She skimmed the article and her eyes widened. "They're owned by the Trillium Group and are operated out of BTI."

"BTI?" Kenneth pursed his lips. "Isn't that…"

"Pout," they both said in unison.

Martha picked up her bag and headed for the door.

"Where are you going?" Kenneth called after her.

"To see a friend who might have some insight into this," she said, calling up Google maps on her phone.

Now, what was Buzz's address again? she mused.

Reuben—Friday, February 10, 4:01 p.m.

Reuben and Aki arrived back at CIA headquarters. Aki sat at her computer, and Reuben leaned against her desk as they looked over their newly found evidence.

"I gotta admit," he cleared his throat sheepishly, "you sure looked good when you were sweet-talking Julian."

She laughed. "He's certainly cute."

"So you're attracted to stoner dropouts, huh?" Reuben smirked. "So I guess I should take up weed."

"Oh, God." She laughed. "You'd be terrible to smoke pot with."

"And why's that?"

"You'd get too jumpy." She shuddered.

"And Julian's better?" He pursed his lips.

"No, Julian's a dumbass," she whispered.

They both dissolved in laughter.

"Like, I, uh…" Reuben imitated Julian's voice.

"Oh, God." She rubbed her face. "Well, what do you have here?"

He showed her the photo of the pot baggies. The serial number was for a Canadian dispensary.

"So," she wrote down the number, "we call the Canadian secret service."

"There's a Canadian secret service?" Reuben asked.

She pulled up a number and dialed it on speaker.

"Canadian Mounted Police," the voice answered. "This is Heath."

"Hi, Heath," Aki said. "This is Aki Yamashiro in New York."

"Oh, my God," Heath answered. "Aki, damn. How long has it been?"

"About five years?"

"You mean I've been stuck in this ice box for five years of my mid-thirties? Christ. What has become of my life?"

Aki laughed hard and turned to Reuben. "Heath used to work in this office."

Reuben could have gathered that but appreciated the heads up.

"How's everybody?" Heath asked. "How's Mike?"

Aki's mood changed. "He's good. He just got back from Cairo. We're on a bit of a break right now."

"Sorry to hear that." Heath didn't sound sorry at all. "Tell everyone I miss them."

"I will," she chirped. "Hey, listen, can you run a background check for me?"

"Absolutely."

"I need to find out about a marijuana dispensary. I've got a serial number here."

"OK." The sound went muffled, and Heath typed for a moment. "Go ahead with that serial number."

Aki read it off, then waited.

"Yeah," Heath finally said. "That's registered to CM—Cannabis of Montreal. The contact there we have is Yuri Brenton. He's a big player out here. He owns Brenton Shipping, a multi-million dollar enterprise. So whatever you're up to, and I know you're onto something, be careful. These guys don't play."

"Oh, you know I won't, Heath," she teased.

He laughed. "Yet somehow you manage to survive. Tell me, what are you up to these days?"

"Oh, keeping it fresh," she evaded, with an eye roll at Reuben. "Heath, I'm going to have to let you go. We're pretty busy down here."

"All right, well, you know I always like to hear from the old New York people. Look me up, you know."

"Will do, Heath," she said. "Bye."

"Bye."

She ended the call and made a face. "Poor guy, he's lonely."

"What's his deal?" Reuben asked.

Aki leaned back and toyed with her pen. "He was an agent here for a long time, a good one, too. But he got out of his depth and got double-crossed by a contact. He was tracking a big player in a drug trafficking ring. He had a contact that was giving him great information, and so he went out there, alone, and thought the contact had his back. As it turned out, the contact was relaying everything back to the drug lords. When Heath got out there, it was a trap. They kidnapped him, tortured him for information, and held him hostage for a week".

"That's terrible!" Reuben exclaimed.

Aki nodded. "Sven sent a team out to get him, and they were able to rescue him. But the whole operation was trashed beyond repair, and they had managed to crack him. Invaluable knowledge about what the agency knew got into the wrong hands. Probably single-handedly changed the drug war forever. Once they got him back to New York, he wasn't the same. Sven arranged for him to work undercover as a Canadian Mountie. He feeds us information from the inside when we need it. But it's low profile, not risky."

Reuben shook his head in sympathy. "Damn. That's sad."

Aki nodded. "Yeah. I can tell he's lonely. He was kind of a larger-than-life party guy, too."

Reuben couldn't imagine being sent to the ass-end of nowhere for the remainder of his career. "Man, is that what happens to disgraced field agents?"

"Sometimes," she answered softly. "All right, we've got to find this Yuri Brenton with Brenton Shipping."

"Reuben." Sven approached them. "Great work on the Schaeffer case. The doctored CCTV footage, huh? Where do you think that came from?"

"We think it might be Pout," Reuben answered.

Sven scoffed and gave a long whistle. "Well, if we've got to take him down, we've got to take him down. I've worked on more than one presidential impeachment, so I can handle taking down Pout if we have to. But we've got to have our ducks in a row." Sven winked and then went back to his office.

Reuben's mouth dropped, and Aki nodded with approval.

"Keep this up, you'll get promoted." She smiled and playfully punched his arm.

"Let's not go that far." He laughed. "I'm going to write up what we've done today."

"Yes." She nodded. "The interview with Julian, make sure to upload those photos, and the Canadian dispensary. I'll look into Brenton."

Reuben smiled, glad to have her on his side. "Sounds good."

He went back to his desk and started the write-up. In vivid detail, he entered all the information he had. But all he could think about was Aki. How she had looked at him and how her teasing touch had sent a shiver down his spine. If he could just save the world and not have to die again, he could hold on to all of this forever.

Aki reappeared at his desk. "OK. Here's what we know about Yuri Brenton, and Brenton Shipping. He's a 'naturalist' healer type."

Reuben grimaced. "Oh God, not one of those."

"Yeah, he's all into natural growth and chakras. He lives off the grid, and he's got generators running off the Hudson River. He is firmly convinced that the apocalypse is upon us."

"Which apocalypse?" Reuben smirked. "Hindu, Christ, Muslim, Buddhist—assuming they have one."

"All of them." Aki registered no humor. "This guy is a real nut job. We're going to have to be careful getting in with him. These kind of guys, they've got nothing to lose."

Reuben knew the type. "Anything else we need to know?"

"Yeah." She looked down at her notes. "Brenton Shipping's major investor is BTI."

Reuben and Aki locked eyes for a moment, and then his phone went off.

"Let me..." He gestured toward his pocket as he pulled his phone out.

It was Martha.

"Knock yourself out." Aki smiled. "There's plenty to do here."

He answered the phone as Aki stepped away from his desk and walked back to hers. "Hey, Martha."

"Hi. So I know you're busy, but we're working this Pout angle."

"Who's 'we?'" he asked.

"Buzz," she said.

"Hi, Reuben," Buzz chimed in from the background. "We miss you."

That was Buzz's drunk voice. Martha must be in hell dealing with him alone.

"Shut up." Then Martha's voice got louder as she spoke into the phone. "I just wanted to fill you in on our progress."

"We!" Buzz yelled.

"Fine, *we* wanted to update you. Seems Pout got a speeding ticket at the Canadian border in Detroit. Three hours before the shootout on Wednesday, the eighth."

Reuben smiled. "So he was definitely there."

"Yep, his business empire is a maze of different groups. It's hard to pin it all down."

"I know," he said. "It's all companies within companies."

"Exactly," Martha agreed. "But he owns the maple syrup company, basically."

"What's the maple syrup company called?"

"White Mountain Foods," she said. "What have you got?"

"Not a lot," he lied. He wanted to get back to Aki before going down the rabbit hole with everything he'd found. "Right now, I've got that he owns a Canadian pot dispensary and he picked up some from a small-time dealer outside Mr. Sudds."

"He was at Mr. Sudds, then?"

"Yeah, he was definitely there three days ago at 3:14pm. But the CCTV footage has been doctored, so you can't tell. You have to check the cameras from Hurley's Chicken next door."

"Hurley's Chicken, huh? Maybe I can get a search warrant."

Reuben was glad he was able to give her that much, at least. "That would be awesome." Right now, most of what he had was from hacking in and manipulating contacts. If they could get some legally seized evidence, it would sure make things easier in court.

"Buzz and I are going to work on hacking into the security cameras so we can uncover anything else," she said.

"Great." He decided to give her a tip on Schaeffer. Not too much. "The small-time dealer was an Iowa kid named Julian Schaeffer. He met him at Mr. Sudds and delivered Canadian pot that's produced at a Pout-conglomerate shipping company called Brenton Shipping."

Pout had done a good job of setting up Julian as being involved in the experimental weapon heist. The radioactive materials and microwaves in that dumpster had probably been planted by one of Alister's men. Julian was just a pot dealer.

"Great." Martha's voice was muffled as if she were taking notes. "We'll rendezvous later."

"Yeah, let's have drinks tonight," Buzz yelled. "My place."

"You don't need any more drinks, Buzz," Reuben told him. "Go sleep it off."

Buzz laughed, and they ended the call. Alister was definitely at the Detroit-Windsor border, huh? He pulled up the Detroit-Windsor police department, and within a couple of minutes, had a copy of the speeding ticket.

This guy's definitely dirty, he typed to Aki. He uploaded the ticket to the case file and linked it to Aki, with Martha's notes about the time stamp.

We're closing in on him, she replied instantly. **Let's go out there tonight, see what we can find out.**

You mean, a stakeout? he typed back.

She sent him a winky face. He reread the message thread several times. There were definitely worse ways he could think of to pass the night.

CHAPTER THIRTY-THREE

Reuben—Friday, February 10, 5:09 p.m.

Reuben sat with Aki in her darkened Porsche outside of Alister Pout's Upper East Side mansion. They had watched him go in, and it seemed like he might be in for the night.

He stared up at the lighted window. "I wonder what he does up there."

She smirked. "I can think of a lot of things."

"He has a reputation, I'll give him that," Reuben conceded. "I don't understand what women see in him."

"The bad-boy image is complex." She sighed. "It's like, you know he's all wrong, but it's exhilarating and fun and wild and free."

Reuben let the comment hang in the air for a while. "Is that how you felt about Mike?"

"At one point," she whispered. "But, I don't think he ever understood me."

"Why is that?" he asked.

"I always got the impression that he looked right past me," she said. "He saw what he wanted to see, and that was enough for him. He didn't look any further. You know he made me feel so insecure that I got work done?"

Reuben couldn't believe it. "Work? You mean, plastic surgery?"

She winked.

"Why would you… Look at you; you're perfect." His words were genuine. "Why would you ever want to change?"

Aki shrugged. "He always made me feel like I had to conform to his expectations."

Reuben hated Mike with a passion. "Why would you be with a guy like that?"

"It's complicated," she said. "Because when you do meet those expectations, he can make you feel like the queen of the world."

"You did not have work done. You're lying," he teased.

"No, no." She laughed. "I had a nose job." She fingered her nose. "It used to be flatter. I had it raised. Plus, I had padding added to my butt."

He raised an eyebrow and peered at the seat, and she laughed. "Don't look!"

He shook his head and pursed his lips. "I'm going to have to inspect this so-called padding."

She laughed harder. "It's bad. It's like these silicone bags inserted into my ass cheeks."

"What the?"

"Yeah, it's like having a gel pad inside your body. They squish around; they move when they're pressed."

Reuben thought his eyes would burst out of their sockets. "Your butt squishes?"

She nodded. "Yeah."

"Oh, I'm definitely going to have to see this in action," he told her. "You can't leave me hanging on that one."

She chuckled. "I shouldn't have told you."

Reuben failed to hide his joy. "Oh no, you *definitely* should have. That is information I couldn't live without. One simply hasn't lived until they find out about shapeshifting silicone butt pads."

She laughed so hard she laid her head on the steering wheel. She sat back up, and her face was still red in the dark, low lamplight. Their eyes met. His heart quickened, and Reuben felt a lump rising in his throat. Was he really in this moment? Did he really have a chance with this woman? Or was he completely delusional? There was nothing more in this world he wanted than to kiss those lips. And it seemed like, there in the darkness, that's what she wanted.

But that wasn't true, he decided. There was one thing he wanted more than to kiss her. He wanted to not ruin what he had with her. Maybe he could ask her. That would be a chivalrous move, right? He took a deep breath and had just begun to form the words when his phone went off.

Aki's tone was casual, friendly. "Who could be calling this late?"

The moment was broken.

He grabbed his phone and sighed. "Of course, it's Martha. She's a friend of mine," he told Aki before answering the call. "Yeah?"

"You're not going to believe this," Martha told him.

"What's up?" he asked.

"So, Buzz and I hacked into the Brenton Shipping system."

"Whoa," Reuben said. "Hold on, let me put you on speaker with my partner who's working with me on this." He muffled the phone and turned to Aki. "Martha is NYPD. They're working the Pout angle while we're chasing Schaeffer."

Aki lifted a perfect eyebrow. "NYPD, huh? I guess we could use their help."

He shrugged. "We already have. All right." He clicked the phone on speaker. "Go ahead. You're on with Aki.."

"Hi, Martha," Aki said cordially.

"Is this *the* Aki?" Martha recalled all of Reuben's interactions with the special agent that she'd seen on Buzz's timeline calendar screen. Realizing she was probably embarrassing Reuben, she quickly pivoted. "So, we got into Brenton Shipping's system, and guess what? They're shipping sand."

Reuben was perplexed. "Sand? What does that mean?"

Buzz entered the conversation at this point. He seemed to be sobering up. "I did some satellite testing, and I'm detecting scant amounts of radiation as well as very high-frequency microwaves from the Brenton Shipping headquarters. They need the sand for weapons testing."

"Got it," Reuben said. "So we think they've got an experimental microwave bomb out there, is that what you're saying?"

"Yes." Buzz paused. "Looks like."

Reuben watched Aki. Her eyes blinked fast and hard. She didn't know they knew about Interpol's missing bomb, and he hoped they didn't give it away.

"It's outside of Montreal on the Hudson River," Martha said. "I'm texting you the coordinates, but we don't have an exact address."

The text popped up on his phone, and Aki read it. He immediately forwarded it to her phone. "But we don't know enough."

"And there's not enough time," Buzz said. "We've got to get more time. We need to know more."

Reuben scratched his head, seeing where this was heading. "How?"

"We need to go back a few days," Buzz said. "Which means…"

"Yeah, yeah." Reuben sighed. "I know what that means."

Reuben ended the call, and he turned to Aki.

"Who was that man?" she asked.

Reuben didn't even know where to begin explaining Buzz. "A friend. Look, I've got to go."

Aki's eyes widened. "What? We're in the middle of a stakeout."

"Yeah, about that…" He grabbed the phone out of her hand and tossed it on the floorboard.

"What the hell, Reuben?"

Then he turned to her, and in one quick motion, kissed her.

Hard.

They both panted in the darkness of the car, and she grabbed him and pulled him toward her and kissed him again. Before they knew it, they were at each other like teenagers.

Things were about to get more serious, and that was when Reuben pulled away.

"Aki, we've got to stop," he whispered as he let her go. He realized that this moment would only satisfy his fantasy of her. He wanted more, and being with her now, only for her to forget, would be harder than never being with her at all.

He knew Aki now. She wasn't just the hot agent who worked in the same building as him. She wasn't just a simple fantasy anymore.

She was much more. She was real. Reuben wanted the real her more than anything.

"Why?" Aki sounded hurt. "We're both consenting adults, and you're not an asshole like most guys."

He almost caved. "I know. But after this is done, you won't remember any of this."

"Wait? What? Why would you say that?"

"It's just the story of my life right now," Reuben said as he got out of the car, walking away before she could say anything else.

CHAPTER THIRTY-FOUR

Reuben—Friday, February 10, 7:03 p.m.

Martha, Buzz, and Reuben all sat in the living room of Buzz's mansion. The trio of twenty-somethings lounged amid empty bottles of wine brewed from grapes grown long, long before they were born.

"What we need," Buzz said, "is to send Reuben back another three days."

"Three days?" Reuben exclaimed. "Why three days?"

"If the border attack is going to happen on the eighth..." Martha snapped her fingers excitedly. "That will give us a day to do some investigations and potentially stop the whole damn thing."

Reuben didn't hate the idea. "And stop me from having my blood boiled again."

"Everyone's blood," Martha corrected.

"True," Reuben conceded, "but I'm the only one who remembers it. You two are lucky."

Martha shook her head. "We're dead. The only reason we know anything is because of you."

"And my nanobot," Buzz said.

"And Buzz's nanobot." Martha shrugged.

Buzz stood. "I also estimate that the metal mesh used in the bomb's construction has already come into port. A specialized type of metal mesh is important for these kinds of bombs, trust me. Once I find the details of the port, we'll be able to go back a couple days and follow the shipment. If we can connect that to Pout, then we'd have some evidence against him but not enough."

Martha nodded. "Maybe I could get a warrant and have local PD stake out the shipment. If I can tie the shipment to Alister, then I can get a second warrant to follow him. We can put him at the scene with some hard evidence and not just a flimsy speeding ticket. It's not the best plan, but it's all we've got at the moment."

Reuben considered this. "I could also use that time to hack into RedBook's servers. Might be able to find some dirt there. If we're right, and I believe we are, then they'll be putting extra resources into New York's epicenter to record the fallout from the bomb. Doesn't get any more red-handed than that. Red-handed...or should I say, 'RedBooked?'"

Martha and Buzz groaned before the scrawny scientist said, "You don't have any kids to be making dad jokes. Save it until you spawn."

"Save it even then," Martha chimed in. "Unless you want to rear social rejects."

Now they all laughed.

Even Reuben chuckled. "We also need a way to shortcut getting up to speed if you have to die and warp back in time. I really want to avoid the whole 'kidnap Martha to convince her' routine again."

Reuben turned to Buzz.

"Ah yes. Well, I put a nanobot in Reuben's body that automatically gets synced to my computers when he warps back. All my notes and the timeline details are then updated on my computers."

"Yeah," Martha said. "But isn't there something else you can do to immediately let me and you know the situation? I'm no scientist, but can the nanobot in Reuben's bloodstream record video through his eyes? Maybe we could record a message to ourselves. Vital information only we'd know?"

Buzz nodded. "Yeah, that's easy enough. I like it. It would be very efficient. We can call it the 'Binnie routine.' We watch the video every time Reuben warps back. We just have to be sure that we say the kind of things that a deep fake couldn't know. You'll have to get intimate."

Martha nodded.

Buzz wasn't done. "And Reuben will know."

Martha nodded again, and with a playful jab against Buzz's shoulder, said, "As long as I can keep a few secrets from you, I'm good. So do we have a plan?"

Buzz nodded, but Reuben was hesitant.

Martha must have sensed this because she said, "What I would give to be you, Reuben. Be able to warp, save people, fix mistakes. Stop the bad guys."

Reuben pursed his lips. Why would anyone want to be him? *He* didn't want to be him. But he didn't say anything, he just looked at Buzz and with a heavy sigh, said, "OK, we've got a plan. Videos, dying. Repeat."

Martha shook her head. "No. Videos, some hand-to-hand training, or shooting. Then you die."

"I know how to fight," Reuben said.

Both Martha and Buzz looked at him for a long minute before bursting out in laughter.

"Seriously." Reuben put up his dukes and stood in a ready stance.

"Seriously?" Martha laughed. "All right. Let's do the videos, and then let's see exactly how good you are at fighting."

Reuben—Friday, February 10, 8:07 p.m.

They recorded the videos. Afterward, Buzz assured Martha that they would receive an automated email every time Reuben warped back. All they had to do was watch the video of themselves explaining Reuben's ability in their own words, followed by their personal recorded message. Following that would be a very brief first-person view of Reuben dying and then waking up at a prior time. Following that would be a link to Buzz's timeline calendar with any new things they needed to know.

Buzz's personal message was as expected. He basically repeated a long code that only he could understand.

As for Martha, she recorded a bunch of stuff but kept shaking her head. Nothing she was saying was definitive proof. Not until she thought of something she did that was out of the ordinary.

Out of the ordinary and embarrassing. Sometimes she talked to Petunia, the red toucan figurine on her keychain. Ran police cases by the plastic bird. Bounced ideas off it. It never responded, but the mental process had helped her crack several cases. Not that she'd ever told anyone.

Reuben desperately tried not to laugh.

"Oh, I'm *so* kicking your ass. Come on. Show me what you got." She walked up to him, and before he even understood what was happening, she had knocked him to the ground.

"Ow, my head." He rubbed the back of it. "I slipped."

"No, I knocked you over." Martha scoffed. "It was a basic move. You've got to know how to block and how to anticipate."

"Do you know how to use a gun?" Buzz pulled a handgun out of a drawer in an end table.

Reuben's eyes grew wide. "What are you doing with that?"

"Don't get your panties in a twist," Buzz teased.

"Oh, right, said by a damn Hugh Hefner-wannabe in silk pajamas."

"All right, all right." Martha stood between them. "Enough name-calling. Reuben, you need training. Training for combat, training for shooting. You need to know how to take these guys down alone if you have to. Tell me, what can you do?"

"Well, I'm pretty good at ballroom dancing." Reuben struck a dramatic pose worthy of *Dancing with the Stars*.

"Dancing?" Martha groaned.

"Hey, it's a demanding sport. Check out this Reverse Fleckerl combined with a Solo Spot Volta. I killed at regionals." Reuben spun around an invisible partner before doing another spin with his right arm dramatically shooting out behind him, his middle finger pointing inward.

Now it was Buzz's turn to groan. "So, what? We meet the terrorists, and you're going to challenge them to a dance-off? In ballroom dancing of all things. The sissiest of sissy dancing."

Reuben pouted. "Hey, I am a regional champion!"

"In dance!" Buzz laughed.

Martha put a hand on Reuben's shoulder. "He's right. You need training in skills that actually matter."

"How am I going to get that?" Reuben asked. "We're running out of time."

"What do you mean?" Buzz sipped his glass of wine. "You have all the time in the world."

"So, what are you suggesting?" Reuben said.

Buzz and Martha smirked at each other. Reuben wasn't so sure he liked this new alliance between the two of them.

Buzz stood. "Let's take this into the studio."

"What studio?" Reuben asked, following him.

Together, they ascended the marble staircase. Reuben had only been up here briefly. Most of the time he had spent in Buzz's living room or labs.

But now they approached a bedroom that had been converted into… "A yoga studio?"

"Here," Buzz gestured at the room, "you will learn."

"OK." Martha clapped her hands and took charge. "I'm going to throw a punch at you, and you're going to block it."

Reuben watched carefully, but Martha's move was so sudden that he couldn't think fast enough to block her. The next thing he knew, her fist was in his gut.

"Ahh!" he cried out.

Martha groaned. "This is going to take a while."

Buzz nodded. "Yes. I say we come up with a plan. We train him, then we kill him. Then he comes back, we train him some more. And so on, and so on, until we get back to three days ago."

"That sounds good." Martha stood in a fighting stance. This time Reuben saw when her fist moved, and he instinctively pushed her hand away.

Both Martha and Buzz cheered. "This might work," Buzz said.

"OK," Martha said. "Let's try it again."

Reuben tried to block it but failed. She hit him again and again.

"Hold on," Reuben said, getting to his feet. "I have a plan."

"Show me," Martha said, stepping forward.

As she swung, Reuben shouted, "Henry Cavill. That's what you lit all those candles for?"

The words threw her off, messing up her timing just enough for Reuben to step to the left and shove her to the floor.

Martha looked up. Reuben had won that round. "No fair," she said. "You promised you wouldn't tell Buzz what I shared on the video."

"All's fair in love and war," Buzz said with a leering smile. "I think I know what my next sexbot will look like. Maybe I'll build Henry for your birthday."

Martha stood with a huff and said, "Again." This time she faked him out with a punch, and then when she finally threw one, he blocked it. But, he blocked it with enough force that he could push harder. The next thing he knew, she was on the ground again.

"I like this." Martha smiled from the floor mat. "You're learning."

"Thanks," he said, "I'm getting there."

Martha smiled. "That you are."

She spent the next hour sparring with him. Block. Punch. Knock down. Block.

Reuben dug deep into his psyche to pull out his inner aggressor. He had never been encouraged to let that part of himself out. But suddenly, there it was. He knocked Martha to the ground over and over.

"I think he's ready," she told Buzz eventually. "At least, as ready as he can be after one training session. A few more of these, though, and he'll be proficient."

"Ahh, thanks, I think," Reuben said.

"So three days," Buzz said. "As far back as you can go."

Reuben grimaced. "We're probably going to have to do this a few times. I can't seem to figure out how to control how far back I go."

Buzz shrugged. "I've been thinking about that. I think there must be a way to influence how far back you go each time. It is said that some yogi masters can control their minds so well that they can perfectly recreate a moment from their past in their own minds to the point where they remember every smell, texture, thought. If you can, for lack of a better word, meditate on what you were doing three days ago, there is a good chance you'll warp into yourself then."

Reuben thought about this. "How would we know?"

Buzz frowned. "How would we know what?"

"How would we know that these yogis are able to perfectly replicate a moment in their mind? It is in their mind, isn't it? We kind of have to take their word on it."

Buzz pinched the bridge of his nose. "That's not the point."

"Isn't it?" Reuben said. "I mean, your whole theory on how I can control my warps is based on something completely unsubstantiated. I think it is very relevant."

Buzz sighed. "Look, what were you doing three days ago?"

Reuben thought about it. "Um, it was a pretty boring Tuesday. I was at work, updating some surveillance software the agency uses."

Buzz shook his head. "No, get specific. What are you thinking about, feeling, doing, sensing? Focus on a specific moment three days ago. A single thought, a single action."

Reuben threw his mind back three days. He thought about his day, everything he had done, and nothing stood out. It was a mundane day…except for when he saw Aki at the end of the work day. She looked so tired from whatever badass shit she was up to. She was going over a report by the window, deep in thought, when all of a sudden, her face lit up.

She had figured something out. What? Reuben had no idea. But she had seen something…a clue, a lead, *something*… and her whole face had just lit up with pride.

Reuben remembered wishing he had the courage to ask her what she was so proud of. "Yeah, I got something."

Buzz smiled. "Good."

Reuben turned and saw Buzz had a handgun.

"No!" Reuben screamed as the bullet pierced his flesh.

CHAPTER THIRTY-FIVE

Reuben—Friday, February 10, 8:09 p.m.

Reuben came back to the yoga studio. So much for focusing on Aki's smile.

He stood in front of Martha as she turned to Buzz.

"This is going to be harder than I thought," she told him.

With that, Reuben reached out and knocked her over.

Buzz whistled, but his victory wasn't for long.

Martha grabbed his leg and dragged him to the ground. They wrestled on the floor for a moment, and then she pinned his arms down. "Give?"

"Give," Reuben managed through the pain.

She got off him, and they both panted.

Then Buzz and Martha received their emails from themselves since Reuben had warped back. The emails also contained a link to Buzz's timeline calendar and anything they had previously learned.

"Woohoo!" Buzz cheered. This verified that the "Binnie process" worked. No more awkward explanations for Reuben to have to make to them regardless of if he warped back before they knew about his ability or even if he warped back just twenty minutes.

Buzz grinned. "A pretty good process we developed."

Martha turned to Reuben then. "Yep, now let's try that again." This time, she roundhouse-kicked him square in the face.

"*Ow!*" he cried out.

"Stop being a little bitch." She reached up and high-kicked him again, and this time he grabbed her foot and pushed down. But again she grabbed his leg and dragged him down with her. They wrestled on the floor, and she pinned him again. "Give?"

"Never." He raised his legs and tossed her off him. Then he rolled on top of her and pinned her. "Give?"

She panted and caught his eye, and he noticed a look he'd never seen before. He remembered the thing she had said about him being a handsome man. He suddenly felt very uncomfortable. He'd been so caught up with Aki, he didn't really notice Martha.

At least not like that.

It was at that moment her fist pounded into his exposed gut.

"Never show weakness," she ordered.

"Right." He rolled onto the floor.

"Again." She stood in her fighting stance. Between Buzz shooting him and Martha kicking his ass, he was starting to wonder what kind of friends he had.

"Come on," she yelled.

He threw a punch, and she blocked it. Another, and she blocked it again. Then he tried a trick he had only seen in movies. He threw a punch, but when she blocked it, he immediately kicked her feet out from under her. She fell to the ground.

"Good job, Peet." She smiled as he helped her up. "But you weren't ready for this."

"What?" he asked as she delivered a knee to his groin. He fell back in miserable pain but then saw her in her fighting stance. He suddenly threw a punch that she didn't expect, and he knocked her off her feet again.

"I think he might be ready," she told Buzz.

"Ready to die?" Reuben replied wryly.

"What?" Buzz furrowed his brow. "Never. Let's all go for a swim. I think we could use some cooling off."

"Definitely," Martha panted.

The trio headed down to the pool, and the blue saltwater beckoned to Reuben. He couldn't take it. He just jumped in headlong, the cool water calming him. Later, when he thought about it, he remembered Buzz throwing the hair dryer into the pool.

But that was only much later. At the moment, all he heard was Buzz saying, "Focus on that event three days ago," just before his body became overwhelmed with the jolt of electricity that coursed through him.

Reuben—Friday, February 10, 8:03 p.m.

Reuben came back to Buzz's yoga studio. Again. Part of him wondered why he didn't go back three days, but another part of him was beginning to realize that he needed his training. He needed to get better, smarter, faster, and more capable if he was going to stop the bomb from happening again.

"This is going to be harder than I thought," Martha panted to Buzz.

Then the "Binnie process" unfolded, and Buzz and Martha received their emails with the videos and the timeline updates.

Suddenly Reuben lashed out and threw a punch at Martha and then sideswiped her with a kick. She dragged him to the ground, and he quickly pinned her wrists down. "Give?"

She panted and he caught that same look, but he ignored it this time. He couldn't let emotion ruin what he was trying to do. Alister and whoever Alister was working with could ruin him in one emotional moment.

"Give," she said.

He let go, but then she delivered a two-fisted punch to his gut.

"Never trust the enemy," she commanded as he fell backward.

Reuben and Martha wrestled more in the yoga studio. More punches, blocks, and kicks. Every time Reuben thought he'd conquered one of her moves, she'd throw out another one. Expect the unexpected. Never trust the enemy. Always have a backup plan. Reuben's face swelled with pain, but he noticed that Martha wasn't exactly bursting with energy, either. She had a bloody nose and bruises everywhere.

"You're getting better," she commented wryly.

"I'm kicking your ass is what I'm doing."

"Yeah?" She panted. "Is that right, Peet?" With that, she delivered a hard left hook to his face. Damn, he should have seen that coming.

In all of the commotion, neither of them noticed that Buzz was missing.

"I think we all need to take a breather." Buzz suddenly burst into the studio like a ray of sunshine and passed out drinks.

Reuben was exhausted and thirsty and took the drink. He downed it all in one gulp, and it burned his lungs. He coughed and choked and instinctively reached out to his friends for help. But no help was offered.

He curled on the floor, gasping for air, and swore he saw Buzz taking notes. Oh, no. What the hell was he doing? With what little strength he had, he grabbed Buzz by the leg as the light slowly faded from view. Buzz yelped at Reuben's weak attack as the scrawny scientist tried to pull away.

The last thing Reuben heard was Buzz's muffled voice saying, *Concentrate on three days ago.*

Reuben—Friday, February 10, 8:03 p.m.

Reuben arrived back in Buzz's yoga studio.

"This is going to be harder than I expected," Martha said.

Then Reuben effectively kicked Martha's ass up and down.

"I think he's ready," Martha panted.

Then Buzz and Martha received their emails.

Buzz smirked. "All right, we're ready for the next phase."

"Yeah." Martha rose from the floor and applied a cold water bottle to her face. "The new phase."

"Guns." Buzz's eyes twinkled.

Buzz drove the golf cart loaded with guns deep into the gardens. "Now," he said. "It's dark, but we're going to do this."

"All right." Reuben shivered as he looked at the guns. He remembered the last time Buzz had shot him, and had a sneaking suspicion that was where this was headed. Although,

Buzz seemed to kill him a different way every time. So what did he know?

Martha and Buzz grabbed rifles out of the golf cart, and Buzz tossed one to Reuben.

"You're going to learn to shoot." Buzz patted him on the arm, and Martha rushed ahead of him.

"See the bottle she just set down?" Buzz asked.

Reuben nodded.

"Now, that's Alister," Buzz said. "Kill him."

Reuben pointed the gun and pulled the trigger. He hit one of Buzz's cars ten yards away. Whoops. Well, he could honestly say Buzz was going to kill him for that.

And he did. With one nasty gunshot.

Reuben—Friday, February 10, 8:47 p.m.

Reuben came back to training in the yoga studio. He sparred with Martha and he saw that she was paying closer attention to his moves than she had in the beginning.

"I don't know, Buzz," she told him. "Do we even need to do this? He's pretty good already."

"Maybe we need more equipment from the lab," Buzz said as his and Martha's phones alerted them that they had a new email.

"Good idea." Martha slipped out of the room, and that's when Reuben noticed the little black box about the size of what he imagined a bomb might be.

"Ah, shit." Seeing that he was by himself, he stepped up to the box.

He opened it up. There was a soft click, and he saw that it was indeed a bomb. A bomb with four different-colored wires and a digital display ticking down from ten seconds.

It didn't matter, he figured, if he tripped the wrong wire. He was going to die today anyway. He took a guess and pulled the green wire. The ticking bomb stopped. Reuben stood and cheered for joy.

But it was short-lived. Buzz tore through him with a collector's edition colonial musket.

Damn, he never could stay a step ahead of this guy.

CHAPTER THIRTY-SIX

Reuben—Tuesday, February 7, 5:07 p.m.

This time when he died, Reuben didn't try to focus too hard on Aki's smile. The memory of her standing by the window at work was still on his mind, but the unexpectedness of his death had caught him off-guard.

Death by musket? Really, Buzz?

The image of Aki's smile had been at the back of his mind, though, and he'd reflected on it as his consciousness faded. Her smile calmed him. Calm was good. Especially when your best friend kept coming up with maniacal new ways of murdering you, all in the name of science.

Calm was what he felt when he came to, standing upright under fluorescent lights in a hallway with windows.

So he was back at work. No biggie. But how far back had he traveled? He'd had no control over it in the past. So had he gone back one day? Two days? Three?

Oh shit!

He turned his head, and standing five feet away was Aki, looking as stunning as he'd ever seen her. She was dressed in dark skinny jeans and a tight leather jacket, a mysterious, sexy smile on her lips as she stared out at the city beyond.

Excitement throbbed through his system. This was the moment he'd been trying to warp back to throughout his training at Buzz's. He'd done it! He'd actually controlled how far he'd gone back this time.

"Holy shit," he muttered.

That was when Aki turned to face him.

"Excuse me?" The sexy smile was still on her face. She stood there, mysterious and glorious.

Reuben thought, *If only I can figure out the perfect thing to say...*

But was there any such thing as the perfect thing to say? Maybe. By Reuben's recollection, this would be the first time he'd ever spoken to Aki in the timeline. In her mind, Reuben didn't even exist. He was just another nameless tech guy in a cubicle where she worked.

It was time to make a favorable impression on her.

He recalled the time he'd talked to her before dying from the microwave bomb in the future on Valentine's Day. That interaction had gone amazingly well as he'd fixed her computer. The next time he'd time-warped and tried to talk to her... Not so much. She'd thought he was a stalker. How could he replicate the first success he'd had?

Before him, Aki cleared her throat, her smile starting to fade.

As he saw it, he had two options that might work: act like an asshole like Mike Fury. Or be himself.

What did he have to lose?

Reuben started beatboxing to the sound of a Depeche Mode song that resembled one of Je Ne Sais Pas' songs. Bouncing lightly on his heel, he started to...

He started to dance.

Only just a bit, like the entrance dance a wedding party gives when they arrive at the reception. As he came out of a slow spin, he met her eyes.

"Sorry. I uh…" Reuben scratched his temple. "I just figured out something really important. That was uh, my victory dance."

Aki stood staring at him.

Shit. I messed it up.

He was about to turn and walk away when she caught his sleeve.

"That was impressive," she said, her smile returning.

Reuben stood straight and checked his watch like a cool guy might. "You think so?"

Aki nodded. "Definitely. I've seen you around, but I'm ashamed to say I don't know your name."

He smiled and extended his hand. "Peet. Reuben Peet."

She took it and laughed. "James Bond, right?"

Reuben thrust his hands into his pockets and shifted his eyes off to the side. "Guilty."

She laughed again. "I'm also celebrating something—a smuggling ring I recently took down. It was small time, but you know, we do good work here. Important work."

If she only knew.

Reuben nodded, trying not to have a heart attack. Things were going so well, he might as well try to keep the conversation going. "Hey, I'm just a lowly tech guy, but I bet you've got some crazy stories."

Her eyelashes fluttered. "Too bad they're all classified. Look, it was nice meeting you but I've really got to get back to work. Something I'm working on for Sven."

Reuben reminded himself that Aki still had a boyfriend at

this point in the timeline. He smiled at her, and she smiled back as she walked off.

Needless to say, he was on cloud nine. He now knew how to control how far back he warped: keep calm and warp on, and he also got the girl. Well, kinda.

This was a huge double-win.

Shortly after Aki had walked away, Reuben got a text from Buzz. "Got the email with the video and timeline notes. Dude. You can warp back in time!"

A few minutes later, Martha called Reuben. "This is all so fucking crazy," she said. "But, I believe it."

CHAPTER THIRTY-SEVEN

Reuben—Wednesday, February 8, 7:42 p.m.

Reuben and Martha had gone straight to Buzz's mansion after that. Martha and Buzz had hit it off well. After they had all had a stiff drink, Buzz showed them both to his server room so they could view the timeline calendar and all their notes on the big screen.

Then the training had recommenced.

It was a shit load of training.

As Reuben kept training, there would come a point where he'd get too tired to continue and Buzz would kill him to reset the training. Buzz and Martha would get their automated email afterward, but they no longer made a big deal about it. It was just part of the process.

Buzz watched as Reuben and Martha sparred in the mansion's garden. It was evening now, and the fight between him and Martha was fairer than it had ever been.

He was actually good now.

He should be after all the warps he'd done. Of course, they

didn't just train for combat between all those warps. They'd also done a ton of research, gathering all the evidence they would need to legally bring down Pout and connect him to the microwave bomb.

During their research, the Trillium Group and Better Tomorrows Incorporated kept coming up, and they learned that Pout had recently sold RedBook tech to several foreign countries, among them India, Pakistan, and North Korea. While the activity raised flags, it didn't concern the microwave bomb attack in New York. After Pout was taken down, RedBook would probably follow suit, rendering the tech useless.

On a hunch, Martha had Buzz try to track down the guy who'd met Pout at Mr. Sudds, the one wearing the hoodie with the stripes on the shoulders who'd handed Pout a burner phone. They spent an hour searching for the mysterious guy, but they just couldn't find him. Oh, well, chances were it was just a henchman who'd be mopped up when Pout was behind bars.

But they still hadn't found enough to nail Pout.

Buzz hit the motherlode when going through emails sent to an encrypted email address that Pout used. There, Buzz found diagrams of the completed microwave bomb along with a list of all the parts—a type of specialized wire mesh included—and their expected arrival times by van to Mr. Sudds. The emails clearly stated that the bomb was to be assembled and modified there and then transported to an as yet to be named location for detonation in the city on February fourteenth.

"Holy shit, Pout's done for," Martha said. "How could he be OK with killing so many people like that?"

Reuben gritted his teeth. "This is great stuff, Buzz, and it'll definitely finish Pout. But how are we going to get all this evidence to the proper authorities?" He checked his watch. "We need to stop that bomb before it even crosses the Canadian-Detroit border. But it's the eighth, and it's already happened. When I warp back so that we can stop it, our evidence is going to be gone."

"Not to worry," Buzz bragged. "I'm a genius and have saved all the evidence in a zipped file to the nanobot in your system. Even after you warp back in time, the files will still be inside you. All we've got to do is transfer them to your smartwatch and phone and then forward them to the proper authorities and federal agencies."

Reuben rubbed his chin. "Damn, that's good thinking. I've never been evidence before."

The three of them laughed.

But their biggest mission wasn't the training or the researching, but actually stopping the semis. They couldn't entrust this to anyone else. They'd finish this themselves.

They decided to have Reuben warp back again to allow the events at the border to unfold one more time. The shootout went down while the three of them watched from satellite imagery, listening in on one of Marshall's old police scanners. They got a ton of useful details: truck timing, which officers would be on duty, good locations to stake out the run. All in all, they were close to ready to go in and stop the semis from ever crossing the Detroit-Canada border. The microwave bomb would never enter New York, and no police officers would be wounded or killed.

Almost ready.

Reuben would have to die again to warp back to the time of the border crossing.

Buzz lay on a lawn chair and drank cocktails while he sunned himself.

"You know it's February," Reuben reminded him as he blocked another one of Martha's punches.

"The tilt of the Earth's axis in relation to the sun has no bearing on our ability to absorb the sun's nourishment," Buzz said. "Besides, it feels good."

"Feeling is relative." He blocked a kick from Martha.

"Shut up." Buzz sipped his drink.

Reuben rolled his eyes. "You know, you ought to get up here and try a few rounds."

"I'm a man of science," Buzz said. "Brute strength is of no interest to me."

"So, how do we stop Alister?" Martha delivered a roundhouse kick, which Reuben instinctively blocked.

"I think," Reuben threw a punch, and she blocked him, "that I need to be at the scene of the shootout. I can block the shipment from crossing over, at least I think I can."

Buzz pondered as the two danced around the garden in an even match. "You think he can pull it off?" he asked Martha.

"I think he's ready for at least basic combat," Martha told Buzz.

"You think you're ready?" Buzz lifted his sunglasses over his head and a sly smile played over his face. "Gun?"

Reuben was quiet for a few minutes as he blocked and punched at Martha.

"Maybe," he finally said, "but I think I need to see my dad first." He checked his watch. By the time he got home, his dad might already be asleep. He was exhausted after all that training and dying.

He decided to crash at Buzz's place and then see Marshall in the morning.

Reuben made the long drive home and arrived at the apartment complex before the sun even rose. It felt like it had been so long since he had been here.

Downstairs, Midge watered her plants and shot Reuben a quick smile. This meant that Marshall hadn't really behaved, but he hadn't really misbehaved, either. It was good information for him to know before he entered the fray.

He entered the room, where Marshall sat staring out the window.

"Where the hell you been?" Marshall asked.

Reuben ignored the question. "How you doing this morning, Dad?"

Marshall scoffed. "What do you care?"

"I care a lot." Reuben started toward the kitchen. "Have you eaten and taken your meds?"

"Aw, shut up," Marshall bellowed. "Who died and made you my doctor, huh? I never asked you for any of this shit, doting over me like I'm a fragile little China doll."

"You know, Dad." Reuben turned and faced his father. "Once upon a time, you were somebody."

Marshall scowled. "Once upon a time, huh? Is that what you think of me? I'm a goddamned fairy tale character, huh? Bippity-boppity-goddamned-boo."

Reuben rolled his eyes and took out Marshall's pill box. He started to make eggs. "Yeah, once upon a time, you were a hero," Reuben continued. "Now you're just... Look at you. You're an asshole, and no one can stand to be around you. You know that?"

"Oh, aren't you just a ray of sweetness in the morning?"

Marshall shot back. "Good morning to you too. Didn't I teach you some manners, son?"

"You don't get it, do you?" Reuben continued. "You just don't get it. *I am the only one on this planet who cares about you.*"

He let the shouting hang in the air for a moment, and he stood panting before his father. Marshall just stood there, eyes narrowed, but didn't say a word.

"There are six billion people on this planet," Reuben continued. "Six billion people on this damn rock, spread out over seven continents and mountains and lakes and rivers. It's full of so many people, there's not enough food to go around. Out of all of those people, I am the only one that gives a shit about you."

"Oh, get off yourself," Marshall said. "You think you're a saint? You're no saint. Anything you do for me, you don't do it for me; you do it for yourself. So you can pat yourself on the back at night and tell yourself you're a martyr for your crazy old man. That you're a good son. That way, you don't have to face your pitiful life and that you're still sleeping alone in a twin bed and you're almost thirty years old."

"You know," Reuben's eyes burned hot with anger as he used a tone he had never dared to take with his father.

Maybe it was the lack of sleep; maybe it was facing death a thousand times. Maybe it was learning to fight with Martha. But whatever it was, he suddenly wasn't scared of anything his father had to dish out.

But when he looked in the old man's eyes, he saw the fear, and for just a second, he felt for the man.

"You know," Reuben's voice softened, "I remember when I was little. I remember feeling like my dad was the strongest, bravest man in the world and how I wanted to grow up and be just like him. I remember most of all being on that bus with Martha. That guy Thorne—"

Marshall cut in, "Don't bring up that bastard."

"Goddammit, for once, would you fucking listen to a word I'm saying?" Reuben retorted.

"Don't take that tone with me."

"I'm trying to tell you something," Reuben said.

"Then say it already, dammit." Marshall stood with his hands on his hips.

"I remember how it was when you got us off that bus," he said. "That was the day everything changed. Because that was the day Mom left, and you never wanted to talk about it. You never—"

"Of *course* I'm not going to talk about it," Marshall bellowed. "I'm a man, which is more than I can say for you."

"You know," Reuben told him, "I've changed a lot. I'm working on something. I can't explain it right now, but you're going to be proud of what I'm doing."

"I doubt it." Marshall shuffled back to his room.

Reuben watched Marshall's departing back and started to say something but realized there was no point. He wouldn't remember any of this. He was about to leave the house when Marshall whipped around to him.

"You know," his father stood in the hallway, gray hair frizzing from all directions, "maybe if you'd worry about your own life and stop worrying so goddamn much about mine, maybe you'll grow out of this, whatever the hell this is, stunted man-child, self-appointed nursemaid, and we'd be able to have a real conversation…like men."

"Whatever." Reuben turned toward the door, but the words just bubbled beneath the surface, and he couldn't stop them from flowing out. "I know you're not going to believe this, and it doesn't matter anyway because you won't remember it anyway—"

"Oh, fucking cheap shot, asshole," Marshall interrupted. "Wait until you're my age and you've lived through what I've lived through, then come tell me that—"

Reuben laughed mirthlessly and talked over him. "I have these....powers. I can go back in time. When I die, I go back in time. There's a bomb."

Marshall stood frozen but didn't respond.

"On Valentine's Day, it will go off," Reuben continued. "I've seen it and died by it several times. I'm going to stop the bomb, save the city, save you and Martha and all of us. And no one will know. Least of all you."

Turning to face his son, Reuben saw something he hadn't seen in a long time. His eyes gleamed with the sheen of a tear. "You're not losing it, are you, son?" he asked, his voice soft, almost inaudible.

"No, Dad, I'm telling you the truth."

Marshall put his hands over his ears, shaking his head.

Reuben tried anyway. "I didn't expect you to believe it, but I thought I'd tell you."

Marshall pursed his lips. "No, I don't believe it. I just didn't think you inherited the batshit crazy gene from your mother. Dying and coming back was her idea of pillow talk, and look where that got us all."

Reuben's mouth dropped. What the hell? But Marshall disappeared behind a closed door before Reuben could get a word out.

Whatever.

The "Just Like Your Mother" thing was Marshall's universal trump card. He played it any time Reuben wasn't off-put by their usual rounds and he needed just a little cherry to top it off.

Reuben surveyed the room one last time and then walked out the door.

Guess it was time to die.

CHAPTER THIRTY-EIGHT

Reuben—Thursday, February 9, 7:31 a.m.

After grabbing a snack at Taco Bell, Reuben made the now-familiar drive out to Buzz's mansion. He arrived at the circular drive and noticed Martha's small blue Sentra sitting outside. Great, the gang was all here and waiting for him.

He let himself into the mansion, not bothering to ring the bell. "Buzz? Martha? OK, I think we should do a bullet to the head this time. That seems to hurt the least."

He opened the door fully, and he noticed the rope pulley system too late. "What the..."

A chainsaw came down from the ceiling and cut off his head. The last thing Reuben saw was Martha and Buzz high-fiving each other.

Reuben—Wednesday, February 8, 7:33 p.m.

Reuben reinhabited his body to find himself sitting with Buzz and Martha on Buzz's couch. This had been after all their training and research and just after he'd told them he was going to visit Marshall in the morning.

Well, he'd already done that, but he hadn't gone back far enough. He hadn't died calmly, nor had he had a proper amount of time in mind that he wanted to go back to. He'd need to go back to earlier in the day if they were going to make it to the border before the semis crossed with the bomb. Clapping his hands together, he said, "OK, it's go time!"

Buzz and Martha stared at each other and then back at Reuben. Then they received their emails and nodded in understanding that Reuben had just warped.

Reuben cleared his throat. "We need to go back one more time, before the semis cross the border, to stop it in person. The three of us. Plus Aki. She's a badass agent with lots of experience in these sorts of missions."

Buzz sipped his wine and crossed his legs. "That's not such a bad idea."

Martha looked resolved. "I agree. Let's do it."

"So, how do I get to die this time?" Reuben shuffled his feet.

Buzz steepled his fingertips like a mad scientist might. "I've always been interested in the human body's defenses against hypothermia. It might be interesting to challenge the existing data for medical purposes."

Reuben scoffed. "Uh, calm down, Joseph Mengele. We're talking about quick deaths. This isn't Auschwitz."

Buzz set his drink down and stared deeply at Reuben as he thought. "But for science. Do you see the usefulness of being a human capable of infinite deaths? Can you imagine what we could discover?"

Reuben quipped back, "You've got plenty of data already." He pointed to his wrist.

"I could always get more," Buzz said.

Martha stood and grabbed her purse. "You're scaring me."

"I'm scaring myself." Reuben laughed. "Look, I'm tired of dying. Luckily, I think I've gained control of my time warps now. I just have to keep calm and warp. At least I only need to die once to go back to when we want to go."

Martha considered his words. "Fuck. All that dying you had to do to get to this point." She went in and gave him a hug. "An ordinary guy might consider just forgetting the bomb and leaving the city."

Reuben shook his head. "You know I can't do that."

She smiled. "I know. You're a good man. I hope you know that even though no one remembers what you're doing, I do…*we* do. And I, for one, know that you're a hero."

"We believe you're a hero," Buzz leaned back and folded his hands behind his head. "But, let's take things a little slower. Reuben, why don't you calmly tell us what you're thinking? What's the plan?"

Martha sat back down, and Reuben slowly eased himself back into the couch.

"OK. The plan is I go back in time so we can stop the maple syrup shipment at the Detroit-Canada border. The microwave bomb is in one of those semis. We have the details we need, so let's get to it."

Martha blinked. "Are you sure you're good training-wise?"

Reuben nodded. Well, he had to be sure, and it would be good to prove it to his friends. "Martha, stand up."

Martha slowly stood as Reuben balled his fists. "Try to punch me."

"OK, but you do realize I've been trained for this kind of thing, right?"

"Yeah, so have I. I'm waiting, Princess." He knew the name would irritate her, and it did.

She narrowed her eyes and threw a right hook. With one swift move, he blocked it. But that wasn't all. He twisted her arm, and in a quick sweep, wrestled her to the ground. Within seconds he lay on top of her, and they both panted breathlessly.

"Good job, good job." Buzz clapped, and they both got up.

Martha dusted her pants off. "Not bad."

"I learned from the best." He smiled at her.

Martha eyed him. "You know, you're…different, somehow."

"Good or bad?" Reuben asked.

"I'm not quite sure. More confident, but…" She trailed off.

Reuben tilted his head. "But what?"

She waved him off. "Never mind."

Buzz interrupted them. "As much as I would love to let this little love flower blossom, we do have an agenda here. Reuben brings up a great point."

Reuben sipped his drink and let it numb the sting of whatever Martha's ambiguous words meant. "What's that?"

"You need to die," Buzz said. "But according to our calculations, we have to go back at least five hours so we can hit the border before Alister does."

"Five hours?" Martha glanced at her watch. "It will take about half that just to fly to Detroit. That's if we can find a flight leaving, like, right now, and then if we can get to the airport in time."

Buzz flipped open the drapes to the garden and stood at the window overlooking his domain. "Fortunately, I'm prepared for this very thing."

"What a surprise," Reuben said. "You bought a jet?"

"No. That's so bourgeois." He flipped his hand dismissively. "I made a jet-copter. You ready?"

Reuben turned to Buzz. "Ready for what?"

"This." Buzz pulled a samurai sword off the wall, and with one seamless swing, took Reuben's head off.

Reuben—Wednesday, February 8, 1:43 p.m.

Reuben reinhabited his body. Buzz and Martha got their emails then, and after viewing the timeline and notes, they were all caught up.

Buzz grabbed his head. "Fuck me in a peach tree; we've got everything we need."

"Almost," Reuben said. With the help of the nanobot, they reviewed everything they had learned about the crossing at the border before Reuben's previous warp. Then Reuben turned to Buzz. "You got a jet-copter, somewhere, right?"

Reuben—Wednesday, February 8, 1:58 p.m.

Buzz careened the golf cart through the gravel-lined pathways of the property. He was actually dressed this time, looking sharp in hunter-green trousers, a blue and white striped waistcoat over a white dress shirt, and a baby-blue suit jacket. He had combed his hair and changed his usual silver-rimmed glasses for black-rimmed ones that gave him just the tiniest edge of cool.

"The advancement of robotics in the last thirty years has created an expansion of its application toward aerodynamics," he rambled.

The tiniest edge.

Reuben tuned him out and tried mainly to focus on

keeping both himself and Martha anchored in the golf cart. They drove for quite a while, down dirt backroads that Reuben had no idea even existed.

He tried not to fall on Martha when Buzz made a hairpin turn and they descended steeply. "What's the statistical probability of an object being ejected at this velocity?"

Buzz smirked, in on the joke. "It's lower at higher speeds due to centrifugal force. That's why roller coasters work."

To make his point, Buzz floored it, and he laughed while both his passengers screamed. They finally arrived, thankfully in one piece, at a large open shed with a metal bay door that was pulled up.

Reuben saw nothing anywhere except empty fields and grass. "Where are we?"

"This is the hangar. An old dairy farmer owns this field," Buzz explained as they all disembarked the vehicle. "But he went bankrupt in the early 90s when he tried to sell unpasteurized milk and got sued. He managed to hang on to the land, though. I guess it's been in his family since the 1800s. But he can't afford to do much with it, so it sits here. I rent it from him cheap so I can do experiments, and he looks the other way. It works out."

They all went inside the hangar, and it was exactly what Reuben expected from Buzz. Robotics experiments every which way, and tools, and…

A large missile-shaped device in one corner.

"Is that a bomb?" Reuben asked.

Buzz's eyes twinkled, and he patted the orange, shoulder-height missile. "Yeah, I tinker around a little. Nothing too fancy. What? It's not even radioactive."

Reuben shook his head. "You scare me, dude."

"You know you could go to jail for that," Martha reminded him.

Buzz pursed his lips and shook his head. "Nah, the Pentagon knows about it. I'm doing some testing for them." He threw an orange tarp over the bomb. "It's best that no one else knows about it, though."

Reuben and Martha looked at Buzz for more information, but he wouldn't give it. Instead, he pointed them toward another device.

The helicopter. It looked like it had started with the body of a gutted Toyota Sedan, but it was way cooler. Reuben ran his hands over the shiny red metal that now had double propellers overhead and a homemade nose that he assumed had been welded onto the body. "You did this all yourself?"

Buzz opened the driver's door to reveal the entire front seat had been transformed into an elaborate cockpit. "Mostly. I had a bit of help with the cosmetics. But this baby should get us to Detroit in forty-five minutes, maybe less."

Martha looked at him dubiously. "Under an hour? Commercial flights do two."

"Yeah, half of that's prep and half 'cause they're slow. We can hurry and get there quicker. What are you waiting for? Get in."

Reuben and Martha both shrugged at each other and climbed into the back seat of the makeshift aircraft. Once they were seated, Buzz activated airtight locks from the driver's seat.

Ruben followed Martha's lead and strapped on his seat-belt. "You do have your pilot's license, right?"

Buzz turned a key and yelled over the roaring engine, "Eh, more or less."

"Very comforting," Martha yelled back. "You could have at least lied to us."

"Do we get a safety demonstration?" Reuben asked.

Buzz pulled a lever, and the aircraft lurched to life. "Yeah, don't die. Or in your case, what does it matter?"

Buzz's taxi out of the hangar was less than graceful and made Reuben wish for the golf cart ride. The ascent was quick, and Reuben realized how much movement commercial planes absorbed. As the helicopter rose, the trio was strapped flat to the back of their seats like astronauts in a rocket, and Buzz fought every little breeze and wind from the cockpit. Reuben felt queasy, and a small headache started to form in his temple.

"How often has this thing gone out?" Reuben asked as they hit an air pocket. The impact turned his headache and stomach-churning into full-blown nausea.

"Huh?" Buzz yelled over the noise.

"I said," Reuben tried again, "how often has this thing gone out?"

"Oh, this is the first real trip. I've done a few test rides, though."

With a jolt, the copter leveled, but the last part was all Reuben needed.

"Aw, shit," he whined and felt his breakfast rise.

Martha threw a fast-food takeout bag at him, and he fought the urge to vomit, but it was no use. He barfed inside the bag.

"Sorry," he mumbled to his disgusted companions.

Buzz grinned back at him. "I guess I shouldn't do this, then?" Buzz jerked the copter into a sharp nosedive. He laughed as both Martha and Reuben screamed and Reuben threw up again.

Martha smacked the back of Buzz's head. "Stop being a jerk."

Buzz laughed but leveled them out. The ride quieted after that, and after vomiting twice, Reuben actually felt a lot better. Sort of.

He decided to calm his nerves by thinking about what would happen at the border. They would definitely need backup. How could they get it? He could call Aki. She wouldn't have any knowledge of any of this, so he'd have to be careful how he brought her onboard, but he'd find a way. She would be on board.

He pulled out his phone and, surprised to see service at this altitude, dialed the office. When a CIA receptionist answered, he identified himself with his agent number and asked for Aki's line. It was difficult to hear over the roar of the aircraft, but he hoped that would play into his urgency angle.

She answered on the first ring. *Good sign,* he thought.

"Hey, it's Reuben Peet from the office."

"Reuben? Wait, the tech guy from the window?"

"You got it," he told her.

"With the dance moves?"

"Uh...yeah."

She chuckled. "Wait, where are you? What is that noise?"

"That's what I'm calling about. I'm on a helicopter, heading to Detroit."

"Detroit? What's in Detroit?"

The jet-copter turned, and Reuben gripped the door handle. "I got a lead on something. It's a strong lead. I can't get into it right now. But, it's got something to do with the Schaeffer case."

"Schaeffer? How do you know about that?"

Shit. Reuben knew he had to be careful with what he said.

There were things he couldn't officially know, not without trying to explain that he could warp back in time, which there was no way she'd believe.

"It's not really about Schaeffer. He's a decoy..." Reuben's mind frantically searched for a plausible reason for how he could know all this. "Look," he said. "I know I may just look like an ordinary tech guy. But I'm actually working undercover."

"Sven put you undercover?" Aki didn't sound convinced.

"No." He bit his lip. "Sven's boss did."

"Oh shit. I didn't know. Damn, yeah, no offense, but I thought you were just a tech guy."

Whew. Reuben smirked. "And that's the way it's got to stay. But I've found myself in over my head, as these things sometimes go. This thing, we're talking international war crimes. It's big. I need some help."

"OK." Aki's voice took on a grave tone. "Tell me what you need. How can I help?"

"I'm heading to the Detroit-Windsor border. I've got a tip that it's going to go down."

"Canada?"

"Yeah, but our side. I'll need backup. I've got an NYPD officer here, she's in it all the way, but she's out of her jurisdiction."

"Right, I hear you. I actually can make it if you send me an address. But there's no one else here to go with me. Want me to run it by Sven?"

"No," Reuben said quickly. "You by yourself should be just fine." He hoped. Besides, the fewer people he had to let in on this, the better. The jet-copter started to bounce like a buoy in the water; he was starting to feel sick again. "I'll send you the address if you give me your cell phone number."

She did.

Reuben smiled as he saved it in his phone. "All right. I gotta go. Really appreciate the assist."

"No problem, Reuben."

He ended the call and the sick feeling in his stomach intensified. He rummaged around on the floor for another puke bag but couldn't find another bag. In the end, he had to grab a puke bucket—Buzz's autographed Mets helmet. He vomited runny green chunks.

"Is this helmet real?" he asked as the acid rose in his throat for another round.

"It was," Buzz muttered as he stared at Reuben hunched over it.

Reuben's stomach did a full turn, and nothing came out but spittle. It was so unsatisfying to go through all the pain of throwing up and not actually get the release of anything coming out.

CHAPTER THIRTY-NINE

Martha—Wednesday, February 8, 3:40 p.m.

Martha hiked up the road toward the Windsor border crossing, leaving Buzz and Reuben waiting in the rental. The trucks would be coming by in about twenty minutes, and if this plan was going to work, she couldn't smell or look like a woman that had just spent an hour in a fucked-up jet-copter two feet from a puking passenger.

A tiny wooden homemade goods gift shop sat about a quarter-mile before the border, and she stepped off the asphalt shoulder and into the dusty yard. There wasn't much to speak of, although they tried. A Canadian flag waved proudly from the railing, reminding visitors what side of the bridge they were on.

She stepped inside. It was a one-room gift shop with trinkets and troves galore, featuring flags and maple leaves and a Valentine's Day table that showed off red, white, and pink cookies and cakes.

A portly blonde woman in her early fifties greeted her from behind the register. "Hello. What can I get you for?"

"I just need a restroom," Martha said.

The woman made a face. "Oh dear, you do need a little freshening up, now don't you?"

Martha blushed and glanced down at her jeans and V-neck combo. She'd thought she'd done fine dressing for a day hanging with Reuben, but between meeting Buzz and the helicopter ride, she'd had quite the day. "Yeah, it's been something."

The woman pointed toward a wooden door with a flowered wreath on it. "Right through that door. Take as long as you need."

"Thanks."

Martha entered the flowered door, set her bag down, and caught her reflection. No wonder the lady had freaked out. She did look bad. She ran water over her face and fought with a green spot on her pant leg. She knew what it was but refused to let herself identify it. She rubbed the stain out satisfactorily and noticed the perfume and lotion set. Ah yes. She covered herself in perfume and lotion and fixed her hair into the classic damsel-in-distress messy bun. She grabbed her bag, poured out her makeup bag, and quickly fixed her face.

"Great." She smiled at her reflection.

She pulled down her V-neck and plumped up her bra to show a little more cleavage than she normally did. Still not quite right. What was missing? Some leg. She looked down at her jeans and had an idea.

Martha poked her head out of the door. "Ma'am?"

"Can I help you, dearie?"

"You wouldn't happen to have a pair of scissors, would you?"

"Scissors?" The woman looked at her, confused, then shrugged. "Sure." She handed Martha a long red-handled pair.

"Thank you." Martha smiled and shut the bathroom door. She stared at her jeans. "OK, I used to be able to do this when I was a teenager."

She slipped them off and took the scissors to just below the crotch. *This is going to be so cold outside...*

"I hope this works."

Martha slipped them back on and rubbed lotion over her toned legs to make them shine. She stared in the mirror and came up with one last idea. She cut the neck of her shirt farther down and let the cut pieces flap over her cleavage. *Yep, gonna be cold out there.* She sighed. *All in the name of duty.*

"Let's go get 'em," she told herself in the mirror. She grabbed her things and returned the scissors.

The woman looked at her in surprise. "Oh, honey. Why, don't you look...refreshed."

Martha laughed. "I'm from Montreal. My boyfriend is in Detroit, and he's meeting me. It was a last-second holiday getaway. I didn't get a chance to change before I had to get on the plane."

She raised an eyebrow, and Martha noticed the red-and-white rhinestone heels with the Valentine's bears. "Could I get these?"

The woman took in Martha's getup and hesitated. She frowned with disapproval, and Martha's stomach dropped. It didn't occur to her what her plan might look like.

She sighed. "I just want to buy the shoes."

"Uh-huh." The woman stared at her disapprovingly the whole time as she rang her up. She noticed the woman's fingers gravitating toward the phone.

"I'm not a hooker," Martha finally said. "The truth is, I kind of need to look like one." She flashed her badge at the woman. "I'm an undercover cop, and I'm here on a case."

The store owner looked at the badge. "Trafficking?"

"Yeah," Martha lied. "We're doing a sting."

The woman's face lit up. "Tell you what, the shoes are on the house. Here, take these cupcakes, too."

Martha tried to refuse. "I couldn't—"

She shoved a box of cupcakes at Martha. "Give them to the girls you rescue. Now go on, git. Take care of those poor girls."

"Thanks." Martha felt a twinge of guilt as she exited the shop. She wasn't saving trafficking victims, but she was on a trafficking sting. That part was true. Sort of. It was her own sting, but she seemed to be on her own a lot these days anyway. She stopped in the yard to switch her tennis shoes out for the heels and shoved them and the cupcakes in her bag. She checked her phone. Perfect. She plumped her boobs up one last time and took to the shoulder.

The plan was to entice the maple syrup truckers to stop to pick up the hot damsel in distress. According to their snooping, it would be the lead truck that had the incriminating materials. Then she would be in the cab and could circumvent the crime from there, with Buzz and Reuben in the rental waiting for instructions. With long, confident strides in the heels, she sashayed down the road, trying her best to pretend she was on the beach in Florida instead of Canada in winter.

It wasn't long before she got a couple of honks, and then a couple of college guys in a Dodge Challenger slowed beside her.

The driver rolled down the window, and she could smell the pot. "Want a ride?" The driver's glassy stare undressed her, and her stomach turned.

His friend ogled her from the passenger seat. "We could be down for a threesome."

Martha rolled her eyes. "I'm a cop. Beat it, assholes."

"Shit!" The car's tires squealed as they split.

Shivering in the cold February air, Martha rolled her eyes again and turned back to the road. There it was, the convoy of three semis barreling in her direction. She stuck out her thumb and tried to make eye contact with any of the drivers. She swished her hips and jutted out her chest.

A blue Corolla pulled up beside her. "Hey, baby."

She booked it past them toward the trucks, holding out her thumb.

"Forget you, too," the Corolla driver yelled before he pulled back out onto the road. He almost cut off the first truck, and the driver was so busy trying not to hit the Corolla, he didn't see Martha. Martha tried to flag the second truck, but he just raced past her on a mission. A couple of cars behind the second was the third.

Martha resorted to Def-Com-5 for this one. She stood in the truck's certain vision, caught the driver's eye, and pulled up her shirt. Talk about cold weather. The driver smiled approvingly but kept driving. Meanwhile, about five cars honked, and a woman yelled out of a minivan. "I got kids in here. Get a hold of yourself!"

"Ah, they see worse on the Disney Channel," she yelled back.

The trucks were gone. Damn.

She stepped off the highway and called Reuben. "Mission failed. The eagles have flown the coop."

"This means you're not in the trucks, right?"

"Right."

"OK, Aki is close," he said. "She's got a backup crew."

Martha made a face into the phone. Aki. Aki. Aki.

"If the trucks get to the other side—the American side—Detroit police will be on it, and cops are going to die."

Martha felt her blood surge at his words. Criminals and shootouts were one thing, but officers dying in the line of duty...

"I'm on it," she said.

She ended the call and took out her gun. She switched out the heels and slipped quickly into her tennis shoes. Then she ran like hell to catch the trucks. They were almost to the border. With ease, she flagged down a black BMW driven by a young businessman in a suit.

"Car broke down?" He flashed her a sexy smile and glanced around at the shoulder.

She collapsed into his passenger seat. "Something like that. Just book it to the border."

"Whoa," he said. "I'm a lawyer."

"And I'm a cop." She flashed her badge and her gun. "Just drive, dammit."

He held his hands over the steering wheel in surrender. "OK."

He swerved in and out of traffic, and Martha kept her eyes on the trucks. Thanks to the hot lawyer, she was gaining on the trucks.

"So might I ask what you're doing out here?" he asked.

She didn't take her eyes off the semis. "I'm on a case."

"All the way out here from...New York?"

She whipped her head around and then blushed when she noticed she still held her badge in her hand. She shoved it into her bag. "Federal case."

"You're on the other side. This isn't your federal."

"Shut up and drive," she ordered.

He obeyed. They got close enough to the semis, and Martha rolled down the window and stuck her head out. The highway speed hit her full in the face, and her hair blew every which way, obstructing her vision. She finally leaned out enough to get her gun out the window. But there was an Escalade between the BMW and the last semi. If only she could get around it. The semis were almost to the bridge. If she could just get around that Escalade, she could get a clean shot. Martha waved her gun toward the Escalade, and it quickly changed lanes and sped away.

"Thank you," she mumbled. Now she had a clear shot at the tires. She aimed and pulled the trigger. Boom. Boom. Boom. The gunshots hit the tires, and the crippled vehicle slowed.

She sat back down in the car, and the lawyer visibly gulped. "Look, lady, I don't know who you are, but I don't want any trouble—"

"Then just shut up and drive," she repeated. "And get me closer to the other ones."

"You got it."

The lawyer switched lanes and pulled right up beside the other two back-to-back semis. Now on alert, the drivers both looked at Martha and mouthed obscenities. She knew they were armed, so she had a limited time. She emptied her magazine out onto the tires of the two vehicles. It worked, and they both hobbled to the side of the road.

CHAPTER FORTY

Reuben—Wednesday, February 8, 4:23 p.m.

Reuben and Buzz sat in the rental on the shoulder before the border crossing. They had gotten a Kia Sedona because that was mainly what the rental agency had, and they figured they could use the ample space. Now, as they waited for news from Martha, Buzz spent the entire time complaining about cheap Korean cars and how badly they were engineered and how he missed his Mercedes.

Reuben flipped on the heat, and the knob instantly popped off.

"See, that's what I mean," Buzz said.

Reuben laughed and popped the knob back on. There wasn't much he could argue with. He had never driven a Mercedes, and certainly not Buzz's. This was, in fact, a sore point he would rather not revisit.

Where's Aki? Reuben wondered as he called her.

"Yeah?"

He put her on speaker "What's your 20?"

"I'm still in Michigan, twenty minutes to the border. But

the traffic is horrible, so the ETA on my GPS is going up, not down. What are we getting ourselves into here?"

Reuben narrowed his eyes as he kept a lookout for Martha. "My sources show an illegal shipment of maple syrup about to cross the border into Detroit—"

"Maple syrup?" she interrupted. "Then why are we on it? Why not border patrol? Local police? I thought you said this was big. International war crimes-big."

"It is," he assured her. "Look, I can't tell you everything that I know. There are informants with families, and I'm not entirely sure if I can trust everyone at the office." Reuben paused for dramatic effect. "But, between you and me, there's more than maple syrup being transported in one of those trucks." He swallowed, hoping his story had been convincing.

There was a pause, and then Aki came back on the line. "OK. Tell me what needs to be done."

Oh, thank God, he thought. "We've got to stop three semis from crossing the border and—"

Up ahead, he saw the semis. One was out front, and the other two were farther back. But next to the first semi was a black BMW with...

"Is that Martha?" Buzz asked.

"Aki, I'm going to have to call you back." Reuben ended the call abruptly.

Martha leaned out of the passenger side and pointed a gun at the semi.

"Go, go," he yelled at Buzz.

Buzz fired the engine and pulled out onto the highway. Gunfire rang through the street, and drivers scrambled to get out of the way. It wasn't clear what Martha had hit, but the semi shook, and it didn't look good. When she let off another shot, the vehicle swerved and spun in a complete three-sixty.

The BMW raced to the shoulder for safety, and Martha got out. Then the BMW sped down the shoulder at the highest speed the car could manage, disappearing before the semi hit the highway barricade and squealed before knocking the steel barricade completely over. It teetered for a moment, trying to find balance on its broken wheel.

Finally the crippled truck fell flat on its side, hitting the asphalt with a fantastic crash of metal and glass.

Buzz was on the shoulder now, trying to stay away from the scene.

Martha stood on the highway in cutoff shorts and watched the whole thing. Once the truck had finished crashing, the whole highway stood at a standstill. Then, the drivers of the other two trucks started to run toward Martha.

Reuben instinctively jumped out of the car and ran toward her. "Martha!"

But it was too late. The other drivers fired their guns, and he saw her crumple.

"No! No, Martha!" he yelled as he ran.

The drivers kept firing, and no sooner had he reached her body than the familiar sting of a bullet ripped through his chest. He writhed in pain, and then they just kept coming.

Oh well. Better luck next time, he thought as he died.

Reuben—Wednesday, February 8, 3:30 p.m.

Reuben, Buzz, and Martha sat in the Kia on the side of the road. This time, Martha wasn't hitchhiking. Reuben lamented, remembering her skimpy cutoff outfit. *That had to have been cold...*

"We never did come up with a plan," Buzz remarked. "We've spent the entire day discussing how we needed a cheap shit minivan, but we don't know how to stop the criminals. Not that we could with this inferior engineering."

Reuben groaned. "OK, we get it; you hate the minivan. Well, if you could have chitty-chitty banged-banged us here in your Mercedes, we would have been glad to go take it. But since you don't know how to do that, I guess we're stuck with the Kia."

"I know how to make a car fly," Buzz said.

"A Toyota," Reuben said. "But you still have yet to figure out how to make German engineering fit your aerodynamic purposes. It's a work in progress."

"I could. It's just, I mean you know—"

Martha chimed in from the backseat, "Guys, guys. Let's not fight. Let's talk about the plan."

Buzz glanced at her in the rearview. "The fact that we don't have one?"

"I have something," she said.

Reuben sighed. Oh yeah, this wasn't going to work.

"I could pretend to be a sexy damsel in distress hitchhiking again."

"Won't work," Reuben said.

"I'd pick you up," Buzz muttered, and Reuben shot him a side glance.

"We can come up with a better plan than that," Reuben said.

She applied lip gloss. "I think it might work. It's an idea, and I don't see you guys volunteering anything."

"These guys are on a mission," Reuben said. "They're amped up enough that they're planning to shoot cops. They don't have time for hot hitchhikers right now. Besides, we would need to be sure of a closing plan. If we don't have a clear one, it could put you in danger. Again. I have another idea."

He pulled out his phone and put it on speaker. "Aki, where are you?"

"Ugh, I'm stuck in traffic," she told him. "GPS says I'm thirteen minutes away."

Reuben grimaced. "Yikes. It'll be close then. We're on the Canada side, and they should come through here in about twenty, but we don't think we can stop them in time."

"What do you mean, 'in time?'"

Reuben forgot that Aki wasn't in on his powers. "I've got intel that they're twenty minutes away from the border. They're armed and dangerous and ready for a fight."

"They're hauling something other than maple syrup, then?" she guessed.

Screw it. He'd tell her the truth and save himself from the "international war crimes" spiel. "We think it's an experimental microwave bomb."

There was a pause. "Are you serious? Shit. I should've told Sven and got some reinforcements. This is serious."

"It won't be necessary. Sources say that there are only three truckers. They're armed, but with you, we can take them."

"Um, all right. What about local PD?"

"We haven't alerted them yet," Reuben said. "To be honest, I'm not sure they'd believe me."

"I have higher clearance than you. I'll call them and have them alert customs to let us do our thing. I don't care how many hostiles there are; this is too sensitive to have them interfering."

"That would be nice," Reuben said. "But you can't just call up the police and tell them to hold off."

"You can if you're a federal agent," she said. "At least, temporarily."

"Right." Reuben blushed and felt stupid. She was right. She had a higher security clearance than he did and had probably been in countless situations like this.

"I'll put them on standby," Aki said, "and then I'll meet you on the Detroit side."

"That will work." Reuben ended the call and turned to Buzz and Martha. Martha's eyes were narrowed at him. "Security clearance? Federal agent? I thought you worked for the State Department. What is it you do, exactly?"

"I'm not at liberty to say." He strapped on his seatbelt.

"Christ." Martha shook her head.

Buzz started the engine and pulled out onto the northbound lane.

"Aki wants to meet us on the Detroit side of the border," Reuben said.

"I know, I heard," he said.

"Then where are we going?"

"I'm not at liberty to say." His eyes twinkled, and Martha laughed.

"Come on, you've got government clearance, too."

Buzz raised his eyebrows and kept driving.

"Really, we've got to meet her," Reuben said.

"Uh-huh, I know."

"Buzz? Really, where are you going?"

"I'm not at liberty to say." He pulled into the McDonald's drive-through.

"I guess I don't have security clearance for lunch, then?" Reuben said.

"Nope."

The Kia covered in discarded fast-food wrappers, they met up with Aki on the other side of the border. They met her in a parking lot, where she arrived in her Porsche.

Buzz didn't waste a beat on that one. "See, how come she gets a sports car and we get a car named after some voodoo town in Arizona."

Reuben wasn't listening. Aki stepped out of the car wearing skintight leather pants with studs down the front, matching high-platform lace-up boots, and a crop-top vintage t-shirt from the band KISS. Her asymmetrical pixie cut had fresh purple highlights.

"OK, I get it now," Buzz muttered to Reuben.

"Yeah," Reuben whispered back.

Martha scoffed. "She dresses like that for work? How unprofessional."

"No, she doesn't. Just when she's doing field work." He stepped out of the car, and Buzz and Martha followed him.

"Hey," he said to Aki.

She simply nodded.

"Aki, meet Buzz and Martha. Guys, Aki."

"Cool," she said as Buzz and Martha nodded to her. "Let's get down to business. PD's on standby, but we're going to intercept the semis as they come across the border. Three semi drivers, four of us including a getaway driver. Everyone armed?"

"Uh..." Reuben scratched the back of his head. Wow. He hadn't expected Aki to go full Rambo. It was a good thing he'd done all that combat and shooting training with Martha at Buzz's mansion.

"I'm NYPD," Martha said.

Aki nodded with approval but wasn't impressed. "Cool. You guys packing?"

Reuben and Buzz looked at each other.

Aki reached back into her car and pulled out a duffel bag. "These ought to do." She passed out handguns.

Reuben took one, but Buzz held up his hands.

"I'm not comfortable carrying deadly weapons. I'm a staunch advocate of gun control."

Reuben looked at him sideways. Buzz had killed him so many times. But now, when it was time to go after real criminals, he went all anti-second amendment pacifist?

Aki had little patience for his shenanigans. "If you're going to be on this op, you've got to be armed. I'm not going into a high-danger situation with an unarmed crew. Too much risk for several reasons, one being the possibility of a hostage situation. I'm trusting you because Reuben obviously does. Either take the gun or take a hike."

Aki's no-nonsense manner sent Reuben's heart racing. Damn, she was hot taking over like that.

Buzz took the gun silently.

Martha loaded hers. "I think we need to establish a command post. Buzz and Reuben and I have been working this case if you want to fall in with us."

Aki didn't falter. "NYPD, you're out of your depth and jurisdiction here. This is a federal operation. I'm cutting you in because you've got intel and we can use you."

"Oh." Martha blushed.

"Having said that," she placed her hands on her hips and studied Reuben, "where are we?"

He checked his watch. "They should be crossing right about now, if you want to jump in the van?"

Aki nodded, and they all boarded the van. It suddenly felt much more crowded with Aki in the back seat.

Buzz turned onto the highway, then pulled out onto the shoulder right on the other side of the bridge.

"We can stand outside and get a good angle from there," Martha said. "Maybe we could pretend to be hitchhikers."

Aki shook her head. "It's too dangerous. We need to be prepared to leave the scene. Also, this first customs lane is the one for declared goods, so it's likely to be the lane they're in. We need to block them off, taking over two lanes as soon as they come across. Then, before they can switch lanes, we're on them."

"This is pretty aggressive driving," Buzz said. "I'm not sure this Kia is engineered—"

"Shut up, Buzz," Reuben said.

This was not the time for Buzz's complaining. Aki would not be impressed.

Aki pointed toward the semis barreling through customs. "There they are. Go, go!"

Buzz pulled into the first lane and parked on the highway, half in the first and half in the second lane. Traffic from the second lane backed up, perfectly creating a wall that wouldn't allow the semis to get away.

Aki yelled, "Go, go!"

Buzz stayed in the Kia, set to move it as soon as the rest of them were safely inside the semis.

The other three jumped out of the van, brandishing guns. Aki reached the first one and talked to the driver. He wasn't sure if she was using charm or violence, but he moved on to the second one.

He approached the driver, about twice his size. His palms

felt sweaty and his mouth was dry. Who was he kidding? He couldn't hold up a semi-truck.

In his periphery, he saw Martha confidently jog up to the last semi. How could she do that? He couldn't let her show him up. So he steadied his gaze on the driver of the truck. Now that Aki had halted the driver, Buzz moved the Kia and was gone. There was no turning back now. That was when he heard the gunshots.

He instantly turned to see Martha stumbling toward the asphalt. The three truckers got out, all with their guns, and the next thing Reuben knew, Aki was on the ground.

"Aki." He ran over, knelt on the ground next to her, and accidentally dropped his gun. One of the truckers kicked it away from him, and Reuben stood. He held his hands up and was surrounded by three burly truckers.

In the distance, police sirens wailed. No cops were coming to save him.

"Get on out of here, boy," one of the truckers slurred.

Reuben knew he needed to go back in time and fix all of this, and this was the perfect way to do it. "Just kill me already."

The trucker furrowed his brow. "You want to die, son?"

"Yeah, sure, why not?"

The three truckers stared at each other.

"Why? I don't need to kill you. You ain't done nothin'. And by yourself, you cain't do nothin.'"

"I just want to be like the cool kids." Reuben gestured toward the dead women in the road.

"Dead?" the trucker asked.

"Yeah. Dead is the new black."

"Damn millennials." The trucker shook his head. "I never will get your generation."

"We were raised in an era of tolerance and diversity. No one is better than anyone else. So now we're a generation of conformists." He gestured again to the corpses.

The trucker looked at his friends.

One of the other truckers reasoned, "Well, two murder charges. It's not like we're ever getting out if we get busted."

The first trucker shrugged in agreement and cocked his gun.

Reuben closed his eyes and waited for it. Then, boom. The bullet pierced through him, and he fell to the ground in agony.

"You asked for it," the trucker yelled as they all got in their trucks.

Reuben—Wednesday, February 8, 2:01 p.m.

Reuben came to in the helicopter hangar. Buzz opened the driver's door and showed off the cockpit.

Reuben felt sick just looking at it.

Buzz and Martha got their emails. Then Buzz continued answering Reuben's question about whether he had created the helicopter by himself. "Mostly. I had a bit of help with the cosmetics. But this baby should get us to Detroit in forty-five minutes, maybe less."

Martha looked at him dubiously. "Under an hour? Commercial flights do two."

"Yeah, half of that's prep and half 'cause they're slow. We can hurry and get there quicker. What are you waiting for? Get in."

Martha shrugged at Reuben, and he cocked his head dismissively. "Doesn't surprise me. I'm not looking forward to a bumpy ride in this thing."

Martha boarded the aircraft. "Eh, maybe it won't be so bad."

Reuben spotted a pail on the side of the room. "Trust me, if Buzz's golf cart driving is any indication, this will be hell."

"I know what I'm doing," Buzz said.

Reuben raised an eyebrow and grabbed the pail.

Buzz watched him deftly enter the helicopter and strap on his seatbelt, pail at his knees. "We've done this before, haven't we?"

Reuben just nodded, and Buzz jumped up into the pilot's seat. "That is so extraordinary."

Martha strapped in and glanced over at Reuben cuddling his pail. "I guess I should get one."

"No, you'll be fine," Reuben said.

"This time thing is so weird," she said.

He stared out the window as the plane lurched into motion. "You think it's weird? Try living it."

The plane took off, and Reuben pulled out his phone to call Aki.

CHAPTER FORTY-ONE

Reuben—Wednesday, February 8, 4:25 p.m.

Reuben and Buzz met up with Aki in the parking lot. Aki passed out guns to the guys. Reuben grabbed his, but while Buzz protested, Reuben cocked his. Then, he saw a beer bottle lying on the ground about ten yards away. He aimed and shot the bottle, which shattered.

Aki handed the second gun to Buzz, then raised her eyebrows at Reuben. "Not bad for a tech guy." She ran her tongue over her lips.

"You know, I have a few skills packed away for a rainy day," he said.

"Clearly." She pulled out her gun and aimed at the beer bottle next to it. She shattered it, too.

"Not bad yourself," he said.

She looked him over. "You know, when I first met you, I thought you were…"

Reuben grinned. "A nerd?"

"Well…yeah," she admitted. "But you surprise me. What else have you got tucked away in there?"

Reuben cleared his throat. He wasn't sure if that was an innuendo or a reference to his earlier comment.

Martha cocked her gun and shot a tree. "Can we get moving before these thugs kill innocent officers? I mean, you're on federal government time and all."

"Or should we book you two a room instead?" Buzz teased.

Reuben blushed, and Aki cleared her throat. "Let's get moving."

The group piled into the Kia and set the earlier plan into motion. They would block the vehicles and hijack them.

Reuben used the drive to advise the group on the pitfalls of the operation. "These guys are armed and dangerous. They're not going to take being hijacked lying down. We've got to be ready. If we approach these guys and they're ready for a shootout, what do we do?"

Aki nodded approvingly. "Good thinking. What should we do?"

Reuben pursed his lips and played the scene back in his memory. What could they have done differently? "Let's not try to get into the vehicles with them," he said. "Make them come to us."

Martha frowned. "How do we do that?"

"We stick together and hold them up," Reuben said. "Disable all the vehicles first, but don't separate. Keep an armed wall. Buzz, don't leave. Stay behind as backup."

Aki stared at Reuben. "I like your thinking."

He winked. "I've been around a bit."

"Ugh," Martha groaned softly.

They arrived at the border crossing, and Buzz blocked off the two lanes.

Reuben got out and instructed the ladies. "Remember, an

armed wall. Buzz, stay behind us for backup, and for God's sake, don't be afraid to shoot. I've seen you shoot dozens of times."

"Not humans," Buzz said.

Reuben smirked. "Believe me, you're fully capable of it."

The three friends stood as an armed wall, and together they approached the first trucker.

"Keep me covered," Reuben said.

He walked up to the driver's side, and Martha pulled the trigger and shot out the tires. Reuben remembered back to college when he'd trained to be a door-to-door phone salesperson. He lasted an entire day, but they taught him a technique he'd never forgotten. They were supposed to knock on a door, and in a bored, perfunctory manner, demand to see the homeowner's phone bill. When the owner retrieved it, the salespeople were to compare the rate with the rate they were offering. If their rates were lower, they were supposed to say, "OK, I'm with the phone company, and I'm going to sign you up for a new rate plan. If you can just fill out this sheet for me here, please."

It worked. Well, for everyone else. Reuben couldn't get a single person to switch. But he'd always remembered that technique. It came to him now as he prepared to hijack this vehicle. He affected a bored, perfunctory demeanor and tried to open the driver's door. It was locked.

He banged on the window with his gun. "Open the door," he said, surprised at how much he sounded like Marshall.

When the driver hesitated, Reuben kept eye contact with him but reached down and shot another tire.

"I said open the door," Reuben calmly demanded.

Martha yelled from the other side of the truck, "Stand back. Stand back."

The other truckers protested. "What the hell?"

Aki yelled, "I said stand back." From her spot on the other side of the truck, she aimed and shot the second semi's tire.

"Christ, lady," one of the other truckers yelled.

Reuben knew better than to take his eyes off the trucker he had cornered. "Out of the truck. Keep your hands where I can see them."

In another lifetime, he would have been quoting a movie line. But he hadn't said it because it was in every shootout ever. Considering his circumstances and his history, it just made perfect sense.

The trucker obeyed and stepped outside. He held up his hands. "What do you want?"

Reuben gestured with his gun. "I want you to join your friends over there, scumbag."

The trucker sighed, and Reuben led him to the group where the women had them cornered.

Once they had the three at gunpoint in a crowd, Aki ordered them to the side of the road. "Our business is with you, not the rest of the border. Move it."

They silently did as they were told. Reuben got up into the cab of the truck and attempted to move it. But semis are a different animal, and everything he did just made the engine roar unhealthily.

"You're gonna strip the engine," the trucker yelled. "Let me help you."

Reuben tried again and finally waved the trucker over. "Nothing funny."

"I'm not trying anything funny. I just want to move this along, and no one's going anywhere if you tear this thing to hell. Plus, it's my rig, and I don't know what your plans are, but I'd like to get it back one day. So it's in my best interest to tell you how to take care of it."

"Fine."

He stood outside the cab. "OK, so the first thing you want to do, is…see that red button right there?" He pointed toward a large red button that hung from the wiring under the console. It didn't appear to be connected to much of anything. "Yeah."

"The vehicle's in safe mode. Means nothing can happen unless you pull out of safe mode."

Reuben frowned. He had never heard of such a thing. But he'd never driven a diesel before.

"To get it out of safe mode, you got to rev the engine and then push the safe mode button." The trucker held up his hands. "I'm not trying nothing funny, and I don't want you to shoot me, so I'm going to step away."

He shut the door, and Reuben revved the engine. Then he pushed the red button. Nothing happened. What the hell?

Then it did.

A high-pitched beeping sounded. The trucker had lied. He had just detonated a bomb.

"Oh fuck," Reuben muttered as the blast tore his skin to pieces.

CHAPTER FORTY-TWO

Reuben—Wednesday, February 8, 5:01 pm.

Reuben came to as Buzz blocked off the border crossing with the Kia. He turned to Martha and Aki. "We're clear on the plan?"

"Clear," Martha said.

"Got it," Aki said.

Buzz's and Martha's phones beeped that they had a new email, but they disregarded them.

Reuben turned to Buzz. "Keep us covered."

Buzz saluted him with his gun.

The trio got out of the car. Reuben stood in the middle, flanked on both sides by the women. He cocked his gun, and instead of going to the driver's side, he stood in front of the hood and pointed the gun clear at the windshield. He stared the driver in the eye and pulled the trigger at the windshield, and then without looking down, shot front tires on both sides.

The driver exited the vehicle. "Look, we're all good."

"No, we're not," Reuben said, steely-eyed. "As long as

you're working for Pout, we are definitely not good."

The trucker's faced paled, and he stammered. "How did you—"

Reuben waved his gun. "Get your ass on the side of the road, dickhole."

The other truckers got out of their vehicles, and without moving, he yelled, "On the side of the road, now. Hit the pavement. On your faces. Let's go, move it."

The other truckers hesitated, and Reuben rolled his eyes and shot the tires off the second vehicle.

"Jesus," the second trucker muttered. "He's crazy."

All three of them hit the ground on the shoulder.

Reuben glanced at Martha and Aki. "Keep 'em covered."

He knew better than to try to move the vehicle, especially now that he knew about the bomb. He jumped in the driver's seat and saw the "safety button." He remembered learning how to disarm a bomb at Buzz's. He fumbled with the wires until he neutralized it. Then, he needed to find out what was in that truck. He grabbed the keys out of the ignition and decided to check the back. But as soon as he got out, he noticed that the tables had turned on the side of the road.

Two truckers now wrestled the two women, trying to get control of the guns. Reuben rushed to help. But before he could get to them, one of the truckers pulled out a giant knife from his boot. The blade glistened and even made the tiniest whistle as it was unsheathed.

He turned to Reuben. "Time for your little sister-wife-girlfriend to die. You get caught up with snakes; that's what happens."

Reuben aimed his gun and pulled the trigger. He hit the trucker in the arm, but it was enough to get him to release

Martha. The other one had Aki cornered with his hands clasped around her throat.

"Where's..." Before Reuben could finish, the Kia drove off. Reuben saw a petrified Buzz held in the driver's seat at gunpoint. Reuben was torn between who to save. Buzz was likely toast. But Aki... Reuben suddenly remembered all the sparring he had done with Martha.

Martha was busy keeping her assailant at bay. Reuben busted out his moves and knocked the trucker off-balance.

"What the..." The trucker released Aki, and she slid to the ground to catch her breath. The trucker turned to him with a toothy grin. "You want some of this?"

Reuben stared him in the face and raised an eyebrow. "No, I prefer to deal the cards, thank you."

He held his gun in the man's face, but not before the Kia came plowing back toward them. "Shit."

Buzz was still driving, and the trucker in the passenger seat motioned for him to stop. Before the vehicle had even come to a stop, the trucker jumped out to confront Reuben.

But Reuben was already there. Using his combat training, he quickly knocked the trucker to the ground. "You OK?" he asked Buzz.

Buzz was clearly shaken, and Aki had recovered. Martha had kicked the crap out of the trucker who had held her at knifepoint. Reuben watched as he lay on the ground moaning. All in all, things were going quite well this time around. Then the moaning trucker grinned and pulled out two small, concealed pistols from his boots.

You've got to be kidding me...

"Run," Reuben shouted.

The Kia was too far away to hop into, so they hit the ground on foot, trying to get as far from the highway as possible. Within moments, all three truckers had fully recovered and climbed into the Kia to give chase.

Reuben spotted an abandoned warehouse on the side of the road. "Come on, guys." He gestured toward the side of the building.

They all stood and caught their breath. He tried a door, and to his surprise, it opened. The foursome stepped inside the warehouse. The first thing Reuben noticed was the smell. It smelled like animals. Buzz clicked the door behind them. They were safe. For now.

It was a large room that looked like it had been used for gatherings but now had no real evidence of the sort. They knew the truckers weren't far behind them, and they had little time. They wanted to take them down, but they needed cover as well.

There was a small storage closet, and Buzz stepped inside it. "I'm going to hide in here. Gun fights are not my thing."

"Someone needs to cover Buzz," Reuben said.

"Martha," Aki said, shaking her head at Buzz, "why don't you establish a post with him?"

Martha pulled out her gun and reloaded it. "I can do that." She disappeared into the closet and the locks clicked.

That left him and Aki. He noticed a high catwalk off to the side with a metal door. "Let's go up there. Might be a window in there where we can watch for the truckers."

"Good idea. Let's check it out."

She followed him up the stairwell. Beyond the metal door was a small office that had a window that looked out at the entry to the warehouse. The room appeared to have at one time been a sound room. An old sound board sat against one wall, and boxes were stacked high on a shelf. They shut the door behind them and locked it.

"I wonder what this place was." She flipped on a bare bulb.

"I couldn't tell you."

She peeked into some of the boxes. "Christmas decorations…and CDs."

"CDs?" He chuckled as he made his way to the window. "I didn't think anyone even had those anymore."

She pulled out a case and laughed. "Garth Brooks, Roping the Wind. You feel like two-stepping?"

Reuben chuckled. "I don't think there's room in here for one-stepping, much less two."

She laughed and put the CDs away. It was quiet up here, and a glance out the window showed it was quiet outside too. No sign of the truckers in the Kia. Where were they? Why were they waiting? Surely they weren't calling in backup to finish off him and his friends. Or even worse—they couldn't be arming the microwave bomb in the back of one of the trucks, could they? They needed mesh and stuff first, right?

When Reuben turned back around, he saw that Aki had found a tiny mirror and was examining a wound on her side. "Is it bleeding?" he asked.

She dabbed it with some old napkins she'd found. "Yeah." She turned to him and grabbed the bottom of her shirt. "Do you mind?" She moved to lift her shirt.

He blushed and looked away.

She laughed. "You can look."

He turned back to her, and she was in a silky burgundy bra, and he saw something he didn't expect to see. Stretch marks and scars from previous battles. They crawled up her sides. He had pictured her topless a million times, and every time, he always imagined an impossibly flat and toned stomach and silky-smooth skin.

She was flawed and more beautiful than he thought possible. Seeing her like this burst a bit of the fantasy and shifted it into something more real. More desirable.

He knew then that he loved her. Not just the fantasy of love, all filled with impossibly perfect sex and a lifetime of never fighting. But something much more real.

Much more desirable.

He gulped and tried to act natural as she tended to another wound.

He watched her, and he wanted to tell her how he felt. "Aki, I…"

She met his eyes then, and her lips seemed to quiver. Or maybe it was just Reuben's imagination. They suddenly found themselves standing very close to each other.

"Reuben," she said softly and continued to take in his eyes. "I can't explain it, but there's something about you. Something…"

Now they were even closer, their lips a few inches apart as they reeled each other in with their eyes.

She shook her head and then the moment was broken, but they were still standing close to each other. "Reuben, I've got a boyfriend."

A loud boom resonated through the warehouse.

"We know you're in there," one of the truckers yelled from outside the building.

Reuben spun toward the window again. The Kia was parked outside the building. They had sneaked up when he and Aki were having a moment, or whatever that had been.

Aki grabbed her shirt and slipped it back on. "Shit. We need to get down there."

Reuben nodded, his heart aching for that moment they'd shared.

Her words had meant there was hope for the two of them.

CHAPTER FORTY-THREE

Reuben—Wednesday, February 8, 5:32 p.m.

Reuben and Aki reached the ground floor of the warehouse just as the guys stormed the building. Reuben fired the first shot. It hit the trucker in the arm and he cried out, and then with eyes full of rage, ran toward Reuben. He moved like a burly machine, but Reuben tripped him, and he fell.

Martha emerged from her closet, and the next thing Reuben knew, the three truckers and he, Aki, and Martha were all dodging each other's bullets, hiding behind doors and barrels. He worried about Buzz but knew he would be the safest in the closet.

Reuben had one trucker cornered—the one he had held up out on the highway. "Where's Pout?"

The trucker grinned, and they danced around the floor, holding each other at gunpoint. "I don't know what you're talking about."

"You knew ten minutes ago."

The trucker feigned surprise. "Pout? Oh, you mean Alister Pout, the one who's supposed to be announcing his candidacy for Canadian parliament this week? I don't know. But I'm sure you could check his Facebook page. He loves to do all the baby-kissing and glad-handing."

Reuben scoffed. "Please, Alister Pout's about as interested in politics as I am in needlepoint crafting."

"Well, then I take it you're quite the needle-pointer. They say it's very relaxing. You could needlepoint some cliché for your wall, like 'God answers prayer' or something."

"What do you know about God?"

"Not as much as you're about to," the trucker said.

"Nah, I don't feel like dying today." Reuben lunged at him and grabbed the man's wrist to keep him from shooting. They wrestled on the ground for a few minutes, then he heard Martha scream.

One of the guys had a gun pointed at her temple.

"Shit."

He scrambled to get up and crushed the man's fingers with his shoe. The pressure was enough to get him to let go of the gun. Reuben grabbed the gun and rushed to help Martha. But, it was too late.

The gunman pulled the trigger, and Martha crumpled to the ground.

The gunman turned to the rest of them. "Let that be a lesson to all of you. Don't mess with snakes. I think we're done here. We done here, guys?"

The other two truckers rose, bloodied and dirt-smeared but fine.

"Yeah, we're done here, boss," one of the others said.

Then they turned and left the building.

Reuben watched as they left. They had gotten away, and he stared at Martha's bloodied body. He thought about the moment he and Aki had shared upstairs and how he didn't want to warp back and erase that from ever happening. But he couldn't let Martha be dead forever. He had to go back and fix it.

Aki yelled to Buzz, "You can come out now."

Buzz emerged from the closet, looking shell-shocked and ashen. "Reuben, I don't think I can do this anymore. This is too real."

He looked at his friend's terrified face. Being held hostage in that Kia must have been the scariest moment of Buzz's life. Before this whole thing, it would have been the scariest thing Reuben had ever encountered. But after all he'd been through, it didn't seem that bad.

"Don't worry. I'll fix it." He took the gun in his hand and dutifully pointed at his temple.

Aki shouted, "What the hell are you doing?"

Buzz grabbed her hand. "He's immortal. Just don't look."

"What?"

Then Reuben pulled the trigger and died.

CHAPTER FORTY-FOUR

Reuben—Wednesday, February 8, 5:19 p.m.

When Reuben came back to his body, he stood with Martha, Buzz, and Aki in the abandoned warehouse. Buzz and Martha's phones beeped. They disregarded them.

"Someone should cover Buzz," Aki said.

Ah, that's where we are, Reuben thought.

This was the moment he'd ended up in the sound room with Aki. He knew then what he had done wrong this time.

Well, not with Aki. But with Martha.

Hiding out with Aki, although it had been the highlight of his year, maybe his entire life...all of his lives combined...had, in fact, given the truckers time to organize, arm, and come up with a plan. This in turn had led to Martha's death. He had felt bad about leaving her there alone in the closet with Buzz. They probably should have stuck together.

Aki called out, "Martha, why don't you do that?"

Reuben's heart sank with the realization of what he had to do. He had to save Martha and couldn't be up in a room with a half-naked woman when he knew his friend's life was on the line. He had to save them all.

Martha loaded her gun. "I can do that."

Reuben pushed the image of Aki and him standing so close together in that upstairs office away. "I don't think that's a good idea."

Martha was defensive. "You don't think I can do it?"

"It's not that. Splitting up isn't a good idea. We only do well when we stay together and have each other's backs."

"All right," Martha said. "Let's stick together."

The threesome, minus Buzz, snuck toward the entrance of the warehouse. From here, they could hear the stolen rental Kia approach.

One of the truckers said, "I think they're in there. I say, let's go kick their asses."

"I don't know. What that one said about Pout scares me. How would he know?"

"He probably don't. He probably don't know jack shit and he's just testing you."

"I want to know who these guys are. Is they police, or what?"

"I don't know. For all we know, they're CIA or some shit."

Reuben, Aki, and Martha continued listening while they slowly snuck out of the warehouse. The truckers had their backs to them as they were trying to force open the door. Reuben held up three fingers to the ladies and gestured back and forth.

Three of them, three of us.

There was a stack of large crates near the truckers, and Reuben motioned for his two friends to join him behind it as they continued to listen. The truckers had stopped trying to open the door and were all facing each other now.

"But I don't like Dunkin Donuts," one of the truckers said. "Their donuts are too cakey."

"They're coffee donuts," another answered with annoyance. "Look, just shut up, OK? I just want to blast these snot-nosed kids before they go off spouting what they know."

These guys sure were chatty. Eh, he had no room to talk. He'd been upstairs with Aki, talking, and had gotten someone killed. He shook his head to clear the image and tuned back in to the truckers' conversation.

The third one scoffed. "We don't know what they know. They probably don't know nothing."

Reuben wondered if these guys were going to say anything useful or not.

The first one answered, "They know enough. They know we're with the Canadian, and that's something."

Reuben whipped around to Martha. Her mouth dropped.

"Yeah, but they don't know who that is."

"Would you two shut up so we can come up with a plan?"

"All right, so how many are there?"

"Four. There's the two chicks. The hot one, and the fuckable one."

The three truckers laughed.

"Then there's the dudes. Couple of dorky dudes. One thinks he's Kiefer Sutherland, the other's a scrawny little nitwit."

"OK, I'll take the ladies, and you two split up and take the dudes."

"Well, that's not fair. Why do you get to take the ladies?"

"Can we not argue? We have seriously deadly shit in the back of our trucks. Let's get these bastards taken care of so we can get the bomb to the boss."

"What does Alister Pout want with bombs, anyway?"

"I dunno. I just do what the boss says."

The guys moved on to strategies for how they would kill them. Reuben decided he wasn't going to get any more information out of them. He motioned to the women, and they snuck forward, one behind each trucker. Then Reuben counted off three fingers.

The plan was to apprehend them with the classic, 'Put your hands up,' but the largest trucker was surprisingly fast. He pulled out his gun and shot Aki in the head.

Reuben sighed before turning the gun on himself.

Reuben reemerged ten minutes earlier as they snuck up on the truckers and listened to their conversation again before trying to subdue them. This time Reuben motioned for Aki to crouch. But it didn't matter. The same trucker got her again. What was it with this guy and killing beautiful Asians? Reuben briefly wondered if he was racist before killing himself again.

Now he came to eleven minutes earlier. This time they'd hit the truckers hard. No listening to their conversation. They just went for it. This time the truckers got both Martha and Aki.

"What the fuck?" Reuben said before killing himself once again.

Again and again, Reuben tried to get the drop on them, and each time the truckers always managed to take one of them down.

Finally, Reuben knew what he had to do.

Reemerging thirty minutes earlier, he told the others to wait behind the warehouse while he went in solo. He tried to get the drop on the truckers, and this time their gunfire was focused on him. He went down, but not before seeing what they did. The largest trucker always went for the head. The middle guy always shot wide and to the right, and the third one always went for the torso.

He repeated this action again, this time approaching with his arms out. He might not be the fastest, smartest, or most deadly agent, but Reuben had something no one else did.

Reuben knew how to ballroom dance.

Anticipating the largest trucker's headshot, Reuben did a Fallaway Rock and Swivel before twisting into a Basic Forward followed by a Basic Backward. All their shots missed, and they lined up for another volley.

No matter. Reuben was ready.

Gun in hand and one Outside Spin, two Oversways, and a Lindy Circle later, he managed to wound two of the truckers. Only the largest trucker remained.

The trucker was walking forward now, pistol right in front of him as he tried to shoot Reuben. But with every shot, Reuben dodged using the Promenade Step before he finally broke into a Reverse Fleckerl, ending the move with a Solo Spot Volta, his back to the trucker, gun in right hand, middle finger on the trigger, barrel pointed behind him at the trucker's leg in his periphery.

He shot the trucker in the leg, and he went down with a bellowing scream.

Reuben stood over him and growled, "Ballroom dancing, bitch!"

Then he looked around. No one was there to witness his glory, and for a brief moment he thought about killing himself again just so that he could have an audience.

Maybe if I position my phone just right, I could record it...

Then he shook his head. He'd died enough for one day.

He'd died enough for a lifetime.

CHAPTER FORTY-FIVE

Reuben—Wednesday, February 8, 5:43 p.m.

With the truckers captured and in the local PD's hands, and with Buzz recovering from trauma, the foursome took the Kia back down to the border highway.

"Are you sure you don't want me to drive?" Reuben asked Buzz.

His face was steel. "I'm fine."

Reuben was worried about Buzz. He hadn't been the same since he'd been hijacked. "Do you want to get a drink?"

Buzz shook his head and stared at the road. Well, it couldn't be solved right now, anyway. Martha was going through the truckers' phones and Aki was on hers.

She clicked her fingernails as she talked. "Right. We have confirmation that customs confiscated the vehicles. Did they get a visual on the explosives?"

Reuben and Martha whipped around to face her, waiting for an answer.

"Well, can you find out for me? No, I'll hold."

Martha read from the phone screens in front of her. "I've

got so many texts on here that if we can connect this number to Pout, this guy is going down. Check this out: '$4,000 for delivery of package by Wednesday night.' Of course, he could be talking about anything, but you know he's talking about the bomb."

"What did Alister Pout want with a bomb, anyway?" Reuben asked.

"That's the big question." Martha kept reading through the text.

Aki came back on her phone. "So, they did find the explosives in the trucks? And it is the missing one?" She raised her fist in silent victory, and everyone in the car applauded.

"We saved the world, guys," Reuben said.

Martha smiled. "Well, it was mainly you."

Reuben would have loved to have disagreed for modesty's sake. But the truth was, it *was* mainly him. He had literally died again and again to save the day.

"I couldn't have done it without you guys," he said. "Victory lunch on me?"

The trio agreed in unison, "No."

"We need showers and beds," Martha groaned.

Reuben cocked his head in agreement. He wanted those things, too. Aki was still on the phone and had been listening for several minutes. "Thanks. Call me when you have an update."

She ended her call and turned to the crew in the van. "First of all, Buzz and Martha, the CIA thanks you for your service."

"CIA," Martha said matter-of-factly. "That's who I was thinking you really worked for. State Department. Ha."

Buzz smiled for the first time since the hostage situation. "Finally, we can talk about it."

Reuben smiled ruefully. "We're not supposed to tell anyone."

"Well, they helped save the world," Aki said. "We can let them in on a little security breach."

Reuben continued, "Not even Marshall knows, and he can't."

Martha zipped her lips. "My lips are sealed."

Aki cleared her throat. "Secondly, they did confiscate the bomb, and…" She eyed Reuben carefully. "A zipped file containing damning evidence against Pout has just been forwarded to the CIA, NSA, and FBI from an unknown sender. Would you happen to know anything about that?"

Reuben exchanged a knowing glance with Buzz and Martha. Buzz beamed.

Aki's phone beeped. "Well, that was fast. Check this out." She pulled up a live news program on her phone, and Reuben watched.

"Canadian investor and tech mogul Alister Pout has been arrested this evening on allegations of drug trafficking and high treason. The former businessman holds residences in England, Canada, and in New York and was planning to run for public office in Canada this fall. He was arrested at a fundraiser gala in New York City. He is suspected of being connected to an experimental weapon that has been missing for a couple days now. No statement was available either from Mr. Pout's office or his legal counsel.'"

Martha laughed. "They're staying far, far away from him."

"Yep," Aki said and then smirked at Reuben and his friends.

"We did it, guys." Martha smiled, already closing her eyes for rest. "Now, let's get some sleep."

"That sounds nice." Aki yawned. "I guess I've got to book my flight home. What flights are you guys taking?"

Martha, Buzz, and Reuben all looked at each other.

Reuben cleared his throat. "We flew out here private."

"Sweet." Aki smiled.

Reuben shook his head. "But I think I'll take commercial. This kind of private is way overrated."

Martha laughed. "I'm with you on that one."

"I'll give you a ride home, Aki." Buzz glanced back in the rearview at her.

"What am I missing here?"

They all just laughed.

Martha, Reuben, and Aki arrived back in New York, and they chatted about the case all the way toward baggage claim. Buzz had flown back on his own, and now it was just the three of them. Aki stood at the carousel, and Reuben waited with her.

"I didn't check anything," Martha said. "So I'm going to head out."

Aki smiled. "Sure. It was good to meet you. See you around."

Martha smiled back. "Good to meet you, too."

She left down the hall, leaving Reuben and Aki. Reuben dug his hands into his pockets. "I'm glad we solved that case."

"Me too," Aki said.

Reuben chuckled. "I was beginning to think it would be like my dad's raw milk case."

Aki tilted her head. "His what?"

"My dad's a retired cop, and early in his career, he had this case about these kids that got sick off this raw milk from a—"

"Milk co-op in upstate?" she asked. "Early 90s?"

"Yeah." Reuben's eyes widened. "You know about it?"

"Sure." She shrugged. "It's classified, but I've read about it."

Reuben frowned. "Classified?"

"Yeah," she said. "It was this company AmeriPharm trying to test a cure for some new virus. The one that eventually came back in the early 2000s as SARS."

"I remember SARS. Wait, the milk thing had to do with SARS?"

Aki nodded. "Yeah, everyone knows. Well, everyone who has clearance," she said apologetically.

"Right."

"But basically, AmeriPharm was testing for a cure for SARS and thought they had a preventative measure. They figured if they could get the population to drink it liberally, then the populace at large would build up antibodies. So as a beta test, they got a bunch of farmers to try it out in their milk co-op. A bunch of people died, and the project was abandoned. AmeriPharm, as you could guess..."

"Was really us," Reuben said.

"Yeah. It was an agency project, basically," she said. "Slightly more complicated than that. It was a real company. But when it came down to it, yes, it was the CIA."

"And when it went bad, they disappeared into the night and let the farmers swing."

"That would be it," she said. "There's my bag." She grabbed a small red suitcase off the carousel and wheeled it toward him to say goodbye. "Well, it was fun."

Ruben shrugged. "Yeah, well, you know, we could make it more than fun."

She raised an eyebrow, and he continued, "Go back to my place, get some beers, you know, talk some more about Canadian milk farmers." With luck, maybe Marshall would be out drinking with some old police buddies.

She laughed. "Well, as engaging as talking about Canadian milk farmers might be, I'm going to have to pass. You're too much of a badass for me."

"You don't like badasses?" Reuben asked.

"I do," she said. "And I shouldn't. It never works out. In fact, I'm in a bad relationship right now. You know what? Life's too short. I think I'm going to break up with Mike as soon as I get home." She stared reflectively at the airport's ceiling while Reuben did a mental fist pump.

Then Aki turned back to face him. "But hey, we could still be friends, right?"

Reuben's heart sank like the Titanic. "Yeah, yeah."

"Cool." She playfully punched him on the shoulder and sauntered out of the terminal to catch a cab.

Fuck. Reuben just stood there, a hand clutched over his chest. Maybe Aki was going to cause him to have a heart attack after all.

How had this happened?

He stood stricken, alone in the airport, until an attendant asked if he was OK.

Was he OK? Of course he wasn't. The woman he loved had just put him in the friend zone, and now he had to go back home to Marshall.

To reality.

As he sat in the cab on his way home, his phone went off. It was Martha.

"Hey," she said. "Just want to find out if you've made it home."

"I'm on my way," he muttered.

She let a silence pass between them. "How did it go with Aki?"

"What do you mean? We just said goodbye."

"Uh-huh, you know what I mean."

He shook his head. "I think that ship has sailed. Er, sunk."

"What? No, that woman was looking at you like she wanted to bang your brains out."

"That's not what she told me."

"Whatever. She's lying."

"She punched me on the shoulder and said 'cool.'"

"Oh...yikes."

A text from Buzz popped up on his phone, and he laughed.

"What?" Martha asked.

"Buzz must have been thinking the same thing. He texted me. 'Beware. If you mess this up, once you're in the friend zone, statistically, it is nearly impossible to get a date. In fact, you're more likely to die from a microwave explosion.'"

Reuben groaned.

"Well, you know, given your history," Martha said.

"Yeah, so maybe I've still got a chance after all." He laughed.

"Maybe. I like her, though. A little snobby, but you go for that type. So, I think she's good for you."

"Thanks." Reuben felt an emotion like hope flutter in his gut. Maybe him and Aki weren't over after all. He grinned fearlessly and made a brave fist. "You know what, maybe you're right."

"Of course I'm right. I'm always right. Call it cop intuition."

Reuben had to admit. He did feel a lot better now. He was

going to fight for Aki and find a way to work things out, even if it killed him—which it probably would. More than once.

Martha sighed. "Hey, want to come over?"

Reuben checked his watch. "Right now?"

"Yeah. To celebrate us being heroes and all. I could use a drink and some company after all of that."

"Sure." He smiled. "It's not like I have anything to go home to."

"Yeah, me neither."

He ended the call and instructed the driver to change routes toward Martha's neighborhood.

"Actually," he said, "you're going to have to get in that lane."

"That lane? Now?"

The lane was crowded, and there wasn't another turnoff for another couple of blocks. "Sorry, you can get in now, now, *now*."

The driver cursed and did a quick turn that sent Reuben flying against the side of the door.

"Geez, man," the driver said. "Are you trying to die or something?"

Reuben smiled. "Nah, I'm done dying. No more for me. All I want is to live for the rest of my life so I can die from old age. Preferably in my sleep. That would be nice."

The driver stared at him quizzically from the rearview. "You do that kid, you do that."

New York State Penitentiary—Wednesday March 18, 9:01 a.m.

"New roommate, Pout," the officer yelled as he opened the cell.

"I'm sorry." He looked at the officer. "My lawyers arranged a private cell for security purposes."

The officer laughed. "Security purposes? Ain't no security in here, Mr. Pout. This here's prison."

The man entered. He looked different without his hoodie on—the hoodie with the stripes on the shoulders—but that scar across his face was unmistakable.

Alister tensed, "How did you get in here? I did as you said, and I didn't say anything to anyone about you."

The man put a finger to his lips, "Shh, people are listening."

Alister shut his mouth.

The newcomer set his things down on his bed and squashed his mattress. "This will do. Do nicely."

Bile rose in Alister's throat. "What do you want?"

"Don't worry. I won't be here for long. I just want a few of my questions answered."

"What do you mean you won't be here for long?"

"Don't worry about it. Tell me which foreign governments invested in RedBook. I need dirt. More specifically, I need to know which leaders are on edge so I can push them over."

Alister frowned. "What? I don't understand."

"Microwave bomb was destroyed. But why have a bomb when you can have a nuclear war instead."

"I wasn't sending a..."

"RedBook was to be the ultimate surveillance tool. Who wanted it? Why? I need information. Or better yet, your files. Where are they?"

Alister's mouth hung open.

The man spat on the ground. "Your plan wasn't a complete failure. It just didn't work. Your files."

Alister said nothing to any of this.

The man sighed. "When I enlisted you as my pawn, I expected more. The files."

"But you're in jail with me. How will you—"

"Just answer my questions," the man kicked him in the gut. Repeatedly. "That's for failing on your mission." He gave him another kick to his face. "And that's just because you're an asshole. Too bad you won't remember a thing about it. The files."

Alister whined in pain, and he held his face. "You broke my fucking nose?" They heard guards running to the cell.

"Don't worry about it. You won't remember any of this in a minute. You One-Deathers never do."

"Where?"

Alister had no choice and told this scarred man where he kept his flash drive of information.

"And the password?"

"But—"

The man lifted a fist, threatening to punch him.

Alister covered his face and said, "You only die twice. No spaces. The 'e's are the number 3."

"Interesting password. And wholly inaccurate. One can die way more than twice."

Alister wiped the blood off his face and laughed. At this point, the guards were fumbling with the cell door. "What are you planning on doing with that information? You're stuck in here with me."

"Am I?" The man pulled a contraband razor out of a toiletry bag, and without hesitation or fear, stabbed himself in the neck over and over again until he gagged and finally died with a smile painted across his face.

To Be…Repeated

AUTHOR NOTES RAMY VANCE

JUNE 8, 2021

"I hope you got this out of your system," Michael yelled at me.

(Well, not yelled – anyone who knows Michael, he doesn't really yell at you. He just gives you a blank stare that lets you know, in no unequivocal terms, that you're in trouble.)

I nodded.

"What did we learn, Ramy?"

Me, sheepishly looking away from the screen, "No more crazy, time-travelling, multi-dimensional stories with mad scientists and underpowered heroes. It was hell getting this through Beta and the editorial teams. Lynne (the editor) wants my head on a stake and Beta thinks I'm certifiable. I get it. Never again!"

Michael nodded satisfied. Beta-readers nodded satisfied. The editorial team nodded satisfied.

Me: "But now that this series is in the can, we need to plan the next and I have an idea… Vampires colonizing space…" Pause. "Oh, with a bit of wormhole travel thrown in, too. And an alien race that gets their food from photosynthesis."

Michael purses his lips, thinks it over and says, "OK, let me have it. What the plotline?"

Vampires Colonizing Space (which is a bit of a misnomer because we don't really have many vamps in it. It's more of a… well, you'll see) will be out in July

So much for straight-forward simple stories.

AUTHOR NOTES MICHAEL ANDERLE

JUNE 8, 2021

Thank you for not only reading this story but these author notes as well!

Now that we have Ramy's version of events, let us discuss my version.

This is how I remember it.

Ramy: I have this fantastic idea where we are going to do something like *Groundhog Day* and Chuck… You know, the tv show where the tech guy is a spy?

Mike: Ramy, sounds good except the whole timey-wimey issue. LMBPN has had a couple of those, and they are always a B@#@# to do and get right.

Ramy: No problem! I'll have the timeline all worked out, and it will be super tight.

Mike: I don't think you are hearing the words coming out of my mouth. Is your ZOOM working? I know it's late there in Scotland. Perhaps the fact that we have done these types of stories and it's been a total shitshow isn't translating correctly through ZOOM? Do I sound like I'm speaking Russian over there right now?

Ramy: Hear you four by four. This is going to be so funny. A guy wants to get the girl, but the girl is a spy-like person and our guy just learned that the world exploded…

Mike: <<Thinking>> *There is no greater teacher than pain.*

Mike: Ok, Ramy, we can try this. I mean, how bad can it be…for me?

The answer to that was, it was fairly annoying for me.

Ramy, on the other hand, was up for almost seventy-two hours trying to do his day job and fix the @#%#!!! errors the first book had coming back from the Beta readers. At one point, I was worried he was losing his hair.

I have on good authority that he isn't going to try and pull this off again.

Right after his next effort.

Ramy is like a teenage collaborator who refuses to see the reality of the problems he causes himself because he gets caught up in the idea. Let's see how wise he gets over the course of the next few stories.

Well, if Ramy was a teenage collaborator with two kids, two jobs, and a mortgage.

As soon as Ramy pitches an idea…hell, as soon as my mind registers that the words *coming out of his mouth* are intended to pitch an idea, my hand involuntarily moves up and my mouth (of its own accord) yells, "NO!"

It's a learned response.

Until next time!

Ad Aeternitatem,

Michael Anderle

OTHER BOOKS BY RAMY VANCE

Other Middang3ard Books

Never Split The Party (01)
Late To the Party (02)
It's My Party (03)
Blue Hell And Alien Fire (04)

Death Of An Author: A Middang3ard Novella

Dark Gate Angels

Dark Gate Angels (01)
Shades of Death (02)
The Allies of Death (03)
The Deadliness of Light (04)

Dragon Approved

The First Human Rider (01)
Ascent to the Nest (02)
Defense of the Nest (03)

Nest Under Siege (04)
First Mission (05)
The Descent (06)
Sacrifices (07)
Love and Aliens (08)
An Alien Affair (09)
Dragons in Space (10)
The Beginning of the End (11)
Death of the Mind (12)
Boundless (13)

Other Books by Ramy Vance

Mortality Bites Series
Keep Evolving Series
Fatebound Series
Welcome to the Dragon Show Series

BOOKS BY MICHAEL ANDERLE

For a complete list of books by Michael Anderle, please visit:

www.lmbpn.com/ma-books/

All LMBPN Audiobooks are Available at Audible.com and iTunes

To see all LMBPN audiobooks, including those written by Michael Anderle please visit:

www.lmbpn.com/audible

CONNECT WITH THE AUTHORS

Connect with Ramy

Join Ramy's Newsletter

Join Ramy's FB Group: House of the GoneGod Damned!

Connect with Michael Anderle and sign up for his email list here:

Website: http://lmbpn.com

Email List: http://lmbpn.com/email/

Facebook:
www.facebook.com/TheKurtherianGambitBooks

www.ingramcontent.com/pod-product-compliance
Lightning Source LLC
Chambersburg PA
CBHW050509110726
47899CB00005B/1381
* 9 7 8 1 6 4 9 7 1 8 5 2 5 *